Running Cold

Steve Zell

Tales From Zell, Inc. ™

ISBN-13: 978-0-9847468-5-9
2nd print edition: October 2017
10 9 8 7 6 5 4 3 2

Cover: *Running Cold*© 2012 by Steven J. Pitzel

Dedication

To Nina and Vicki. Without their love and support there is no way I could manage something like this. It's just that simple...

And to Mom and Dad for the summers in California during those wonderful, if sometimes awkward, childhood years. The magic was absolutely real...and I swear the monsters were too...

Acknowledgements

Special thanks to my good friends, Gina Bovara and Karen Rekate for the final insanity checks on this book!

In Memory of Merl Reagle

Your crossword puzzles were and always will be truly amazing, but some of my favorite memories revolve around your music, and those hours we spent singing our favorite sixties songs beneath the shadow of that vintage Leslie. Thank you for your friendship in times of great need and always.

Foreword

It's Father's Day as I write this foreword and I've eagerly opened my Father's Day gift, a brand new album from *The Beach Boys*! Go figure.

Amazing how cool the timing of things can be sometimes! It occurs to me (as it has that it's about time for me to call my own dad), just how important music is not only as a backdrop, but maybe even as the stage for many stories. I realize now, that even though I rarely have music playing while I work, (unless it's on at the various coffee houses I haunt) that I constantly listen to music in my head while I write, and while this is not a story of the events or politics that shaped the period, the music of the 60s certainly colors *Running Cold*.

I wouldn't say the 60s represented the *best times* ever – while they provided me a trove of sweet, bittersweet, and even heartbreaking memories – I believe the 60s were every bit as turbulent and frightening as they were innocent and naïve.

One thing I can say about the world at that time is that it was a very different world than the one we live in now – and that difference was captured in its music – or maybe the music shaped that world – it's hard to say which came first.

If you didn't happen to live through that era, it may not hurt to set your music search back several decades, buckle up, and let it flow while you read on. If you don't know where to start – thank you to my friend and trivia buddy, Ken Applin, for providing the Running Cold playlist on the following page.

Running Cold Playlist

Pieces of April – Three Dog Night
In My Room – The Beach Boys
Red Rubber Ball – The Cyrkle
Somewhere Along the Way – John Gary
She's Come Undone – The Guess Who
Hard Day's Night – The Beatles
Catch a Wave – The Beach Boys
Once Upon a Time – John Gary
Don't Worry Baby – The Beach Boys
Surfer Girl – The Beach Boys
Wild is the Wind – Johnny Mathis

Chapter 1

Stepping on the Vine

It's a game of hide-and-seek, but Michael doesn't want to play.

It's a game Nicky always starts, and Nicky doesn't play it like other kids. With Nicky, "hide-and-seek" isn't over when you're found. And Nicky only plays when Mommy and Daddy are gone.

The house is big and there are lots of places to hide, but Nicky knows them all. Nicky is patient. He takes his time, checks out every one.

It's dark and tight where Michael hides. His cramped lungs suck tiny breaths filled with turpentine and the stench of pet droppings.

There are few basements in Phoenix, Arizona, but the Helm house has one. There's a tool closet in one corner but Daddy doesn't have time to build anything so it only holds Michael's paintbrushes, canvas, and bags of feed for all his pets.

The unused saw-table is home to the pets that can't stay outside.

Guinea pigs, painted turtles, chameleons and blue-bellied lizards, and Michael's favorite - Long John, his African Gray parrot. His pets are active now, skittering under shredded newsprint and leaves in their boxes; struggling against their tiny prison bars to look out.

Beneath the saw-table is a cabinet with all the shelves removed.

That's where Michael hides, knees crushing his lungs.

Wings flap just over Michael's head. The illusion of night the hooded cage affords broken now, by the rustling of the others. Long John, has woken. Michael can hear Long John's scaly feet grasp and slide over the wooden perch, the scissoring of his powerful beak. Long-John's a talker, but an anxious, "click – click – click," is all he's saying now.

Between the clicks...footsteps. Slow, deliberate footsteps that could be coming from anywhere.

It doesn't matter how well Michael hides. Nicky will find him; Nicky always does.

Something wet splashes his leg –

"Michael!"

"Michael, does any of this look familiar?"

Fog gives way to watercolor dunes, waves of green, tans and gray...

From the radio someone sang about having pieces of something, or someone...*Pieces of April?* What could *that* mean? Michael's sleep had been fitful, his dreams were all bad, and the song just didn't make sense.

Mom switched the radio off.

Michael was in the car with his Mom now, not under the saw-table. The basement in Phoenix was a few hundred miles of sand dunes and bleak desert highway behind them. He was free, *safe*.

He rubbed another splash of cold water from his knee.

The icy drip was courtesy the refrigeration unit slung beneath the dashboard. Condensation on the grill dripped so bad sometimes you had to sit with your knees pressed to the door. Doze for a moment – let your guard down even a little – and the ice water got you.

Despite the bum refrigeration unit, the car was almost new – a 1964, sky-blue Plymouth Fury complete with push-button transmission. The Helms had other cars, bigger ones – Dad made lots of money. But this was Dad's favorite – he liked the push-buttons, said they made him feel like he was driving an "Auto-Mat." Dad use to take time off to be with the family, and they'd go on long drives together. Sometimes, Dad even let Michael push the buttons to shift. But Dad would never be with them again.

"Nice houses up there, huh?"

Mom darted her chin toward a hill dappled with gray ice plant then snapped her focus quickly back to the road ahead, a white-knuckle grip on the wheel. Push-buttons or not, to Michael it often seemed the Fury drove *her*.

With the low fog, the hill she'd pointed seemed to be riding atop clouds. The houses winding up its slope got bigger as they reached the apex, giving the hillside a sort of top-heavy look. To Michael, it was like a Dr. Seuss story he'd read – one about a king turtle named Yertle, who stacked every other turtle in his kingdom below him so he could have the best view in the kingdom. The whole stack of turtles eventually fell over. Michael couldn't recall if Yertle died in the fall. He guessed there were a lot of nasty injuries though. Even turtle shells broke if they fell on a rock or…

"Yeah," Mom sighed, "That's the 'cat-bird seat' up there all right."

The biggest house, and the highest on the hill ahead, looked a lot like the one they'd just left in Phoenix.

Michael figured what a cat-bird might look like – but it seemed like a weird thing, and why the heck would it have a big house all its own and just sit there? He didn't care. He frowned at the big house that wasn't theirs.

The houses they passed now were on a hill too, but a much smaller one. Their neighborhood in Phoenix had been on a mountain.

Not many kids lived here – he could see that right off as Mom threaded their car carefully up the narrow roads – no bikes leaned in the driveways – if you could call the weedy stretches of sand in front of the houses "driveways." No basketball hoops over the carports. In fact, there weren't any carports. The cars were either hidden in ugly stucco garages, or left stranded like dead whales in the sand.

The Fury nosed up a hill so steep all he could see were clouds.

"Do you remember any of this?" Mom re-phrased.

Sure he did. It was nowhere he wanted to be.

"Turn right. Go up the hill."

"It's something, isn't it? The way you remember things…"

It sounded like she wanted to say more, but she didn't. Mom talked that way a lot – half of things. Michael wasn't sure if she just figured he knew what she was going to say – or if she was just too tired to go on.

Mom was tired a lot.

He'd spent sixth and seventh grade at Saint Thomas the Apostle back in Phoenix. He hadn't liked Saint Thomas so much, but he'd been there two whole school years and gotten used to it. "Two school years" was a record for Michael. Before that, it was Saint Agnes. Saint Bartholomew before that. The list went on. In many ways, life had gotten easier since his older brother, Nicky, died. In just as many ways, it hadn't.

Here in LaVista he'd be the "new kid" all over again.

"Well," Mom smiled, but her voice wasn't happy. "We're here."

Granma Helm's bungalow leaned into a sand dune. It wasn't much of a house, but now it was theirs. Dad's parents had moved to California when dad went away to Arizona for college. Dad said the California house was one of a jillion beach bungalows built by the studios way back in the Golden Age of movies when Hollywood was "really cranking them out" and "spending like there was no tomorrow" which, apparently, there hadn't been. *Bungalow* was a big word for something the size of a shoe box. Dad said shacks like this weren't supposed to be anything more than temporary housing for grips and extras. Dad said grips and extras were people who worked on films but weren't stars.

"Let's hope the movers are on time," Mom sighed.

The front door opened with a cloud of dust rank with mildew and the ghosts of cigarettes from long ago. Oppressive smells you could almost feel, like a greasy hand pressed over your face. Gramps Helm was a chain-smoker till the day he died. At least that's what Mom said. Once the old man died, Gram picked right up where he'd left off, apparently forging a chain around her lungs Jacob Marley would have been proud of.

"*God,*" Mom grimaced, trying to wave away the bad air with one hand, pressing her chest with the other. For a moment, he thought she might actually retch. "We'll have to do something about that right away."

Mom rolled up shades and cranked open windows the second they stepped inside, and Michael did the same. The light that spilled in was yellow and thick with motes.

"Get started with the bags in the trunk. I'll see if she left any cleanser."

She handed Michael the keys to the Fury, and for a few seconds as he stood holding the cool metal bits in his hands, he mapped the way back to Phoenix in his head.

-=-=-=-=-

There was a curse on kids in Southern California. At least, that's how Sandy Randall saw it. The haze hadn't left their beach all day and the water was cold. Tom and Pete were fine with it – but Sandy was freezing.

Summer can be weird in Southern California. It's sunny, and the ocean screams, "Jump in!" every morning until school lets out end of May.

In June, when you're finally free, the sun hides and the beach goes cold. They call it "June gloom" and it's cruel.

The three of them carried the long board together, Tom and Pete switching off front and back, Sandy in the middle. The middle was easy, mostly just balancing it. The boys were doing all the work. Tom had insisted that's how it should be since Sandy was a girl and, for once, Sandy didn't argue.

At five foot two, she was taller than Pete, though she was much shorter than Tom now. Tom had taken a growth spurt over the school year and passed her by. The last time they'd wrestled, she'd pinned him. That was a summer ago, before the spurt, and she guessed things would probably be different today.

A Beach Boys song called *In My Room* was cutting in and out of the black transistor radio that hung from a strap on Pete's wrist. The radio had swallowed enough seawater and sand over the years that it played more static than music these days. You could still make out most of the words though.

The song was melancholy, about having a special place of your own where you could dream and be yourself. The song made her feel worse.

They'd stayed too long at the beach. A few hours ago, she'd almost walked home by herself, but she hadn't. Walking back wasn't a big deal in itself; none of them lived more than a mile from the beach. But every summer's day since first grade they'd walked home from the beach, the Cove Theater, or wherever they'd spent their day, together.

Today she'd nearly ended that streak.

She felt gritty, salty, and worn-out. Mostly she was just uncomfortable. Sandy had been the recipient of a growth spurt of her own this winter. Unfortunately, it hadn't made her taller. Her favorite bikini and shorts were stretched to the limit these days. Boys were gawking. Every now and then even Tom would sneak sideways glances at her. At first, she'd thought that was creepy. Now, she mostly ignored it.

Sandy smirked, watching the funny tire-tread marks Tom's Huarache sandals left. Sandy was barefoot, as always. She hated shoes. Tom and Pete had tossed in their blue and white Baggies for these new, insanely bright, trunks called "Jams" with "tropical" patterns. They were supposed to look cool. They looked like dweebs.

"Rocky, come on."

"What?"

"Man you are *way out*."

The static on Pete's radio was annoying now – so was her latest nickname, *Rocky*. Over the course of their friendship she'd been Dusty, Sunny, Salty, and now Rocky – anything but Sandy.

"Ditch the board first? Or hit Big Jerry's now?" Tom asked.

"Big Jerry's – Big Jerry's – Big Jerry's –" Pete lobbied.

Big Jerry's was the market on La Playa. It wasn't much of a market; soft drinks and candy, mostly – a freezer full of Drumsticks and Popsicles.

The owner, "Big Jerry" Duttman was a beach boy from way back – even before Mike Love and the Brothers Wilson were born. He was cool. You could get a Dr. Pepper on credit at Big Jerry's.

But going there meant crossing PCH way over on the north side of the backwater, not the south side where they lived, and that meant carrying the surfboard a good mile more than they needed to. That was stupid.

"Take it back," she said, "we're practically there."

"Big Jerry's!" Pete whined.

"That's nuts," she said. "We can ditch it at your house and hit Big Jerry's after."

Tom considered both prospects, tongue thoughtfully working his cheek, right about where a patch of practically transparent hairs had recently sprouted. Was he ever going to yank those out?

"I'm with Pete," Tom said, finally.

She gave the board a shove, nearly toppling the boys.

"Fine, go with Pete."

"Rocky, come on −"

She whirled on Tom so fast he nearly dropped his end of the board.

"*Sandy!*" she spat. "My name is Sandy!"

"Geez. Rock...Sandy," Tom's mouth hung slack. He stood there, skinny as a pole, so gawky in his Jams. His Adam's apple yo-yo'd. That sudden spurt had simply stretched him out, not added to him − except for those daddy long-legs popping out of his cheeks and chin - his neck resembled a pelican's right now. "I didn't mean − I, uh..."

The boys exchanged a glance then shook their heads. Sandy spun the other way, her face suddenly hot. That heading unfortunately started her in the direction of Big Jerry's market, not her house, but she kept on walking just the same.

The two boys stood right where she'd left them for a moment or two, not sure what to do next. Finally, they followed at a respectful distance.

After a short time, the respect left.

"Such a baby," she heard Pete say, finally.

"You're a whiner," she spat over her shoulder.

"Baby."

"Whiner."

"Baby."

"Shut up," Tom said.

"But she *IS* −"

"Shut it!"

"What're you telling me to shut up for?"

Tom frowned and shook his head, "Just do it."

-=-=-=-=-

The movers had come and Mom knew where everything was supposed to go. Michael was just in the way.

For a while, he stood to the side and watched the parade of boxes as long as that seemed interesting. Eventually, he drifted outside and down the block to the next road, and the next one after that. Before long he was at the bottom of the hill, where the main road ran into another one and died.

Looking back where the moving truck leaned, its black tongue lolling out onto the dirt, he noted the order of things. *Their* house was the pinkish one with the gray roof just past an open lot – the hull of an old truck sat rusting in the middle of that lot, being eaten alive by vines with leaves big as he was. There were three other houses between the empty lot and the end of their block. Every house on the hill sat catawampus in the sand like they'd dropped there from the sky. Nothing looked planned at all.

So different from the perfectly gridded Valley of the Sun, Phoenix, Arizona, where every lawn was framed by irrigation "berms" and sidewalks, with exactly two palm trees and two mulberries to a lot. In Phoenix, even the houses with no lawns and just desert outside were landscaped, often bordered by rows of organ-pipe or prickly pear, maybe a couple carefully placed agaves thrown in for accents.

Michael crossed the road to a weathered wood fence that protected a wide riverbed. He leaned there, dejected, arms hooked over the crossbar, chin in his hands. The riverbed was mostly sand, big surprise there, some tall grass, and tumbleweeds. Blue-gray ice plant took over from the grass and weeds halfway across. The ice plant had managed a sprinkling of red flowers, enough to make the riverbed look like some giant with a bloody nose had run across it. On the other bank, the ice plant died away to ropy, gray knots that stretched up a yellow cliff to more houses. Much nicer houses than theirs.

A tall bridge off to his right carried the highway that brought them here. Beneath it, the sand and brush blended quickly to reeds and water.

Beyond that was the one cool thing they'd gained by moving here – the ocean. And that could lift the spirits of any boy.

The fog had broken enough to give Michael his first, awestruck, glimpse of surf since way before Nicky got killed and Dad went away, and he stared at that wonder beneath the bridge for a long time.

Whucck!

Cold, wet goo splattered his face, yanked him from his reverie. He slipped off the fence, and landed squarely on his butt in the sand. At his feet, a clam oozed quivering, salmon-colored meat into the sand. The crossbar where he'd been leaning held a ragged, pink slash, dotted with bits of black shell.

A mottled and dingy white seagull shrieked as it circled high overhead.

Michael jumped to his feet, swiped the slimy globs off his cheek; a mixture of anger and disgust in his gut.

The gull banked, then dropped sharply, landing heavy and loud on the fence just a few feet from Michael. The gnarled wood creaked beneath its odd feet. It was the biggest, scariest bird Michael had ever seen. The gull turned an evil yellow eye toward him and shrieked again – louder than before.

Michael stepped over the gore at his feet.

"It's not my fault you threw your lunch at me!" A gust of wind threw sand into the air.

It was an old bird, Michael figured, weathered as a crusty, old pirate, with chips of gray enamel flecking the edges of its worn beak. It worked that beak like it wanted to say, "back-off kid, or the next clam lands on your skull." Shoulders hunched, it sidled along the fence toward him. Michael couldn't take his eyes off the creature.

But he wasn't backing down either.

"You threw it right at me!" He scolded, even adding a word Mom would have washed out of his mouth with soap had she heard.

The gull flapped its wings angrily, glanced at the foamy meat in the sand, guarded now by Michael's deck shoes. It turned accusingly back to Michael with a shriek so loud it skinned Michael's teeth.

Walk away, a dim voice inside Michael said.

Just walk on home and let the grizzled old fart finish its stupid lunch.

But Michael had already lost his home, his school, his whole life today. He wasn't taking diddly-squat from a stupid bird.

"You don't scare me. You don't win the game."

He had been scared, yes, Michael had, and this wasn't the first time, not by a long shot.

Nothin' but a little scaredy-cat. Little crybaby!

"That's what you think, isn't it?"

I win again, Mikey! What are ya' gonna do about it, baby Mikey? You gonna cry some more?

The gull hunched its shoulders, flicked its wings - eyes narrowing, head bobbing and darting, sizing up Michael from every angle. It was ready now, ready to take what was rightfully its own whether Michael backed off or not.

But Michael had no intention of backing off.

"I'll show *you*. I'll show you – that's what I'll do!"

A cool breeze sent the tall grass waving along the ravine. Michael closed his eyes, felt the breeze gently wrap around him. A breath of it sank deep into his lungs. A familiar tingling in his toes and fingers, the cold had come, and once it had taken a sure hold there, sucked back through him like ice water through a straw. The orbs rolled back beneath his lids, ticked left and right, as if they too were searching for the word, for just the right word.

What was it? What would fit? Something Mom had said.

Blackness. The hiss of fang's suddenly bared.

Found it.

Michael's eyes rolled forward again, the lids opened.

On a breath that could have frozen white as it left his lips, he whispered,

"Cat-bird."

The gull's head flicked back. It slapped the weathered fence pole with the side of its beak, as if dislodging some unseen sludge. Then that ugly beak opened wide, but the shriek didn't come this time; couldn't come. Michael saw a tongue within, spotted gray and pink. The gull's yellow eyes seemed the size of boulder marbles now.

And then the seagull was gone. What stood gasping in its place made Michael swallow hard, his own eyes wide now. The cold had drained away, in its place, a hollowness, *a horror -*

"It's not my fault!" he shouted.

His knees buckled – if only to remind him he still had legs. Legs ready to run, *to run like hell.*

He screamed, whirled away, pounding the sand with each step as he raced his fear up the hill.

"It's not my fault!"

He shivered when he reached the house, that familiar tingle racing over him again. The sight of his own, blue-tinged fingertips, made him catch his breath. He forced himself to breathe. The feeling would pass, sure it would.

Nothing had happened. *Nothing real anyway.*

And it wasn't his fault even if it had.

He jammed his hands deep in his jean pockets before he walked inside.

The movers were finishing up. Only boxes remained.

The bits of their old life too large to be packed – china cabinet, cherry wood dinner table, and the leather sofa from dad's study – were already inside, looking as out of place within these cigarette-stained walls as Michael felt.

The stale odors were still there, cut now by the sting of cleaning fluids in the air. When he swallowed, the taste was a mixed bag of Pine-Sol, bleach, and cigarette butts.

So much old stuff in this house. A lot of nautical crud: hurricane lamps, cork floats, pictures framed with porthole covers. On the mantle sat the main two things he really remembered from their trip out for Grandpa Helm's funeral – a big ugly egg-shaped piece of rock and the odd combination clock and barometer thing set in what looked to be the steering wheel from the world's tiniest schooner.

Everything else was unfamiliar, and all was caked with dust and mold. Mom had already removed a couple pictures from the wall, ghost frames of smoke and dust remained in their place.

The grunts, small talk and the odor of beer-filled sweat added by the moving men didn't help matters.

He wished the movers would just finish already and leave. The den and living room were already piled high. So much had been left in Phoenix; there couldn't be that much more to go.

When he passed a wall of boxes he saw one mover who wasn't actually moving anything. The man's overalls were a patchwork of oil stained denim, a few strands of yellow-white threads left to hide his grimy knees. A cross tattooed on one arm looked like it had been scraped into his warty skin with a melted blue crayon. The cigarette dangling from his hand spiraled gray smoke between fingers browned with nicotine.

The man seemed fascinated with the label on one of the boxes piled in front of him, even though it only said Del Monte Baked Beans – and that wasn't even what was inside.

Then Michael saw what the mover was *really* looking at.

In the kitchen, Michael's mom was scrubbing black shoe scuffs off the linoleum next to the fridge. She wore shorts that were probably too tight for housework, and one of Dad's work shirts that wasn't nearly tight enough.

That's where the mover's eyes were.

The man straightened when he noticed Michael, gave Michael a stupid, yellow grin, then went right back to staring at her, only now he plunked the cigarette in one corner of his mouth and actually picked up the Del Monte box.

"Mom?"

"Honey?"

She stood. The man set the box down not two feet from where it had been, and walked outside.

"I don't like that guy."

"What's wrong, my little man?"

"I just don't like him."

She dismissed Michael's concern with a shrug, but her hands automatically went to Dad's shirt and fastened one more button.

"Well, it's not like we'll ever see them again." But when she rubbed his forehead, she did look concerned. "Mikey, *are you all right?*"

"Uh huh." He shoved his hands deeper in his pockets.

"You've been *so good.* It's been a long day and you've been real good the whole way here. I saw a market on the way up. We'll get some ice cream, okay?"

Chapter 2

"We could walk, you know."

Brit Helm studied the last bit of family she had. Mikey's huge blue eyes could be innocent and piercing at once. They were not his father's eyes, and not exactly hers either.

"It's a mistake to think a kid's half you and half somebody else." Her father had warned when Nicky was born. "They come in with a plan all their own. Got very little to do with you."

The idea that kids came into this world with some sort of Divine program was one of many unsolicited bits of parenting advice he'd bestowed. The one she hated most:

"Spend too much time watchin' 'em and you'll never see 'em grow."

She bristled every time he said it, she wasn't a worrier, wasn't controlling, far from it. She simply didn't believe that children should raise themselves. She'd suspected that her father's advice had been little more than a rationale for spending as little time with his own family as possible.

Then Michael was born, and Brit came to the awful realization that, just maybe, her father knew what he was talking about.

From the moment they'd placed Michael in her arms, she knew *this one is different*. She'd felt inadequate and weak, that something much larger than that tiny bundle had been placed in her care. His eyes had been wide and alert from the start. Something so powerful in those eyes...

Those eyes watched her now; studied her right back. *Looking for any sign of weakness.*

Brit had headed for the car on impulse – you just didn't walk in Phoenix, not in the summer you didn't, and it was *always* summer back there.

"Yes," she opened the driver's door, slid in and popped the button on his side in one continuous motion. Her voice was carefully firm, "But we're still driving."

Mikey rolled his eyes, "We've been in the car all day." He stood his ground, testing her. She leaned over, swung the passenger door open, and adjusted the mirror, mindful not to celebrate her small victory when he finally relented and climbed inside.

Brit eased the car away from the deep sand near the gate. The roads here were little more than an extension of the beach. You could get a car stuck big-time in La Vista.

But you could walk here in summer, and Brit liked that. You could walk forever. You could, in fact, step right off the edge of the U. S. of A, if you wanted. *Just hike out into that overgrown lake and leave this big bad world behind.*

In truth, the ocean was the world's ultimate escape route.

Brit grabbed the wheel too tightly. The car lurched.

A ribbon of pain tied silvery knots behind her eyes. Soon the afternoon sky would be filled with colorful little flying saucers. Half an hour later she'd be blind with pain.

The seven hours of desert road had been too much. Riding Mr. Clean's white tornado through Granma Helm's dumpy little house had made *too much* even worse. Her fingers reeked of ammonia. She shouldn't be driving now. They should have walked to the market, just like Mikey said.

But she'd made a decision, a small one perhaps, but she'd made it and now they'd stick with it. With Mikey, you didn't have the luxury of second thoughts.

Mr. Clean's white tornado followed her as they coasted down the hill.

Two turns and several more yards of sand, and she pulled into the market's parking lot - railroad ties and a worn-out hawser set off the market's patch of sand from all the other sand in La Vista.

"We're here." Brit smiled through her headache, even managed to sound perky. "So what'll it be –"

"50-50 bar!"

And Mikey was out the door.

She began to tell him not to slam it, but too late. With that violent *"whump!"* the alien spaceships in her head doubled their numbers, hovered before her. Brit slumped over the wheel, closed her eyes and counted slowly to three. Then she pushed herself out the driver's side.

Big Jerry's, not really much more than a big plywood box covered with palm fronds and driftwood, perched at the edge of the ravine. Several sun-bleached shark jaws, mostly toothless, and some sad-looking starfish, each minus an arm or two, hung from a badly frayed fisherman's net stretched above the front door between cork floats. The whole market looked to have been washed up from the Pacific and beached at low tide.

It looked nearly as bad as Brit felt.

Mikey had already disappeared inside; a jangle of music pouring out the open front door before it swung slowly back on its post. Thankfully, she caught that door just before it made contact with the frame. The song that crackled from a speaker way too near her head was *Red Rubber Ball* by a band called The Cyrcle.

Through the pain and the crash of distant waves, The Cyrcle tried to convince her the bad times were over and everything would be okay; that the blazing sun was just a red rubber ball.

But the sun wasn't a red rubber ball; it was the fiery launch pad for a thousand alien ships with lasers locked on Brit's temples. And the bad times weren't over for her. Not by a long shot.

She hauled herself across the lot, feeling very tired now, and so much older than her thirty-two years. Maybe the inside of her skull was a handball court and her brain was the ball. A *red rubber ball*, she smiled grimly.

"Is that real?"

"Real as you and me, Sport. Go ahead and touch it. Can't bite you now."

"Wow!"

Mikey's hands hovered over a set of shark jaws on Big Jerry's counter. This set was a whopper, at least two feet across. Big Jerry had obviously saved the best for his paying customers.

Big Jerry himself sat beneath a mop of hair as sun-bleached as the shark jaws, his huge callused, sandaled feet rested on the counter. A faded Hawaiian shirt hung open to reveal the white wool of his chest. He winked at Brit as she came in and greeted her with an innocent, "Hi, Mommy," but the look-over he gave her breasts, legs, and face (in that order) was thorough. Brit shrugged it off. He was a boy in his fifties. She sensed no harm in him.

"*Boss!* Isn't it *boss*, Mom?"

"Very boss. Did you find your ice cream?"

Mikey glanced around, no longer sidetracked by the shark jaws.

"Oh, yeah."

Jerry tipped his chin toward a big red chest with a Coca-Cola logo on the front.

"Freezer's against that wall, Sport."

The logo blazed fiery trails across Brit's aching eyes. She watched Mikey fish around inside. *He was taking forever.*

"Mikey —" she said, finally.

The door cracked back and slammed home another winner against Brit's skull, but it had opened to familiar scents, Coppertone and cocoa butter. Aromas that brought good associations for Brit: sweet summer days and swimming pools, hot dogs with mustard. Rare, happy moments.

Jerry's smile grew even broader as the girl stepped in.

"How they breakin,' *wahini?*"

"Hard right-to-left this morning," the girl said. "Man, it was *glass* midday, but it's *closed-out and dumpy* now."

She was probably Mikey's age, but looked older. Sun-streaked blond hair, long and silky the way Brit's own hair had once been (*was it fifteen years ago, or a thousand?*). The girl's skin was bronze with just a sprinkle of golden teen down covering it. Pretty, heart-shaped face, not a knockout maybe, but a woman's figure was dangerously asserting itself beneath the baby fat.

The girl looked directly at Brit now, and Brit amended that impression. The girl's *eyes* made her a knockout; deep hazel, nearly green, and flecked with gold. Very bright. Very sharp.

Trouble.

A brand new spike of pain made Brit's flying saucers flash and spin.

She paid for Mikey's ice cream quickly, and for the quart of milk her steadily weakening fingers had nearly sent tumbling from the shelf. The spaceships were circling in for the kill.

Big Jerry said something in the way of thanks, something Brit could barely hear and couldn't hope to understand. Her senses, painfully sharp only moments ago, were soft and dull now as the dunes they'd passed outside Yuma.

But she did see Mikey take notice of the girl, yes, she did see that, and she saw the girl looking back.

Brit's scalp shrank three sizes. She practically shoved Mikey out the door before he could protest.

They passed two boys waiting sullenly outside next to a surfboard that probably outweighed the both of them. It didn't take much for Brit to connect the surfers with the girl inside - the taller boy straightened when he saw Mikey, ropey muscles of his abdomen and arms tensing; the sense of some private territory illegally crossed was palpable; a dark and ugly cloud.

Chapter 3

The first night was tough. When the smell of mold didn't threaten to suffocate him, the noxious mixture of Comet cleanser and Mister Clean came close. Twice he woke, choking.

To make it worse – it was way too quiet here. In Phoenix, he'd hear birds, or people talking, at least the occasional car winding its way up Camelback Mountain. It was like something sucked sound right out of this place. Maybe it was the sand piled up in every nook and cranny, or the dumpy hills surrounding them. It was dead here. Sometimes he thought he heard the ocean, but the sound was so slight, so far away, he was pretty sure that was only wishful thinking.

When a sharp "bark!" finally broke the still air he sat up fast and switched on the lamp next to his bed.

The lamp was an old cast iron thing that came with the house. The switch looked like the handle of a skeleton key. Michael and his mom had found a whole ring of keys like it in a kitchen drawer. Most didn't seem to open anything in particular, others seemed to open everything.

His room, like everything else in the bungalow, was small. Enough space for a twin bed, the lamp, a small roll-top desk with a folding chair, and a closet with a frilly crystal door-knob he'd get rid of one day. Several of the skeleton keys fit that door too.

After dinner he'd covered the room's scarce wall space with familiar things. Mostly black and white panels from *Famous Monsters of Filmland* magazine, but also a big poster of Rat Fink, whose bulbous, bloodshot eyes still made Mom flinch when she saw it. His record player sat in the closet on a stacked set of *Encyclopedia Britannica*. The power cord barely stretched to the plug over the baseboard. He was sure he'd be tripping over that cord all the time – but so would any *real* monsters that happened to wander in...

His bedroom window was just above his pillow. He switched off the light and looked for the moon. There were stars, and lots of moonlight, but the big silver ball itself was nowhere in sight. A sand dune leaned halfway up the wall to his window. That was a mixed blessing. It meant monsters could climb in pretty easy, but it also meant he could crawl out and escape if they came in through his door and that was pretty cool. If he leaned out and stretched a bit he could see the rusted-out truck in the next lot. Beyond the other three ratty houses on the block, and on the other side of the ravine, was the high hill with all the *nice* houses.

The girl from the market probably lived in one of those. Some of them still had lights on. He wondered if she was awake too.

She had a pretty name that sounded sort of Indian: *Wah – hee – nee.*

He'd already thought about her a lot that night. She was the first girl he'd seen in California. In Phoenix, you'd hear about California girls. All the songs and stuff. California Girls were supposed to be pretty wild. He supposed that meant they'd let you touch them. What would it be like touching her? How would that feel? Soft, like a mess of flower petals probably. She would feel pretty good, he was sure of that.

His brother, Nicky, would have been up all night painting her. Nicky could paint anything or anyone he wanted to - as an artist, he was amazing.

What he mostly painted though, were monsters.

Michael put Nicky away, swapped him out with something else.

Swapping was a trick he'd taught himself. He had a problem with being angry, and mostly that came from being scared. He'd known that *way* before the stupid doctor told his mom. When something scared him bad, he didn't tend to run away like other kids did. When something scared him bad enough he just got *mad at it*. But he couldn't even get mad the way other kids did, the way you were *supposed to*.

People talked about getting "hot under the collar" when someone got mad. On the playground, when kids fought, or someone got too rough in sports, adults would say, "Cool it before someone gets hurt!" or "Simmer down!"

Heat supposedly went with anger like milk went with cookies.

But not with him. When Michael got mad it was more like thunderclouds forming, like the air around him had braced for a sudden rain. And when it got really bad, if he couldn't stop it, that ice water feeling ran headlong through his veins. They called some things "cold blooded" and maybe that's what he was when he got angry. The only thing he knew for sure was w*hen that feeling happened, bad things came with it.*

Gramps had taught him a way to stop it.

"The toy makes the game doesn't it? Different toys are made for different games."

Michael hadn't seen him, had no idea he'd been followed, and now he was too frightened to care, too shattered to even think.

"Michael!"

Michael could feel his grandfather's strong hands on his shoulders, could feel himself being shaken. But he couldn't face his Grandfather.

Couldn't take his eyes off of -

"Michael – look at me!" Slowly, he did.

There was no anger in Gramps' eyes. No blame.

"You play catch with a ball, you play soldier with a gun. Different toy, different game. That's the way it is, isn't it."

"Uh, huh."

"Life is like that. You don't like the game – you just swap out the toy – before you know it, you're playing a different game."

He eased Michael's fingers open, dabbed away the blood with his kerchief and, without so much as a grimace, wrapped the awful thing he'd found there in it.

Gramps placed a baseball in Michael's hand and closed his fingers over it.

"You just forget the game you were playing, the one that made you angry, and go find your friends. Play a little catch, okay? From now on, you don't like the game, you swap out the toy, play a new game. You understand what I'm saying, don't you Michael?"

He did. And little by little, he'd found a way to stop it – before the numbing cold slipped into his veins and ran headlong through his heart, he imagined himself grabbing whatever that scary thing was, he'd put it away like a bad toy, and swap it out with a good one. But he had to do it fast.

Now he took the girl, Wah Hee Knee, out of that toy box in his head and closed the lid on Nicky. Like that, Nicky was gone.

A sigh he barely heard left him as he pondered the houses on the hill again. Maybe she didn't even live here – maybe she was only vacationing with her folks or something.

He didn't like that thought much.

The dog barked again, and Michael remembered why he was up in the first place. Just one hoarse bark and that was it, but it made his hair stand on end. Dogs didn't usually bark once and stop, did they?

The sound was odd too. It had a wet, metallic ring to it – like the springy echo of a shout inside a tunnel, or against a rocky cliff wall.

But there was no tunnel or mountain outside to echo off of. Sounds died quickly out there.

Out there the moonlight transformed the sand into a wide river of mercury, and the vines strangling the rusted truck flexed and twisted like the tentacles of some radiation-mutated monster.

There was no dog.

Michael plopped back onto his pillow and closed his eyes. He brought the girl out again.

She had pretty eyes. And her skin was brown everywhere except at the edge of her bathing suit. It was almost white there. A secret place not even the sun saw very often. There was something at once thrilling and embarrassing about that.

The house creaked. Michael sat up again, but didn't turn on the light.

A dirty, scraping sound. Something was moving inside the house.

Mom would be out cold. She had headaches sometimes, real bad ones. The pills she took for them were strong. If anything happened, if someone broke in, she wouldn't even know it.

"Mom?" The sound barely crept out of him.

The mold smell had fought its way back to the forefront, and right now that was okay. Right now it smelled better than the cleaning stuff.

Sometimes Michael would smell things that weren't there, like the smell of a copper penny you've held in your palm for a long time, and he'd get pictures in his head he didn't want. *Bad toys he couldn't put away.*

His bedroom door opened to a jumble of dark, unfamiliar shapes.

He had to get up, had to get out, warn his mom, *but he couldn't move.* When he tried, he saw mutated monsters with long black arms and wide leafy hands, he lay stiff and still as a corpse.

Monsters unfurled mutated tentacles toward him over the mildewed carpet.

"Mom?" a croak swallowed by darkness the moment it left his throat. From out there — a series of snorts and grunts — not dog sounds this time — more like the sounds a bull would make,, snout down, hooves planted and ready to charge —

Michael summoned all the strength and courage he had, willed himself up, raised himself over the window ledge and looked out again.

Nothing out there but sand and vines.

The animal sounds weren't coming from his open window.

They weren't coming from *out there* at all.

He slid down beneath his covers, drew himself into a tight ball, only allowing one small tent of space, enough for one eye to peer into the shadows down the hall.

Deathly silence. Nothing.

His breath stopped cold when a pale oval appeared in the darkness. It hovered there in the center of the hallway, then floated slowly toward him through the inky blackness. He drew his covers tighter, felt them catch and tear at the tiny hairs along his neck.

The pale oval became his mom's face, she was just coming to check on him, to let him know everything was okay and there were no monsters in La Vista. He let out the breath it seemed he'd held forever.

And watched her move blindly past his door, shuffling out of sight toward the bathroom.

Pipes groaned in the walls, the splash of water in the basin followed moments behind. The medicine cabinet snapped, then whined open. The rasp of pills shaken from a bottle, clattering onto porcelain and then scattering over linoleum.

At least those sounds were familiar.

Mom. Just Mom.

Relief gave way to sleep.

-=.=-=-=-

In the morning sun, the vines next door weren't nearly so monstrous.

Just the same, Michael took out his Sonic Blaster with its over-sized, black barrel. He pumped it twice, arming it with deadly compressed air, and slipped out his bedroom window. Feet firmly on the sand, he reached back inside and placed his sentries – two green army riflemen – on his pillow, their sights in crossfire. He placed two more on the windowsill. If anything happened to him, his men would protect his room.

Two hops and he was at the base of the hill, but what he saw there nearly brought the night horrors back.

Round tracks in the sand.

If they'd come from a dog – it must have been a really big one, but the sand was soft, and he couldn't make out any toe marks. Hooves?

Last night, he'd thought he heard a dog at first, but the sound had changed. Later on whatever it was had snorted and grunted like a bull.

Bulldog, he thought. Not the pet kind; a real bull-dog. A *half-half.*

He kicked off his shoes and made his own footprints. The sand filled in around them. When it came right down to it, his tracks didn't look much different from the others; hooves, paws, feet, it was all the same. In this sand, anything could have made them. And they could have been here awhile, probably had been. The house had been empty for months. Every neighborhood kid had probably tramped around to take a peek inside at one time or other. Michael sure would have.

He swapped the bulldog in his head for another monster – the one he'd set out to attack in the first place. Bare-footed, feeling the cool grains of sand squish between his toes, he stalked the dreaded *vine-monster* – the many-armed Dark Lord of the vacant lot.

Michael crouched, his left hand cradling the Blaster's sonic chamber (the part Mom called a toilet plunger, much to his chagrin), his trigger finger securely in place. He carried the gun with its business end pointed up and away from his body and his men, the way Sergeant Saunders from the WWII TV series *Combat* would have carried it, (that is, if Sergeant Saunders would have had something as neat-o as a *Sonic Blaster* to blow Nazis away with).

Engagement with the vine-monster would follow strict *Combat* rules.

In *Combat*, when the platoon moved forward, one man would sprint forward to cover, then stop-and-drop. When all was clear, he'd wave the next commando on. A lot of times it would be Frenchy taking the point, sometimes Little John. Today, it was Michael.

The mission was a dangerous one. Michael guessed the vine monster's head was deep in the middle of the rusted-out truck's cab where it was probably still slurping meat off the driver's bones. Somehow, he'd have to sneak close enough for a kill shot without detection. The best cover would be right up next to the left fender. That would mean a naked sprint all the way to the truck. From there, he could reach through the shattered windshield hole and blast away.

A wave of his hand signaled to the unseen allies in his bombed-out bedroom, that he was ready to roll and needed cover. He counted silently, *three...two...ONE!* And took off, sprinting full tilt toward the enemy.

The sprint part didn't go well. Running through sand was a little like running through marshmallow crème. He had to throw himself headlong to get anywhere at all, and by the time he got close enough to try it – he ended up blowing the "stop-and-drop" part completely. His feet stopped okay, but the rest of him slammed right into the truck carcass. A big chunk of flaky rust cracked off and powdered at his feet in an orange dirt-slide that billowed up and made him sneeze.

So much for surprise.

The vine-monster uncoiled several of its deadly green hands through the empty windshield and Michael stepped back, Sonic Blaster ready.

"You're not so tough in the daylight!" He barked.

A huge leaf curled back to reveal not a weapon but a dewy flower that looked like a big orange star. The peace offering didn't fool Michael. *The beast was deadly.*

A quick squeeze of the trigger and his *Blaster* let loose a mutated-monster-plant-smashing sonic boom! Of course, the actual sound was more like a loud "poop." A few moments later the flower shuddered from a near lethal hammer-strike of compressed air. It coughed out a shell-shocked honeybee. The bee buzzed and twirled, crashed headlong into a leaf that must have been two feet wide, and plopped to the sand. It woozily crawled for cover inside a rusted can.

Michael blew invisible sonic smoke from the barrel.

"Hey, kid! Don't kill the pumpkins!"

Michael spun toward the shout, shocked and embarrassed. You always looked funny when you made-believe on your own. Worse yet, it was *a girl's voice – they NEVER understood make-believe combat. Even worse than that – it wasn't just any girl.*

Wha Hee Knee's hair had been pulled neatly back into a ponytail today; she wore Levi cut-offs with white thread beards all round, and a short-sleeve Madras shirt - the kind where the checks bled together when you washed them. He couldn't see her eyes through her dark Wayfarers, but it was definitely Wha Hee Knee circling out in the middle of the road on silver Schwinn Sting-Ray.

He caught what she'd actually said a second later.

"Pumpkins?"

She planted a bare foot in the sand, curled the other around the kickstand and snapped it down.

Cool. She'd be staying awhile.

"Sure. Big Jerry threw pumpkin seeds out here back in the fifties.

Now they just keep coming up every year."

"It's his field?"

"It's sort of everybody's."

Before he knew it, she was standing beside him. Michael nearly passed out. She slid her shades up onto her crown. Those hazel eyes were nearly gold now and looking straight through his, and they were so pretty he couldn't really look right back into them. Michael had a crazy image of Gort, the robot in *The Day the Earth Stood Still*, death ray pulsing beneath its visor, gathering enough strength to zap and melt the Army tanks. It wasn't exactly like Wah Hee Knee was scary or anything, at least not the way Gort was scary, but that's what Michael thought of.

"Take a look," she said.

She stepped past him, trailing the sunny scents of Coppertone and Johnson's Baby Shampoo, and as he followed her into the heart of the dreaded vine-monster (which was looking less and less like a monster all the time now), he felt an excitement building inside that was every bit as powerful and scary as Gort's ray.

She moved the leaves aside, and the sweet, earthy aroma of Halloween Jack-O-Lanterns rose up from the plants, mingling with the suntan lotion and shampoo. Halloween was his favorite time in the world. Suddenly it wasn't sand beneath his feet, he was floating on clouds. Just yesterday he'd seen her for the first time. Today he was exploring a new world with her, *her* world – all this and the smell of Halloween too -

Something stung his bare legs, breaking the spell.

"Ow!"

"Watch it. Pumpkin vines have got some mean needles."

He nodded, and thought quickly of a tougher parallel. "Where I come from, there's cactus all over." He hoped that would make him seem less like a wuss for squealing when the vine poked him. But all she said was that he shouldn't step on the pumpkin vines anyway, "'cause it's really bad luck."

She swept back a group of leaves with a sun-bronzed forearm and, lo and behold - the biggest pumpkin Michael had seen in all his life lay at their feet.

"Wow!" He was genuinely impressed. "But it's green."

"Now it is. It won't be forever. Most of 'em start out like that. But some start out snot-yellow."

"There's different kinds?"

"Oh yeah. Even white ones. Those are Luminas; Big Jerry knows all the names."

Suddenly pumpkins peeped from every shadow and hollow. He hadn't even noticed them before; now that he knew what to look for, he saw them everywhere amongst the leaves. *The whole field was filled with them.* Some were oblong, big and green as watermelons, but some looked like big yellow light bulbs.

Michael was awed. Not much but cactus grew in the one-hundred-twenty degree "dry heat" summers of Phoenix. The idea you could actually grow your own pumpkins hadn't even occurred to him. They just sort of magically appeared at the Bayless Grocery Store every fall just in time for carving.

"Don't kids try to break 'em open or anything?" Something akin to horror in her eyes.

"Why would they?"

The horror seemed to fade to disappointment, and Michael wished hard for a *take-back.*

He shook his head, made the fatal mistake of trying to explain himself. "I mean. B-because they're there." He stuttered. "You know? Right out there in the open."

She just stared at him and Michael swallowed. He wasn't making much of an impression. At least not the one he wanted, and more than it ever had before, making a good impression was suddenly important to Michael.

Instead, he was getting a stab of cold, gold-hazel eye that nearly cut him clean in half.

"But *you* wouldn't break one, would you?"

Michael wanted to crawl into a hole – or swear never to do that or anything else she didn't want him to do, never *ever*. He hadn't wanted to hurt the pumpkins. It had just seemed *someone* might want to do, like on a dare or something, or just out of meanness. There was always a bully or two in every school he'd gone to.

He wanted to tell her all that, but his tongue suddenly wasn't moving so well – the last thing he wanted to do was stutter again. He said nothing. When he thought back on it later, he figured maybe that was exactly the right thing to do.

The sunglasses (Gort's visor) slid back down in place; no light pulsed from them; death ray stowed for now.

She laughed.

"Yeah, course they do. Breaking 'em open's the whole point!" To prove it, she popped one with a single stomp that spurted seeds and green guts two feet past him. "Usually we wait until they're really ripe. We always leave some for Halloween though. Go ahead and do one."

He chose a whitish one and flattened it with his heel – a gush of yellow green paste plopped satisfyingly into the sand. But not without a price – apparently the vines weren't the only parts with "mean needles."

"Cool!" He said, forcing a smile even though he knew he'd be picking fuzzy spines out of his heel the second she was out of sight. And squashing them wasn't nearly as easy with bare feet as she made it look. He could feel the bruise spreading.

"I'm Sandy," she said, which confused him.

He almost said "Mikey," in reply, but got "Michael" out just in time.

"That guy, Big Jerry called you something else." Sandy considered that; she laughed.

"Wahini?"

"Yeah."

"That's Hawaiian. Means 'pretty surfer-girl.' You just moved out here?"

The house he'd had in Phoenix was big and new. He'd left a swimming pool with a slide, and Camelback Mountain, overlooking the best part of town, had been his backyard. Now his house was the cruddy little shack he'd literally crawled out of moments ago, and for the first time in his life he felt something worse than pain. *He was mortified.* But what could he do? No way he could lie to her.

"Yeah. Just moved over there yesterday." He glanced toward the bungalow and shrugged.

He couldn't see her eyes through the shades, but the rest of her face didn't show disgust. She just mirrored the shrug he'd made but toward her own house; of course, in her case, it was one of the nice houses on the hill, but she didn't look any more impressed with her house than he was with his.

Michael decided right there and then, that Sandy was the coolest girl he'd seen in all his twelve years.

They walked back to her bike without another word.

Sandy glanced toward the niche in the hill with the nice houses. The fog was clearing, and now you could just barely see where the ravine cut down to the bridge, and finally, to the ocean.

"Do you surf?"

Surfing had never even occurred to him. At least *real* surfing. When he was seven they'd driven all the way out to Mission Beach from Phoenix. He and Nicky had these little Styrofoam boards Dad bought for a buck each at Skaggs Drugstore. All you could do was lay down and ride the waves in. Nicky had the great idea of spray-painting them all sorts of cool colors. Unfortunately, the paint ate right through them. They broke in half the first day out. Michael decided not to tell her that.

Miserable, he shook his head, "no."

"I've gotta go." She slipped easily back onto her bike and kicked up the stand. She started downhill and his heart dropped. But halfway to the main road she looked back at him.

"See you, Michael," she said, "Teach you to surf, if you want." His heart leapt right back up, all the way to his throat this time.

Their whole exchange had lasted only three or four minutes, but Michael felt he'd just hit every hill and dip on the biggest roller-coaster he'd ever seen at Mach 5.

Teach you to surf, if you want. Wow!

He watched Sandy coast down the road, and wondered what the heck had just happened to him. He knew one thing; in that short span of time his life had changed.

From here on things were going to be very different.

-=-=-=-=-

Brit's eyes opened to swirling dust motes. Beams of light poured through pinholes in the disintegrating blind.

She was in the bed her mother-in-law had slept in. For a self-defeating moment she entertained the notion that the disagreeable biddy had died in it as well. She hadn't, the final hospital bill had come last February.

Her last resort...

The house felt cold – and empty.

"Mikey?"

Brit tugged one water-stained corner of her blind and it rolled back into itself with a snap that rocked her like a cold slap in the face.

What she saw outside was an even worse shock.

A gasp escaped before her hand could reach her mouth and block it.

Mikey was in the middle of the field next door – and standing close, far too close, was the little tanned hussy from the market.

Only one day and the little tramp had already tracked Mikey down.

Brit shook her head and sighed. They were kids, what did she expect?

Kids had a magnetic attraction to other kids. The girl obviously lived nearby.

It was only natural they'd meet eventually. Still, heat flushed Brit's cheeks, and pulsed in her throat.

But only one day. Why couldn't this have happened a few weeks from now, a few months? Why couldn't they have just a little time on their own?

Time to get used to this place, to sort it all out and start over.

A remembered scent, fetid, cloying and suddenly very strong now, and with it an image of her first son's face. Not the beaming, scrubbed face in Nicky's school photo, *but the broken mask he would forever wear in her memory –*

She clamped the grisly image off, the awful odor gone now. Never there.

She almost called Mikey back to the house right then, nearly became the mirror of her own tyrannical, over-protective mother screaming for her only child to escape back indoors.

Before that scream found wings, the girl from the market climbed onto her bike and pedaled away.

Brit smoothed her hair back behind her ears. Her hands came away wet.

Mikey waved when he saw her at the window. He was holding the big toy gun she was positive she'd thrown away just before the move, the one that blasted eardrum-bursting, compressed air.

God, he's got a toy, Brit. He still plays with toys.

He was still a little boy after all; way too young to care about girls.

She was thinking way too far ahead.

The invisible sandbags fate had hung from her shoulders with Nicky's death, seemed to lighten if only a bit. She actually managed a smile.

Just a boy. A little boy who could grow up as normal as any other.

Brit massaged the blood back into her hands. There were other problems to deal with. More immediate ones. They needed to eat. That was job one. She had some money but it wouldn't last. There were calls to make and doors to knock on. A job was all she needed for now – any job. Later on, once they were secure, she'd find a *good* one. She was educated, she was a good worker, and eventually they'd be in the pink.

You have a good chance here, she told herself. *It's a quiet town, it's safe.* Never mind the past. She and her boy were starting over and everything would be all right.

Later on, she found the catbird.

Chapter 4

Michael didn't see Sandy again for a week.

That was bad because he knew she could find him if she wanted to.

Maybe the shack he lived in had bothered her after all.

Nothing was going right.

The only work Mom could get right away was waiting tables at a diner in town. It was beginning to sink in that all those things like houses and cars and swimming pools and nice neighborhoods came from somewhere. And they didn't come from Mom. They wouldn't be getting a new house any time soon.

He didn't like that thought much, and he put it away as she poured his orange juice and they sat for breakfast.

For the first few days, Mom woke him before the sun and fed him pancakes. Michael's chest ached when he got up early – like his heart didn't want to wake up with him. But he knew the stuff Mom took for her headaches made waking up even harder for her.

She wore a short turquoise dress and a white blouse for work, and tied her hair under a white cap. Michael thought she looked pretty, but she didn't say a lot in the mornings, and what she did say sounded tired and sad; phrases like, "just for now," or "once things open up."

Michael wasn't sure what things would open up. Doors, he guessed.

She was always talking about doors opening for women. He didn't know where those doors were for women, or where they led, and she never explained the statement. She was smart, he knew that, even though she acted tired and slow sometimes. She'd gone to college in Boston and had a degree.

Before she left for the diner she always told him to stay around the house and be careful. The harshest rule of all was that he could never go near the beach without her. He always nodded. He'd be careful, sure, but he couldn't really stay around that house. And there was NO way he could stay away from a beach.

The first couple days, he'd only walked the neighborhood – his eyes always returning to that patch of blue just *beyond* the bridge. But he obeyed, and didn't go to the beach. It wasn't that he couldn't get there safely, or anything. The highway ran over an old concrete bridge that spanned a lot of rancid backwater the ocean didn't seem to want. He saw a marked crosswalk over the bridge, and there was sand bar next to the backwater you could walk if you were too much of a wuss to use a crosswalk.

Mom *had* to figure he'd do it eventually. He'd come to understand the rules parents came up with were sort of a game they played with you – a game Gramps had called, *"Being Ready."* He told Michael some rules didn't have so much to do with right and wrong as they did with *being ready* to break them. Sometimes parents put up a fence just so you'd get strong enough to jump it.

But he wasn't quite ready to make this particular leap. Not yet. Mom had a lot on her mind now. Without totally understanding it, he sensed the desperation in her, knew it was something best not trifled with.

Then there was Sandy. He wanted to see her, and she was at the beach for sure. But all her friends would be there too – and they'd all know how to surf. He knew he'd have to try surfing too, and he'd be probably be a "spaz." So, for a while at least, Michael stuck to the hills east of the highway.

But it didn't take long for him to tire of the sandy paths bordered by the funny flat houses – even though some of those houses were pretty amusing. Windows framing glass mermaids and shells, yards filled with broken down boats and ancient fishing nets. One even had a big, rusty old whale harpoon nailed over the porch. Maybe some people really did fish for a living here – that wasn't such a stretch – but whaling? Michael was pretty sure Moby Dick never swam the waters off La Vista, California.

Eventually his explorations took him to the sand bar below the main road. Next to the beach, that sand bar turned out to be the second coolest place in La Vista.

Once you climbed down there it was all hills and hollows hidden by tall grass and reeds twice his height. There were paths beaten through it here and there that you couldn't see from the road above – some you wouldn't find until you were walking right on top of them. Jagged stumps of charred wood poked from circles of rocks, and here and there empty beer bottles and piles of cigarette butts gave testimony to all sort of *big-kid* conjuring and wild goings on that took place far from the watchful eyes of adults. That made it even more exciting. And everywhere, there was that thrilling, briny essence of the sea.

It hadn't taken long to settle on his first order of business in a place like this. He set about building a secret fort.

Finding a location was easy. He probably wouldn't stumble on every cool hollow or cave if he played out here every day for ten years. He finally settled on a depressed hole in the reeds that was hidden from just about every angle. Toward the back end of the hollow, the reeds and grass opened just enough to make a window looking up at the houses on the hill. He widened that window a bit and spent some time weaving reeds into a sort of shutter for it so monsters and bad people couldn't look in.

The next two days he spent foraging for furniture. He spent an entire morning roll-dragging one big piece of driftwood across the sand for a table. Old paint buckets became chairs. He decorated the reed walls with the best shells he could find and a rusted sign with bullet holes in it that read, Barbasol. A cracked glass insulator he pried off a broken post became the centerpiece of the fort. It was ocean blue with a dead black widow spider stuck inside.

He nearly washed the spider out before deciding it was pretty cool having her in there. When the light hit the insulator just right it cast a blue green shadow full of spindly spider legs. All it needed was a legend to go with it – like *The Sword in the Stone* or something. The story formed quickly – his insulator was his magic crystal, and the spider inside its cold, black heart. He wasn't sure what sort of magic would happen in his fort, but whatever it was, it would be righteous.

The crystal needed something equally cool to sit on, like an altar or maybe one of those big crosses that carried the blessed hosts in church. So he set out into the wetlands beyond the sand bar, crystal in hand, sure the spider's power would protect him from evil spirits – even guide him to what he was looking for – whatever that might turn out to be.

The wetlands were mucky and smelled bad, exactly like a dragon's lair would. He imagined it full of quicksand; maybe even tar like the stuff dinosaurs got stuck in. It was exactly the sort of place to find what he needed.

The wetland wasn't that far from his fort, but getting to it was slow going with all the washes that crisscrossed the sandbar and by the time he got there he had the legend of his crystal and its black heart just about figured out.

The way he saw it, the Black Widow wasn't really a spider at all, at least she didn't start out that way. A long, long time ago she'd been a boy. Michael figured the boy was about eight years old when he came to be a spider – eight hundred in human years, so his soul was very old and wise.

The morning haze had burned off by the time he reached the mucky water. He could hear the surf crashing just past the bridge. Now and then he caught a glimpse of the ocean through the reeds. He saw white sails, an aqua sky framed by the slate-colored arches of the bridge pylons. Against the drabness of the wetlands the ocean looked more beautiful today than anything he could have imagined, like someone had painted a dream. A dream that lived and breathed and moved and had a beauty like no painting ever could.

And that brought him back to his imprisoned spider. Michael decided the little boy had been an artist. He painted very cool and beautiful things. And whatever he painted came to life. So the world became full of amazing animals and bizarre wonders.

A cold breeze rippled the reeds, when it hit him he shivered.

And then he heard something odd.

He stopped walking, his legend of the spider temporarily on hold.

It was a radio playing somewhere, barely audible over the sound of the surf. Michael walked toward the sound. He knew the song it was playing, although he didn't know the name. A pretty song, and sad. The singer wasn't familiar, but he was really good. Then Michael realized something really weird – it was only a voice, no piano or guitar or anything.

Someone was singing right there in the wetlands.

But nobody was that good. At least, nobody who wasn't on records or on the radio.

He slowed down, and tried to be quiet. Anyone who'd come all the way out here to sing probably didn't want anyone to hear, which was weird.

Why wouldn't you want to be heard when you could sing like that?

Something deep inside of Michael felt bad about that. If *he* could sing he'd make sure everybody knew about it. But Michael had no such talents.

He couldn't do anything cool.

The song was about a guy in love with a girl – but the girl was getting married to someone else. It was sort of an old-folks' song and Michael could tell the singer was too young to be marrying anybody – the voice was high and sweet, it could have belonged to either a boy *or* a girl, and there was so much emotion in it. Michael really thought the singer might cry, and he almost wanted to himself.

He moved around a thick knot of reeds and when he saw the kid, he nearly blurted out a laugh.

To say the kid was fat would be like saying the *Corn King Giant* was a wee-bit tall. The kid's eyes were closed, but Michael honestly didn't know if he was doing that on purpose or if it was just that the fat from his forehead and cheeks was pinching them shut. A thin brush of glowing orange hair no Crayola could hope to match jutted from a head that was more a bubble of flesh easily white as cotton balls where it wasn't freckled. His shapeless, striped T-shirt had given up the fight to contain him long ago, you could see where one seam had split awkwardly down the side, barely holding on for dear life, and his worn-out jeans had completely lost their grip on his butt – they hung beneath it like a sack and God only knew what kept them from dropping to the ground.

As the boy soared into the chorus, Michael squinted for a better view of the kid's neck to make sure it really was him singing; the kid's throat puffed and gulped with every word. Hard to believe that amazing voice came from this fat freak.

The fat kid held one last note for an impossibly long time, then went right into *Somewhere Along the Way*. That was an old-folks' song for sure, one off a John Gary album Michael's mom played a lot. Michael liked John Gary, although he'd never say so. Johnny Mathis too. The Beach Boys were the greatest, but Johnny Mathis and John Gary could really sing. This kid was just as good as they were. Maybe even better cause those two always had a whole orchestra backing them up. This kid was singing against pounding surf with no help at all, and he was awesome.

Michael felt bad he'd almost laughed before. He felt even worse thinking the kid was a freak – *but Jesus, he was fat!*

Now Michael wasn't sure what to do. He wanted to keep listening, but he was sort of spying. Not cool. And he was cramping up trying not to move and make noise. He couldn't stand there forever, and once the fat kid got tired of singing, the only path out, barring a plunge into smelly dog water (which was what Michael and his friends had come to call the stagnant pools left when the canals were drained in Phoenix), led right past Michael.

So he did the only thing he could – he backed out fast – and nearly fell over. He'd been standing so long in the muck his shoes had sunk in. He was stuck! One shoe plopped off in the smelly yellow goop. He bent to grab it, and the crystal practically jumped out of his hand. It landed with a sharp *splat!* near his foot.

"Crap!"

"What!?" The fat kid yelled. He blinked fast as if waking from a dream. His eyes popped when he saw Michael and he bolted straight into the ankle deep sludge toward the water without a moment's hesitation, thundering through the reeds like a frightened moose.

No one that size can move that fast! That was Michael's first thought.

"Wait! Kid!" he yelled back. "I'm sorry!"

Both Michael's shoes were gone now. But he managed to scoop up his magic crystal without stopping. He ran after the fat kid, socks pulling up muck, flipping it up the backs of his calves. Then the socks left him too. His feet made *ploopy*, sucking sounds as he ran.

"Hey kid, you sing great!"

Maybe the kid heard, maybe not. But he barreled right into the waist deep bilge like it was a clear mountain stream. No way Michael was going to follow him there. As the boy splashed away, the reeds flattened around him.

Halfway to the concrete bridge pilings the kid dragged himself out; he lumbered up the hill toward the houses with his stark white butt loaves glaring over his sopping jeans. He slowed, gulping breath after breath when he reached the road, but never really stopped and never looked back.

Eventually he trotted behind a group of houses and Michael lost him.

Michael collected his muck-covered shoes and squeaked them on his muddy feet, minus the socks, which he figured for a total loss. In the cloudy water, he rolled most of the mud off his crystal.

His treasure was no worse for the wear despite its tumble - no new scratches or cracks he could see, its eight-legged soul still firmly cemented to the web inside. They say a black widow's web, weight for weight, is stronger than steel cable. Despite his mom's warnings, Michael had yanked on enough to figure that was probably true. He wondered if the spider ever thought she'd be stuck like this when she'd spun it. He supposed if you were going to spin a web, you'd better be careful where you stepped.

He made a few detours on the way back to his secret fort but that was okay. He'd barely explored one small tip of the wetlands yet anyway, and it wasn't like he had to get anywhere soon. There were tons of shells that would have been pretty cool at one point, but now they were pitted and scuffed from being out in the sand and sun so long. He collected a few promising ones, but left a lot where they were. The best shells, of course, would wash up fresh on the beach every morning. A shiny new shell would be another good reason to jump Mom's invisible fence.

Runoff and tides had hollowed out little caves and canyons in the mud and sand, and Michael made a game of tramping hard on them as he ran, just to see if they could hold his weight. Many collapsed as soon as his heels hit, turning his forward progress into a series of mountain goat leaps off crumbling ledges. Before long he was breathing hard, running hard. And just when he figured a boy couldn't have more fun than he was having right now, a huge chunk of the bar gave way and – he found *it!*

It was a treasure that eclipsed the glass insulators – even the spider crystal itself. Sliding down the cascading sand was a set of shark jaws like the ones Big Jerry had.

Michael slid down into the wash and snatched them up. They weren't big, and not in as good shape as those Big Jerry kept inside the market. A few rows of teeth had jumped ship – maybe they were still stuck in a meal that got away - and the sand had done a nasty job pitting those that remained. But to Michael, the jaws were just about perfect – just wide enough to hold the blue insulator. *The magic had begun!*

-=-=-=-=-

That night Michael dreamt of monsters.

Sometimes when he slept Michael knew he was dreaming, but this time he wasn't sure. He remembered going to bed, laying down the *Famous Monsters* magazine, and clicked off the lamp – which always made Rat Fink's bulbous phosphorescent eyes and teeth pop out and glow green for a while.

He imagined his cool dark crystal treasure, snug in its magical shark jaw tabernacle back in his fort. And as he drifted, he thought of the fat kid with the amazing voice and that made him a little sad…

And then he was back home in Phoenix. It was dark but Long John, his parrot, was wide awake, Michael could hear him shuffling back and forth on his perch, heard the hamsters rustling beneath their shredded newspaper nests. Rafael the iguana, lifted his head high, darted his tongue, tasting danger in the air…

Nicky was coming…

Michael wanted to scream, to run, but he could do neither –

And then he wasn't in Phoenix anymore, he was in the wetlands, but now they were shadowy and dark, a darkness that twitched and crawled around him like the impossibly long legs of a spider. He was traveling fast, faster than human legs could ever take him, reeds whipping away, snapping as Michael ripped through them. Wind howled past his ears as he rocketed over the marsh; and carried on that wind he could hear the fat boy's voice so clear and sweet.

When the fat boy saw him, his song choked off, his mouth splitting his moon-wide face in a scream –

-=-=-=-=-

Michael woke to the ringing snort-barks of the *Bull-Dog*, and a feeling of falling!

He caught himself, heart racing.

But he wasn't falling he was lying in bed. It was still dark.

Rat Fink grinned its glowing, veiny-eyed and toothy grin from the wall.

The bark came again. But it was a *real* bark this time, just someone's dog somewhere. He took a deep breath, his heartbeat slowed. *The bark still wasn't quite right.*

His chest ached. When he tried to get up, his arms and legs were numb, lifeless things. Then the tingling came, needles stabbing the cold flesh of his limbs. And even more than the bark, more than the dream – that feeling scared him.

His heartbeat quickened again, beat hard against its bone cage. He was wide-awake now. Because other things came with that feeling. Bad things. In his sleep he might have done...something.

He put that thought away.

He stared at Dracula on his wall, at Frankenstein and Wolfman; fake monsters, movie monsters that went away when the film ended and the curtain closed. Eventually the tingling faded. Eventually fatigue closed Michael's eyes. He didn't dream again that night.

Chapter 5

"We'll go to the beach when I get home, okay?"

"Yay!" Michael jumped, socked the air with his fist, and landed so hard on the linoleum the pots clattered in the kitchen cupboards. It was early, and as usual, getting out of bed had not been easy. But he'd woken to the sweet aroma of cinnamon rolls, and found his mom practically chirping in the kitchen.

Whatever caused the mood change, Michael was ecstatic – finally they were going to the beach!

"You've been good? You haven't been there by yourself?"

He almost said, "Not yet," but stopped himself in time. Michael downed his morning orange juice in one gulp, and nearly choked on the pulp. He felt so good, he almost told her about his fort. But he didn't. A boy's got to have his secrets. And if she saw where he actually had been spending his time her hair would probably stand straight up and she wouldn't let him out of the house at all.

Elsie the Cow smiled from a big daisy on the milk carton. The morning sun was just beginning to slant through the kitchen window, and the whole house smelled of cinnamon and bacon.

Then he heard the *Bull-Dog* bark and the sweet fabric of "home" began to tear away, his pulse raced and the tiny hairs rose on the back of his neck. The sound was echoing, far away, but definitely there. And now it wasn't one quick bark – it was many.

"Don't you hear that?"

Mom turned off the water she'd been running and dried her hands on a towel.

"What, honey?"

It was coming from the stove. Actually from the big iron frame over it – the part that took the smoke out of the kitchen.

"Can't you hear that? Something's in there!"

Mom smiled, "It's just the hood."

The hood over their stove in Phoenix was copper, shiny and spotless. This one looked like it belonged over a fireplace in some old castle or something, coal-black and filthy. Looking up into it, Michael saw years of griddle-fried bacon and dust had turned the inside into a greasy tunnel of soot and fur. The fan in the center was pitted with rust, twisted and evil.

"Yecch," Mom said, inspecting it with him. *"There's* a weekend project."

The barks echoed around their heads. Only now, it didn't sound so much like one huge dog, it was a lot of sounds together: surf and wind, a few dogs barking, birds, even people talking – but the sounds echoed and rang, as if all those sounds were ricocheting off the tile in the world's biggest, wettest shower stall.

"When I was a girl," Mom said, "we had one like this in the house in Albany. The way they're shaped...like a big ear, when you think about it...from the kitchen you heard *everything* on the boulevard. Kids playing. Dogs barking. The hood takes out the smoke – but it takes things in too." So that explained the *Bull-dog's* bark. It wasn't just a bark – it was a bunch of sounds put together. The metal walls of the hood made them echo.

That's all it was.

Or was it?

Michael stretched on tiptoe, leaned in deep, with his small ear cocked up into that huge iron one and *really tried to believe it.* In a way the barking sound matched the one he'd heard at night, but in a way it didn't. At night, the sound had been deeper, scarier. Of course, everything was scarier at night. That's why midnight horror features on TV were so cool.

He had another thought, though, and this one was a little harder to dismiss. The fact was, he slept with his head right next to an open window – the kitchen was all the way at the end of the hall. The "hood" explanation was starting to unravel.

And just like that, there was no sound at all. The hood had gone silent.

Somewhere in whatever world that "big ear" was plugged into, those voices had hushed. Michael stepped back on his heels and looked, quizzically, at his mom.

Out there, that world had stopped to listen to *them.*

Once again, the tiny hairs began to prick up on the back of his neck.

Mom touched her fingertips to the black iron, placed her cheek against the back of her hand. Tiny lines creased her forehead.

"When I was a little girl, I really thought the hood was picking up something else. Something that wasn't there at all. A conversation from another world."

He wanted to tell her *she was right! There was something else out there.* Something you couldn't control, that didn't go away like the monsters in the movie houses did when the lights came on. Not just voices, but something big and scary. But his throat went tight, squeezed the words straight back down him. When he finally began to speak, his mom started laughing, and then he couldn't tell her anymore.

"When I was little, I imagined all sorts of things," she said once her laughing jag had died. "Fairies and sprites – you know, little girl things." Her eyes were sparkling, shiny. She brushed a small tear from the corner of one of them and laughed again.

All Michael could do was nod.

=.=.=.=-

It was nearly four in the afternoon when Mom nudged the Fury onto the narrow shoulder above the beach, but it was still sunny and the air was warm.

Mom wore a two-piece navy blue suit tied at the shoulders with flat strings she called *spaghetti straps*. Michael had his green Baggies on, which he thought were pretty cool, but the new thongs Mom had picked up for him in town were a size too big for his small feet. The rubber piece kept sliding off his big toe, and the soles kicked sand halfway up his calves as he ran excited circles around the Coleman ice-chest Mom had packed. The Coleman was sort of a waste today – it wasn't like she'd packed dinner for a family of four, and they each had a Shasta cream soda wrapped in a towel to drink which was probably enough for the hour of decent sun they still had. It would be a tough balancing act getting the Coleman, their towels, and two fold-up beach chairs between the concrete "boulders" heaped at the side of the road, then across the beach to the water.

On top of that, Michael had brought an old empty Purex Bleach bottle with him. The plastic bottle had a good strong handle that ran all the way up to the top and when he'd cut the spout away he'd built himself a perfect shell basket.

Somehow they managed to lug it all down there without a hitch. The beach was a lot longer and wider than it looked from the highway. There weren't many people on it. Old couples parked under umbrellas, some little kids building castles, a few more racing the surf up and down the sand. A handful of surfers paddled their boards lazily beyond the breakers.

Sandy was nowhere to be seen. He felt disappointed and oddly relieved at the same time.

Smelly nets of brown kelp clumped around the high tide line ejected waves of sand fleas and flies as they stepped over them. The surf was sliding up close to the high mark and Michael realized his shell holder wasn't going to get much use. He'd have to get down here early to find any good ones.

Mom claimed a hill a wave-safe ten yards from the high water stain, unfolded the chairs and laid a towel over each.

"This is really nice," she said.

But Michael was in no mood to sit. He flipped off his thongs and bolted straight for the waves, cream soda in hand. He took a mouthful that tickled his whole face from the inside and went down sweet and cold.

The water was nearly cold as the soda when he hit it. He shivered and let the waves break up to his calves to get used to it, enjoying the feel of sand melting like wet sugar beneath his feet. And then there was something new and odd underfoot. The sand sliding back to the sea had left dozens of tiny sand crabs tickling his feet as they dug furiously back down to safety.

He'd definitely be digging for those soon! But now he just went for it, waded up to his waist straight into a big swell that knocked him, laughing, onto his butt. He managed to keep the can upright and over his head just the same.

That first wave slammed the great new reality home: *He actually lived here! They were not on vacation! He could do this all the time!* And, swimming pool or not, when you're twelve growing up in the middle of the Mojave desert, living by the beach was like going straight to heaven without even dying.

The next wave was high enough to splash his face, and he let out an excited "Whoop!" as it did. His pop was more saltwater than soda now but he didn't even care.

He was dizzy with the tang of salt air, with the sweet ringing the pounding surf left in his ears. He waved at his mom up the beach. She waved back from her chair.

Two girls walked along the beach between them. They interrupted their conversation to look Michael's way, and one of them kept looking. The other, who had really ugly glasses, giggled and pushed her friend forward.

He realized he still had the stupid pop can in his hand. *What a doofus!*

The girl without glasses smiled. She was cute, *but she wasn't Sandy.* Heck, they were both at least a grade younger than he was anyway and totally flat.

A short way down the beach a father dropped a match onto a pile of wood inside a donut-shaped concrete barbecue spit that looked sort of like a Morlock hole from *The Time Machine.* The flames leapt high in a blue, lighter-fluid "whoosh!" Two boys chased each other down to the waves as their mom dug foil-wrapped goodies from a Coleman ice chest exactly like the one Michael's family had. Smoke floated across the beach, carrying the promise of grilled burgers and dogs...and a pain something like hunger twisted deep inside Michael.

But it wasn't hunger, at least not the kind a hamburger would help, and when he looked back up the beach again he couldn't see the family anymore.

The current had taken him south along the beach. And when he got his bearings and found his mom again, she was looking straight out at the water, not at him, just out at the sea; at the red sun beginning to settle into it.

Michael tried to find the family again, without luck. The Morlock hole barbecue pits were spread some fifteen yards or so apart as far as he could see in either direction. But none of them were lit.

The wind against his back had cooled and something deep inside; slipped away like the sand beneath his feet.

Just that fast, the day wasn't fun anymore. The sky was growing dark and hardly anyone else was around.

The waves slapped his calves as he trudged, shivering, toward dry sand and back to his mom.

Despite the blasts of wind blowing in from the sea, and the crashing of the surf only a few yards away now, a zone of calm had settled around her. Mom's hair lifted in the breeze, floated back from her face. Her eyes were half-closed, her skin smooth as glass.

Dark sand and ice next to the cooler; she'd emptied their chest right next to their towels! A small gray feather lifted from the dark stain in the sand and fluttered away in the breeze.

"Mom?"

"It is wonderful isn't it? The ocean..."

The wavy line of the watery horizon had nearly doused the sun, a flat red cloud of steam seemed to stretch across the world. The sunset was something to see all right, awesome, maybe even frightening, but her eyes weren't focused on the sunset.

She was staring only at the water.

"It's always there for you. No matter what."

"Mom. You okay?"

She nodded, but the lines had come back to her brow, taking the calm from her face.

"I've seen the way you look at *them*. The way *they* look at you."

He shook his head. No clue what she meant. Mom lifted her chin toward the two girls, far off, but heading back this way again.

"You're at that age, Mikey. You want to know girls. To touch them."

Heat flushed his face. Now he knew what she meant. She knew exactly what he'd been thinking before, and what he'd been thinking was sort of dirty. Not about these two girls, so much, but definitely about Sandy.

Mom's eyes locked on his and even though he knew he didn't want to hear what was coming next, whatever it might be, there was nothing he could do about it.

"Girls aren't like you are, Mikey. They don't think the way you do."

"Awww...Mom –"

"Be quiet and listen. We don't have much time."

And that was weird. They had as much time on the beach as they wanted from now on. They had nowhere to go tonight but back to the stupid little house.

"You're going to fall in love with their bodies, Mikey – without any idea what's going on in their heads and in their hearts. And when you do that, they'll hurt you. Do you understand that?"

He was shaking his head "no" and he didn't even realize he was doing it until his mom grabbed his wrist so hard he saw stars. The can of cream soda-seawater he was still carrying, dropped from his hand. It rocked, gently gurgling its contents into the sand. *She had never, ever touched him that way before.* He stood completely still. Shocked.

She released his wrist. Small points of pain faded like ghost images from a bright light.

"You dropped your soda, I'm sorry," she said. "Go ahead and get another one."

Michael wasn't thirsty. He wasn't anything now but numb. He just wanted to go home and he told her so.

"Then get *me* one...okay?"

He nodded and even though he didn't want to stay long enough for her to finish a can of soda, popped open the chest.

The foul, sickly sweet stench that burst from it nearly dropped him.

But that wasn't the worst of it. Inside were blood-soaked feathers, small bones strung with wet ribbons of soured meat, he could make out the ragged gray beak of an old seagull, a patch of what might have been fur... And then Michael did fall away, knocking the ice chest completely over. Its putrefying contents spilled to the sand.

"It wasn't my fault!"

His mom whirled him back by the shoulder, that normally cream white face fiery red now, eyes narrow. She yanked his face toward the monstrosity in the sand but he closed his eyes.

"Did he fly too close? Did he call you names? What did he do to you, Michael? Did he hurt you?"

And before Michael could stop himself, before he could even think better of it – he answered her. *Actually answered her.*

"He – he hit me with a shell."

Flashes. Quick bright, like the white-hot blasts of pain when a fist smashes your nose. Between the flashes, the splash of wet meat on his face, the broken shell foaming pink in the sand near the post, the hiss of a frightened cat...the ragged seagull flying away, or trying too, suddenly unable to fly again.

When Michael opened his eyes the fire had drained from Mom's face.

What remained was so pale and lifeless he had to look away.

Her lips trembled, almost fluttered.

"Oh, my god," she said, finally. The words, little more than a breath, barely escaped her lips.

At that moment Michael saw the world of difference that lives between thinking a thing is true, and *knowing* it is. He had no idea how she'd found the gull, or when, but as sure as she must have thought he'd been responsible, she hadn't *really* known until that very second.

And he realized, with numbing horror, *that now she knew a lot of things.*

And if trust and love are things you can see, if they're even so much as shadows, he saw them in his mother's eyes, and then he saw them leave.

When she put her arms around him again, there was a finality to it. She hugged him as if drowning, holding the one thing that remained to her - the stone dragging her inexorably into the abyss, and if Michael could have cried, he would have.

His gut twisted so tight against his lungs he couldn't breathe.

Over her shoulder, he found the family he'd seen before. Dad grilled burgers. Mom busily flopped potato salad onto paper plates for her two rowdy boys.

The image faded and left. There was only sand and seaweed where they'd been.

The family was gone, and it was never coming back.

-=-=-=-=-

As she stared over the splashing arms and legs in her pool, out over the redwood fence and across the valley, Sandy yanked her swimsuit in place, a feat that was becoming ever more difficult these days.

June Gloom was beginning to lift. The sky was still tombstone gray, but the color everywhere else was acid sharp. The bluffs over the ocean were a screaming rust where the steel-blue ice-plant ended. The lawns below flared neon green and the brick school buildings at the far side of town were red as fire engines.

Tom and Pete were getting in their last licks for the day, wrestling each other off the huge inner tube in her pool. Chlorine-laced water sloshed across the pink terrazzo and all the way into the flowerbeds. The filter glugged and hissed.

Hers was one of only three swimming pools in La Vista — and one of those was the big public one on Prospect. With La Vista's mild summers and the Pacific Ocean barely a half-mile down the road, a pool was hardly a necessity in these parts. Her mom had always wanted one though, and Dad was a pushover. And, to tell the truth, it was a great way to get rid of the grit and salt from a day at the beach — even though you were *supposed* to shower in the cabana first.

Her mom wouldn't be pleased with the rough-housing (not to mention all the chlorinated pool water soaking her hydrangeas), but her mom was golfing with the other Sodality women today. She wouldn't be home for a couple hours at least.

"Sandy, come on. Try an' knock me off!" Pete balanced precariously atop the tube. King for the moment.

Sandy didn't waste much thought on that challenge. A second later, Tom's legs scissored Pete's waist, ripping him off the tube easy as kicking a snail off a brick. Pete belly-flopped, his wake surged across the pool deck and slapped the concrete under the sliding windows. Another burst of chlorine filled the air.

"Yay! King again!" Tom howled, fists in the air, ribs flaring beneath the brown dots of his nipples. "Come on, Sandy!"

Sandy scanned the ravine below. There was the backwater and beyond that she could see the tin-roofed box that was Big Jerry's market. A couple blocks up the hill and one over from Big Jerry's a splash of green that was Jerry's pumpkin patch, and just beyond that, Michael's house.

Sandy frowned.

Michael knew she surfed. He knew *exactly* where she'd be every day.

She'd even offered to teach him. The beach was half a mile from his house at most. But days had gone by; Michael never showed up.

"Yeah, *Rocky!* Come on!"

Pete had surfaced again. He wrestled Tom's legs, pulled the tube toward the stairs, and then blasted off the top step straight at Tom's chest. Tom slipped effortlessly to one side and back-slapped Pete straight down the donut hole in the center of the tube. The tube tipped high into the air, dropped back with a loud *p-taang!* slapping another wave across the pool deck. The echo rang in Sandy's ears as the tube spun lazily back toward the deep end, with Tom still perched on top, cheering himself. Now he pushed off with his skinny arms, sat into his knees, and then he was actually standing on it, surfing, really showing off.

Sandy rolled her eyes. Down in the valley, the haze was beginning to burn off. Some hope that the sun might just get all of it before crawling off to sleep for the day.

She looked back at the human mantis perched atop the great floating leaf in her pool. *Someone* had to knock him off his high horse.

Of course, Tom had great balance. He could surf like no one else she knew, but he took a lot of dumb chances too. When he wiped out he really creamed. She scooped a grainy dollop of cocoa butter onto her palm, rubbed the sweet-smelling goop onto her legs. She dabbed more oxide over the pink and perpetually peeling bridge of her nose.

Pete scrambled up one slippery side of the great black inner-tube for all he was worth, but then Tom just flopped spread-eagle across it, and palmed Pete's forehead all the way back underwater until Pete let go. Tom was back up in a flash, rocking back on his knees.

"I am Kurok, Son of Stone! None can defeat me!"

Balled up at the ends of his long arms, Tom's fists looked like eyes bulging from a snail's antennae.

Pete cheered when Sandy stood and tossed her towel back onto the lounge. Pete honked a blast of water and snot out his nose.

"Go get him, Sandwoman!"

Tom jutted his chin at her and grinned.

"Yeah, come and get it, Rocky! Better bring an army!"

She dove, parting the cool water with barely a splash, feeling its cool world fold around her, a world with its own sounds, its own light.

Pete's legs bull-frogged just overhead, his colorful Jams billowing as he fought Tom for position. She saw his thing when he kicked, and it looked like one of those little sausages that came in cans. She almost laughed and choked.

The underside of the tire tube loomed over her, crisscrossed by dancing aquamarine diamonds, a shaft of light raining down through its center broken by Tom's shadow. Sandy stretched her arms, tented her fingers over her head and aimed for the light. Two powerful dolphin kicks and she popped up through the middle.

Tom swung away from Pete to stop her, but not in time. She shoved off from the valve stem and in a flash she was straddling the tube, facing him across the hole.

They leaned in, slapping and splashing, Pete haplessly slipping and sliding at their feet. She and Tom locked arms; the real tug-fest had begun.

It felt good. Sandy's arms and shoulders were strong for a girl; she was proud of that, liked the way it surprised boys - but her real advantage was the balance low in her tummy, her powerful hips, and legs. Tom laughed as they grappled, but his eyes were narrow and focused; he strained, tried to muscle her off the tube with his upper body. *Big mistake.* All she had to do was wrap her legs tight and wait for him to burn out.

Behind Tom, Pete had quit trying to climb up the tube, exhausted he wasn't doing much more than hanging on for dear life now.

Tom's laugh wasn't coming out quite so easily now. More like little stutters of gunfire. Every time he got a good grip on Sandy, the cocoa-butter made him slip. His forehead creased and his breath came hot and loud. The little winded laughs stopped altogether.

He shoved *hard*, harder than a friendly game should dictate, and nearly uprooted her as much from surprise as the power behind it. But Sandy held, and now Sandy realized she was breathing pretty heavy too and she wasn't laughing at all.

Locked in battle, they shifted their weight and pushed, shifted and pulled, neither able to wrest a clear advantage. The harsh smells of rubber and chlorine cut through the sweet ones of cocoa-butter and Coppertone, heady as smelling salts, making everything else sharper, clearer.

Tom's scalp was pink and shiny beneath the blond nubs of his crew cut. A wet "V" of fine white hair accented the ropy muscles of his upper arms. The sky painted bright blue patches that spun behind him, tiny rainbows flashed in the glittering water drops on his neck and shoulders. The tube thumped and rang beneath them. The song, *She's Come Undone*, rang from Tom's transistor on the deck.

Little by little the shoving stopped, the movement stopped. Only hot breath and pressure now.

A grin cracked Tom's face and, slowly, made its way over to Sandy's as well. He was trying to psyche her out, but that was a dead giveaway. He was wearing down, slipping. And right on cue, Tom took the chance Sandy had known all along he would; he shifted his weight to his shoulders again for a better hold, and that was all she wrote.

Sandy threw one knee over the tube, nailed him just under the armpit, and Tom dropped like an empty scarecrow. Water exploded into the space where he'd been. The tube bucked but Sandy caught herself and stayed on.

She thrust her fists into the air the same way Tom had before.

"Yeah! King again!"

Pete pushed off the tube and glided to the diving board. He hung, panting, beneath it. Finally he croaked.

"Hear Ye! Hear Ye! Rocky's king again! *Long live Rocky!*"

She didn't even mind her nickname this time.

"Rocky Rules eternal!" She beamed.

But Tom rocketed up through the big donut hole, water flying. He grabbed Sandy's legs, yanked her roughly down into the water with him in the center of the tube.

"What's the deal?" she laughed hoarsely, shocked and half angry at him.

Tom was grinning. At least his mouth was. But his eyes weren't laughing at all, there was something snarling and fierce behind them. He slid his arms under hers, gripped the valve stem behind her. He pinned her hard against the tube.

She felt gut-punched, breathless.

"Come on, Sandy."

What did he mean? A cold knot twisted inside her. Something was wrong, very wrong. *And now she was scared.*

The world had narrowed around them, screwed itself down to a tight focus that held nothing but the water lapping against the tube, echoing and ringing softly.

Sandy's mind raced through the last series of events. She had been playing with her friends in the pool, with Tom and Pete, her best friends in the world since kindergarten. The sky had gone from gray to blue. There had been some roughhousing. She'd wrestled Tom and won. *And then something happened but she didn't exactly know what that was, and now she was standing on her tiptoes at the edge of a cliff, and to fall off was certain death because she was up very high. Very, very high.*

"What?" She heard herself ask. But that was someone else asking wasn't it? The question had no context and the tiny voice couldn't possibly have been hers.

"You know!"

But she didn't. She had no clue.

One of her best friends in the world since kindergarten was pressed way too tightly against her, hip to hip. Something suddenly uncomfortable there, his skinny legs had become distorted beneath the water. He shoved himself hard against her. And then the realization at once laughable and frightening:

He's going to stick his thing in me!

The slowly turning wheel revealed Pete standing on the steps at the other end of the pool now, his head cocked to on side like the dog on the RCA logo, the one who hears his master's voice on the Victrola.

"Hey..." Pete's voice was uncertain, she saw him look around uneasily.

He's looking for my mom, she thought dully. Because something bad is about to happen...

"Hey...Tom. Come on," Pete said. "Don't..."

"Get out!" Tom shouted over his shoulder.

Pete started toward them down the steps. He stopped, and then the great spinning wheel on the water took him out of her sight.

Pete's on my side. *On my side.* Why doesn't he do something?

Something was thudding, pounding; her heart, she realized. The cold knot in her gut went liquid and loosed a spreading warmth inside her. Water lapped into the gutter. The filter glug-glugged.

Tom's eyes were pointed toward hers, yes, but they weren't *looking* at her. They were looking somewhere far away, far past her. His face came toward her, his lips were open. She turned away and his mouth smacked wetly against her cheek. He pawed her suit top. It slid up and she felt herself pop out. A cold ball began to rise in her belly.

"No," she heard herself say, shaking now, shaking so hard the word barely stumbled out. His hand slid roughly down.

Her scream turned the fabric of a warm summer afternoon to crystal.

It broke roughly, shattered over them all.

Tom blinked. The world had gone suddenly silent. The great rubber wheel lazily turned and she, pinned upon it like a butterfly on display, turned with it, blue shadows on the pool bottom became a jellyfish with a hole in the middle and four long, slender tentacles.

Tom's eyes were wide open now, the fierce animal wasn't behind them anymore. *Gone.*

"Jesus..." he said.

"Get out of here." The voice was calm, not her voice. Not the shriek she had meant it to be.

She covered herself.

"I –" His jaw flapped uselessly.

"Leave!'"

Tom slipped under the tube. He walked up the steps past Pete who hadn't moved an inch since the whole thing started, and grabbed his towel.

Then he turned, angrily.

"You do it with everybody else! Everybody *knows* that!" She blinked, gut-punched once again.

"Get out of my yard!" She screamed.

"I...mean...it's...just that – we –" Tom's voice was suddenly very thin and small.

"I said, get out!"

He did this time – foregoing the gate, leaping to the fence, crashing over the top.

Pete seemed frozen to the pool steps, his mouth gaping stupidly.

"Get out!" she spat. *"Get out! Get out! I never want to see either of you again!"*

It took a second for that to sink in, when it did - Pete leapt from the pool in a gout of water. He slipped and fell, smacking his knees on the terrazzo, leaving blood. He found his feet and raced through the gate like a kicked dog. The gate slapped its post then locked behind him.

His brother's long board leaned against the fence. *Should have dropped it at Pete's house like I said,* she thought. Once again she'd been overruled.

It would be the last time.

Sandy crouched low, she took the board in both hands, threw everything she had into it and heaved. It pivoted atop the fence, turned once then nosed over. She leapt onto the fence, stood on the crossbeam, and watched the board flip, then slide down the bluff with a sound like wet sandpaper on concrete. She wanted it to snap, to explode in a million jagged pieces. It didn't. It just surfed the ice plant until it rolled belly-up, on the side of the cliff, scratched up but maddeningly whole. But there was no way to get to it. It could hang there forever.

They'd have fun explaining that to Pete's brother.

Tom's transistor, still sitting on the deck chair, was playing the Beatles now. It had been a *Hard Day's Night* for somebody. A moment later the radio, and the Beatles, followed the surfboard over the bluff and went silent.

The filter glugged. Sandy's towel lay bunched on the lounge. She wrapped it around herself. The inner tube had floated to a corner in the deep end. She stared at it, alien now, something that might have dropped from the sky.

Her head was floating, floating like that thing on the water.

She'd kissed boys before. *Yes,* she had. But never... What had she done? What?

Goosebumps roiled over her flesh. It wasn't until she saw the gold stream running into the drain on the deck that she realized she was peeing.

Chapter 6

"Come on! Come on, Mikey..."

It had taken forever to drift away that night. He'd wrapped himself deep beneath the covers, down deep in the thick and enveloping darkness, searching for some small space where nothing but sleep could find him – not his mom, not the seagull, not even his thoughts. He wanted to sleep and never wake up, not ever. Especially not here in this ugly shack with its dank, moldy air, in the middle of the night when it was even more creepy. He didn't want to wake up for anything or anybody. *Especially not for Nicky.*

But there Nicky was, floating over Michael's bed; all white-faced and cruel gray eyes.

Nicky stretched a waxy stump of a hand toward him.

"Get up, Mikey, come on...let's go!"

"Okay. Okay."

And then he was gone.

Only shirts and pants hanging in Michael's open closet – scarecrow shadows and nothing more.

Rat Fink winked from across the room.

"Over here, Mikey...come on." Nicky's voice had the hollow, ringing sound of footfalls on wet concrete.

There were few enough places to hide while Nicky was living. Now that he was dead, there was nowhere at all.

So Mikey followed Nicky's voice out of his room and on down the hallway. It was so dark he had to feel his way along the cold, dirty walls until, finally, Nicky stopped in the kitchen.

A silvery line of moonlight shimmered across the tubular steel frame of the kitchen table. Mikey touched it, and the light rose up, a snake of sparks slithered over his fingers.

Nicky sat on the stove now in the dark blue suit he'd worn only twice – once for his Confirmation, and lastly for his funeral. Mikey wanted to turn up all the burners, let the blue and yellow flames torch Nicky like the stupid old scarecrow he was. But it wouldn't do any good. You couldn't burn something from Hell.

The iron hood over the stove, that mysterious ear to the outside world, moaned, then howled with a distant burst of wind. And even as Mikey felt himself shrink away from its coat of sludge and dust, from the evil, slicing fan he knew was spinning inside; he was *drawn* to it, to its promise of another world somewhere far from his own.

The wind keened, the dishtowels his mom had folded so neatly over the oven door flapped.

Nicky's hand beckoned him, tendons popping beneath the translucent flesh, working fingers that weren't there.

"Come on Mikey. I wanna show you something I made!"

Michael couldn't say "no." His lips wouldn't move, and now he could feel the ring of icy pinpricks where a mortician had sewn them shut. His feet slid forward across the kitchen floor on their own, he lunged for the table but his fingers wouldn't close. He flew toward the stove –

– and straight up the greasy black throat of the hood. The wicked fan spun inside, rusted scythes whirling toward his face. He tasted bitter rust, the sourness of several lifetimes of spattered fat and filth. The copper taste of blood as the howling wind sucked him into the blades.

He burst into the still night air.

"You have to see this," Nicky said.

A crow soared past, wide black wings tipped silver-blue with moonlight, and Nicky's voice flew with it.

The night air pressed against Mikey's skin like cool satin as they flew faster over the rooftops.

But it wasn't La Vista passing beneath them; they were flying over Phoenix now. The humps of Camelback Mountain rose ahead, and to the southeast, the sandstone mounds that formed the Papago range and the ancient Hohokam holy place known as *Hole-In-The-Rock.* Shingled rooves, neatly bordered yards and swimming pools; the sleeping valley flowed below them like a wide, slow river. Somewhere, in one of those yards, a dog barked, then howled.

They passed their house on Camelback Mountain, over the wide ranch houses of Arcadia, an older and fairly well to do subdivision. Now he knew exactly where they were going, and there was nothing Mikey could do about it.

The neighborhood opened onto a broad him meadow of grass and stones. Just past the wrought-iron gates of Saint Francis Cemetery. A ragged black horseshoe of mourners stood around the grave. Nick's grave.

Michael fought to twist, to turn away, but his entire body was numb, his limbs useless.

"Not a chance, Mikey." The bird spoke over its wings to him, only now it had no wings, it wasn't even a crow anymore, it was the "cat-bird," a *half-half* creature that couldn't survive and hadn't lived long, and it was barely more than dull, gray bones now, even the fur and most of the feathers were gone. The bones fell from the sky, returned to dust and sank into the grass below.

Nicky's head rested on a pillow of blue satin, his Butch-waxed hair shiny and black against it. The flesh of his face contrasted starkly where it met the wax filler, nearly half his face glowed like a lit candle in the moonlight. So did the one hand they'd repaired, or replaced enough of to fold over his chest.

Nicky was still, absolutely still in his coffin. Mikey prayed he would stay that way, *but even dead, there was no telling what Nicky might do.*

Nicky's voice flew by —

"I want to show you —"

It came from a grackle now. The black bird dropped to the lid of Nicky's coffin, took one quick peck at the shiny brass.

"Get closer. You scared or something? Take a look."

In Michael's head, he screamed, *"NO!"* but the sound never made it up his throat.

"It's like nowhere talking through a stupid bird, but saying anything myself's pretty tough with my lips sewn shut. I hate that - they sew your eyelids too. Did you know that? See, your nerves get all crazy, man. People don't want you grinning and staring when all your friends walk by. Bitchin' right?"

The sutures stood out thickly against his nearly transparent flesh now. Blue shadows of thread creasing his lips, puckering the thin flesh between his eyelashes. They were everywhere on his face, holding it together, dark spider webs of cords thick around as worms. What couldn't be sewn together was filled-in with that hideous, glowing wax...so much wax.

"Yeah, that stupid thing ate just about everything — even my eyes. But I'm giving you yours, Mikey, 'cause I'm making some really cool stuff now.

"Best stuff ever. Look at *this.*"

Nicky's lips twitched, tremored, shredding against the threads that tried to hold them, purplish fluid oozed between them, globs of wax clumping sliding, the thick sutures twisting. And then his voice broke free.

"You made this happen, you little weasel. You made it happen 'cause you're a weak little weenie and you got mad! And I'm not the only one who gets you mad.

"Mom pisses you off too! You know she does."

His lips tore wide open, a grin that ripped all the way from his cheeks to his ears. The dark fluid splashed over the pillow, bled outward onto the satin-lined panels of the box.

The hand they'd hidden at his side, the one with no fingers, rose up, gestured to their mom. But Michael wasn't going to look.

"I did some really nice art, Mikey. Made something just for you."

But Michael couldn't close his eyes, as hard as he fought, he couldn't stop his head from turning. *And he was fighting Nicky as hard as he could.*

Still, in the end Nicky was right. Mikey was too weak, and there was nothing Mikey could do.

"Look at her, Mikey. Take a good look."

Mom stood over them at the edge of the grave. Her black veil gone now. The head she wore wasn't her own, and it wasn't alive; a fiery, puckered line crossed halfway down her throat, where it had been tied in place with black shoestring.

"She's perfect now."

Michael woke in his bedroom in La Vista, his room silver blue with the promise of coming dawn.

His mom's face hovered above him, pale as the moon. Her eyes were closed, a network of thin blue shadows just beneath her transparent skin.

The scream died in his throat. He shut his eyes. When he opened them again it was morning.

-=-=-=-=-

Uggh. Diner stench.

It was an odor two parts sour milk, one part old egg whites and greasy dishwater. And it greeted Brit early today. The sun hadn't even considered rising yet, but she was on the job. An MBA and here she was.

Have skirt, will wait tables.

"Joe?"

The stockroom door wasn't locked. Behind the five-gallon Crisco barrels, a ribbon of light glowed beneath the door of Joe's broom-closet of an office.

"Joe?"

Brit snapped on the storeroom light and pulled the door shut against the fog.

"Come on Joe, you're starting to scare me."

The toilet flushed. Brit's shoulders loosened.

"Brit, that you?"

"One and the same. You're in mighty early."

Water splashed and the pipes groaned behind the door. The endless towel ratcheted and slapped the bathroom wall.

"Thought I'd get the books balanced for once."

Brit pulled her apron off the hook in the kitchen and slipped behind the counter. The apron was a frilly little thing, not practical in any sense, with blue piping and three inches of lace all around. The top strategically ended at the nipple line, where, thankfully the blouse took over.

"I keep offering to do it. It's what I went to college for."

A box on the second shelf held all the ketchup bottles, she hoisted it onto the counter, uncapped the half-empties and stacked them neck-on-neck to fill. Tomato clots oozed and chunked slowly down as the gray morning light began to filter in.

After a seemingly endless silence, the bathroom door clicked open.

She heard Joe shuffling back to his office as she got the coffee brewing.

"'Shaw, the day I let a woman into my books..."

At least he'd used the slightly less abrasive 'shaw' expletive rather than 'piss-shaw.' She had no idea what either word actually meant – something Midwestern, she guessed. Either way it burned a little. Because at the heart of that feigned anti-female sentiment, she was sure there was some very real anti-female sentiment.

Brit shook her head. She could forgive him for now. Jobs weren't dropping off the jacarandas in La Vista and Joe was a decent guy, just paranoid about his books like most guys running a small business – probably embarrassed by how sloppily they'd been kept. Joe was a first generation Italian raised in Hibbing, Minnesota of all places. Fifty going on fifteen. He'd been a navy man in the Pacific, and still kept himself in shape. To Brit, he resembled a silver-haired, Victor Mature.

Brit's toe hit something soft and she shuddered to see two tiny furry legs poking from beneath the counter.

"Congratulations, Joe. Looks like you trapped another one."

A year ago the sight of a dead mouse in a kitchen would have sent her shrieking out the front door.

"I'll take it outside." Joe hollered from his office.

"Never mind, I've got it."

She bent down, not quite able to ignore the recent popping in her knees, and stopped cold halfway down.

It wasn't a mouse. The hindquarters were furry and soft – all mouse, but at the ribcage the fur faded to green scales.

Brit shut her eyes, took a calming breath, and looked again.

It was a mouse all right, with tiny black button eyes – might even have been cute if it weren't a disgusting, disease-carrying rodent; if it's back weren't broken, if a kidney-bean shaped drop of blood weren't leaking from its snout.

God, what had her life become?

Brit lifted the trap like a precious memento, her fingers carefully avoiding the strange fruit dangling from it, as she backed toward the door.

She popped the lock, pulled the door open.

"My God!"

A man stood in the doorway. He was tall and lanky. He was filthy.

The trap clattered to the floor, bending the broken mouse nearly in half.

The man leered. A tobacco-stained, jack-o-lantern grin.

"You okay in there?" Joe appeared from the stockroom, a fountain pen wedged behind his ear.

The man's grin faded when he saw Joe – he looked almost sheepish now.

"Excuse me, ma'am. I smelled your fine coffee."

"We don't open for half an hour."

The man bent toward the trap.

Brit stopped him – wincing from the reeking cloud of body odor and stale cigarettes that billowed from his clothing. A tattoo snaked out beneath his tattered shirtsleeve: three small crosses on a hilltop, The Crucifixion rendered in dull blue ink, drawn as ragged as the clothes he wore.

Now she remembered him – he was one of the men who'd moved them in. He hadn't been with the driver in Phoenix – only here. The driver must have hired him for the day. God, *he lived here.*

He straightened, the tattoo slithered back undercover.

"We don't open for –" she repeated.

"Come back at six-thirty, and we'll fix you up," Joe said.

"I'll do that. Y'all have y'selfs a fine morning."

She watched the fog turn him into a flat gray silhouette and then, thankfully, swallow him whole. Like he'd never been there at all.

How long had he been out there?

Finally, she remembered the trap at her feet, and gingerly retrieved it. The mouse left a crescent of blood the size of a fingernail clip on the yellow tile.

Joe took the trap, emptied its awful treasure into a paper bag.

"Have you seen that man before, Joe?"

Joe shrugged; he folded the bag neatly as if he'd just packed a cold lunch inside, then stepped out the door and drop-kicked it into the trash bin across the parking lot.

"Yay - hay! Field goal!"

Joe shut the door behind him and locked it.

"Drifter. We're a block from the highway. You know how it is. Lotta guys pass through."

"You're sure he doesn't live here?"

"Naw. *That* I'd know. Why? You seen him around?"

"One of the men who moved us in. I think the driver hired him."

Joe grunted. "Day labor."

"He's a creep."

"He's a guy looking for a slug of Java. If they're not downright hobos, we call those folks '*customers.*' Long as they're paying. Seemed friendly enough."

Brit shook her head, "Only when he saw you."

Joe rolled his eyes and for just one second Brit saw her fingers wrapped like baling wire around his throat.

Her eyes must have mirrored her thoughts, because Joe took a sudden, deep breath.

"All right. All right. Maybe I'll make a habit of getting in a little earlier. That be better for you, princess?"

"I'd like that. It's spooky here in the morning. Especially when it's foggy like this."

Joe's tongue probed the inside of his cheek.

"Let's see now...how's this go now? You work for me? Or is it the other way around? I just can't seem to get that straight sometimes." He winked.

"You're a prince, Joe."

The fog outside was steady, but brightening now. A spicy tang in the air from the coffee as Brit switched out the full pot; a pinch of cinnamon kept the bitterness away. The beans Joe used weren't exactly prime, but the coffee was passable, and she took a cup with her as she inventoried the pantry.

The man didn't live in La Vista. Did he pass through often? Was it just chance he came by this particular coffee shop? Joe's wasn't the only place to grab breakfast in town. There was even a *Sambos* on the Interstate.

She didn't like the way he'd looked at her. He'd done time – you didn't buy tattoos like his.

What if Joe hadn't been here?

She worked blood back into her temples with her fingertips. A spot deep in her skull throbbed like a bad tooth. *A migraine was all she needed.*

Brit shut her eyes. No flying saucers. Eventually the pain dissipated. Maybe she *was* just being paranoid. She'd find out more once he came back for breakfast – if he did come back. With Joe there, she wasn't betting on it.

Sure enough, the breakfast rush came and went without him. And by the time the waves of regulars had run her ragged, it was a sunny day and all she could think about was a good, hot bath; that, and the pills in her medicine cabinet.

Chapter 7

The Quest

It was another cool gray morning, the air swirled with tiny grains of water that weren't quite rain. They flew just hard enough to make Michael blink, and they stuck wherever they landed. By the time he arrived at his fort in the badlands, he had a shiny new skin of water.

It didn't feel bad. He liked the idea of a new skin. Michael's pets had included lizards of all sorts, blue-bellies, horn-toads, a chameleon, and of course, Rafael, his iguana. Every now and then their skin would get all dry and crackly. Eventually he'd find an old skin standing on its own empty as an old suit of armor. Mom said that when lizards lost their skin it was called "molting." The first to molt was Joey, the chameleon. When Michael found Joey's empty skin he'd been scared out of his wits. It was eerie, like finding a mummy. But it wasn't just that it looked so weird – he was afraid the lizard had just withered away and died. *Nicky, of course, confirmed that indeed his pet was dead.* But Michael eventually found Joey all glossy and happily alive sporting the coolest shade of green Michael had ever seen.

Shiny and brand new.

There were times Michael imagined himself sliding out of his skin and getting brand new again. Sometimes he wished he really could.

The fort was mostly dry inside even though it smelled wet. In Phoenix, after a rain, the desert sent up a sweet scent of new growth that was like nothing else Michael knew. *This was different too.* In his fort, the smell was a mixture of wet timber and the sea. The way he imagined an old ship would smell. And that was pretty cool.

He began what had become a sort of morning ritual. First, kneeling in front of the grass and driftwood tabernacle he'd built, he reached inside, grasping the shark jaws firmly on each side. He placed his prize possession near the window where the sun made the blue glass blaze.

He asked the black widow inside what they would do that day.

His days in the badlands usually started out with a theme – desert island, treasure hunt, fearless hunter, jungle warfare, or such. He was leaning toward *treasure hunt* today. That usually meant digging for shells and stuff. He'd begun to appreciate shells out here in the badlands – they were old and weathered, sculpted into really bizarre spirals and twists.

He still hadn't been to the beach on his own. There would be new shells there - shiny and complete. He knew that. But since that afternoon with his mother, the invisible fence between himself and the ocean had become a high concrete wall. The beach was the last place he wanted to go.

Things had changed at home. These mornings, he woke to find breakfast waiting, but he wouldn't find his mom, even when he tried extra hard to wake up early. He made sure he was home by three-fifteen in the afternoon when Mom would come back, hair tangled around her hat and smelling of cooking grease. He would show her the best shells and oddities he'd found that day.

She would listen, and sometimes even help sort the shells, but it wasn't quite right between them, and she never talked about the diner or what her day was like. The nights passed with television and books – he'd started reading James Kjelgaard and Jack London – cool stories about dogs that made these incredible journeys - joining up with other dogs to fight wolves and cougars and all sorts of things.

The books his mom read all had the same stuff on the cover; usually a big-bosomed woman in some sort of silly lace dress and a guy that had a lot of muscles but looked pretty queer just the same. The books looked really stupid.

Every day, Michael hoped Sandy would ride by on her bike, but she never did. He wondered if she ever hoped he would go to the beach.

He couldn't help thinking what Mom had said about girls; how you could fall in love with their bodies and how they wanted to hurt you because of that. He didn't think Sandy wanted to hurt him, and he wasn't sure how she *could*. He did think about her body a lot though, and he knew that was bad. The nuns and priests at school said boys went to Hell for thinking that way. But nuns and priests were scary and strange anyway.

He knew his mom didn't like Sandy and that wasn't fair because his mom had never even talked to her.

Michael pushed out the reed and grass shutter he'd made; up in one of those nice houses on the hill, *maybe Sandy was searching the ravine for him.*

That's when he saw the writing on the wall.

Michael knew 'The writing on the wall' wasn't necessarily a bunch of words, it was a *sign* that made sense of things. Sometimes it told you what to do. He'd overheard Mom telling Gramps that Dad walked out when he saw 'the writing on the wall.'

Of course, what he'd really seen was Nicky. And Dad hadn't just *'walked out;'* that was just Mom making the best of it. It was much worse than that.

Michael swapped out that thought - but this was an especially bad one, and it didn't leave quickly. Anyone who might have happened along would have seen a small boy staring blankly across the badlands. What Michael saw was Nicky's casket perched on a brass frame. And over the casket, the image Michael hated more than any other: Dad staring straight at *him,* wide-eyed, horrified...

Michael blinked; back now, the bad thought was gone.

Now he saw what appeared to be a long red finger on the cliff, one that pointed up to at a big pink house with a redwood fence. If that wasn't *'the writing on the wall'*, if that wasn't a sign – than what was? The *finger* was really a surfboard hung up in ice plant. Not only was it odd to have something as valuable as a surfboard just hanging there like that – this wasn't just *any surfboard,* it was exactly like the one he'd seen outside Big Jerry's that day he first saw Sandy.

The sign was clear - the house with the redwood fence was hers. It had to be!

His heart beat so fast and hard he felt it banging against his ribs.

But even if he knew where she lived, what could he do about it? It wasn't like he could walk over there and knock on the front door, was it? There was something just *not right* about doing that. What if Sandy didn't want him to come over? She knew where *he* lived and she never came back after that first day. Then there was all that stuff his mom had said about girls. Fences every way you looked at it. Tall ones.

He sought the tabernacle for guidance. Shiny and blue, its spidery heart threw long-legged shadows, but his magic crystal held no answer to this.

The *crunch* of dead reeds just outside his fort nearly sent him through the roof. Another footstep.

Someone had followed him here.

Michael stood absolutely still, listened.

He'd often found beer cans and fresh chunks of burnt wood near his fort in the morning; the badlands were obviously *the hang* at night. But no one had ever come anywhere near his secret fort during the day. He held his breath and waited. The sound had come from beyond the reed wall that faced the ocean. Through the tall grass there were shadows, nothing else.

Moments crept by without another sound. Had he only imagined footsteps? The surf was a dull drone from here, distant. He heard the rumble of cars as they passed by on the Pacific Coast Highway. Hiding was something he'd become very good at, the key was silence. He didn't hold his breath completely - that would make him pass-out, usually just long enough to jerk and bump something, and that mistake was always enough to be found. Instead, he breathed evenly but deeply, his lips parted, letting the air come in and leave silently. If another sound came – it wouldn't come from him.

The sun broke through the haze and lit-up the fort like a hail of fire.

The silhouette of a huge man painted the wall.

He'd been found!

He screamed; fell backwards over his paint bucket seat, his arms pin wheeling. His own scream was joined by another before his butt hit the sand. He shut up- and the *echo* scream kept going.

The shadow was gone – footfalls heading quickly away – a crash like a falling tree.

"Owww!"

Michael practically flew out the front of his now not-so-secret fort. A few feet away he stopped, relieved and amazed.

The fat kid, the singer, struggled to get the thunderous trunks of his legs under him, two halves of a full white moon hanging over his jeans.

"I – wasn't doin' nothing!" The fat boy gasped.

The full bulk of him stood now– at least a whole head taller than Michael, and easily three times as wide. Pink-rimmed gray eyes blinked away the sun, as he turned half-way toward the road. Ready to run again.

"I didn't know anybody was here –"

"I'm Michael Helm," Michael said, more amused now than anything else. "What grade are you in?"

The boy turned back. Then he wiped the sand and dirt from his hands and onto his shirt, carefully avoiding a spot that looked like a mustard landing site, and gingerly offered a huge paw to shake. His hand was thick, pink and sweaty as the rest of him.

"I'm Bruce Stubik. I'm in sixth grade."

"Wow," Michael said.

Bruce's face turned a brighter shade of pink, and Michael felt bad.

The kid was big enough to be in High School; he probably got that a lot.

"I know. I'm...sort of big." He apologized for Michael's indiscretion.

"What grade are you in?"

"Seventh. But I'm sort of small."

Bruce shook his head as he weighed that information. Michael knew the quick calculation the fat boy was making: small as he was, Michael was older. Even if they got to be friends now, they were in different grades so once school started they probably wouldn't be. That's just how it was. Still, Bruce looked a little less like he had somewhere else to go now.

"You sing really great."

"Oh, geez." The pink was a brilliant rose now.

"I didn't mean to spy or anything. I thought you were a radio. Then I saw you. I mean, I didn't think anyone could sing like that. Except on the radio or records and stuff."

The mounds of flesh in Bruce's cheeks moved uncertainly at first, and then creased into a wide smile. It was almost like watching a big chunk of glacier crack and fall into the sea.

"You think so? *Really?*"

"Yeah. You're *boss*, man."

"Dad says singing's for sis —" Bruce's big thumbs fought their way into his pockets, found insufficient cover there and backed out again. "I usually don't like to sing when people are around."

"I wish I could sing like that. I'd sing for everybody. I can't do anything cool."

"Heck..."

"I've got a secret fort. Want to see it?"

"Sure," Bruce said.

When Bruce pushed his way through the front entrance, instantly widening it, he looked genuinely impressed by what he saw. His butt nearly swallowed a paint-bucket when he sat.

"Wow! Would you look at that?"

"That's my magic crystal." Michael handed over his treasure without hesitation. Bruce took the shark jaws with the careful reverence it deserved, and peered into the crystal's dark heart.

"That's a real black widow spider in there!"

"Yeah, that's sort of its soul. You know, Black Magic."

"Geez, are you into that stuff?"

"No. It's just pretend."

Bruce nodded, and he looked relieved.

"That stuff's scary." He smiled. "If it's pretend it's okay though. Hey, I know where there's a whole bunch of those blue insulator things. I'll show you!"

Michael wasn't sure they could find one any better than this one, especially with the spider inside, but having a whole bunch seemed sort of cool.

So they marched off together into the badlands in search of insulators. It turned out Bruce's house was just two blocks from Michael's; of course, that wasn't a surprise – he'd run that way after Michael scared him and the whole piece of La Vista on this side of the hill wasn't more than a mile wide.

Bruce said he didn't have any brothers or sisters and his mom and dad were even bigger than he was - Michael didn't ask that, Bruce just figured it was something Michael should know up front and told him. Michael told him he'd only just moved here, but Bruce had figured that already.

They hadn't walked far before Bruce had to stop and rest.

"Do you ever go to the beach?" Michael asked.

Bruce took a deep, windy breath.

"Sometimes. But I don't like it too much."

"How come?"

"I dunno." Then he shrugged. "I guess I sorta' stand out. I get sunburned real easy anyway."

"Do you know a surfer girl named Sandy?"

Bruce took another deep breath, but this one wasn't because he needed the air. Clearly, Michael wasn't the only boy who'd noticed her.

Bruce's mouth dropped open and his eyes looked straight into Heaven.

"Oh, *Sandy Raaaandaaaall!*" It took forever for her name to leave his lips. *"She's soooo pretty."*

Michael knew the feeling. Just hearing her name made him see the golden streaks of sun in her hair, conjured up the sweet coco-butter scent of her skin. And, of course, he saw all those magic curves that disappeared into little pink lines just where her swimsuit stopped. He was sure that made him turn a little red.

In a way, he didn't like the idea someone else felt the same way about Sandy that he did. At the same time, talking about Sandy with somebody who actually knew her made him feel closer to her. Anyway, and he guessed it was sort of mean, but Michael had a feeling Sandy didn't think the same way about Bruce as Bruce did about her, so it was okay.

In the end, Michael just nodded.

Bruce's forehead tried to crease. "Her friends are *mean.*"

Bruce didn't offer more about that, and Michael didn't ask. He'd been through a few schools. He'd seen enough fat kids get bossed around and picked on. And he'd *never* seen a kid as fat as Bruce.

"You know, she lives right up there."

Bruce gestured toward the house the surfboard was pointing at and Michael's head went light. He'd read the writing on the wall and he was right! Now he knew for sure where she lived!

"Say, what's that?" Bruce said, squinting at the red finger on the hillside, "Oh, man!"

"I think it's her surfboard."

"Naw, Sandy doesn't even need her own board. Guys always let her use theirs. That's Ray Clupper's board!" Bruce pulled himself up, he almost jumped with glee, but his feet couldn't quite part with the ground. *"Ray's gonna kill Pete!"*

"Who're they?"

"Pete's one of Sandy's friends – Ray's his big brother. I mean really big. *Tall.* Ray's in college." The way he said that made Michael believe this Pete guy was doomed.

They could see the surfboard clearly from here, but now Michael saw it the way he had that first time – standing outside Big Jerry's. It was red with a thin blue stripe down the middle. There were two boys standing next to it when he and his Mom came out – now he knew one of them was named

Pete. One of them was sort of tall, but he couldn't have been much older than the other one – definitely not in college.

"How do you think it got there?" Michael asked.

"I dunno. Pete sure wouldn't have done it – not on purpose." Bruce's hands found his hips under a big roll of gut.

Suddenly, Michael had a great idea. At least, it seemed like a great one at the time.

"Let's rescue it! We can give it to Sandy."

"Oh, geez. I dunno."

Michael was immediately blessed with a fantastic image of Sandy meeting them at her door. They'd hold out their prize and she'd be so excited they'd saved one of her friends from certain death she'd kiss Michael right on the lips. He'd never kissed a girl; he imagined the taste of strawberries and the weightless feeling you sometimes get flying too high on the swing-set. He had to admit, he wasn't thinking too much about how she'd thank Bruce.

In fact, he was so wrapped up in that first kiss, he almost didn't catch that Bruce didn't even like the idea. *That was inconceivable.*

"It's sort of on a cliff," Bruce waffled. "How will we even get to it?" Michael considered that.

There it was - his shiny key to Sandy's heart. All tied up in ratty-looking ice plant high on a cliff.

"Heck, I don't know. It got there somehow. I mean, we should be able to get there the same way." The reasoning maybe made sense, and maybe it didn't, but whatever happened, he'd be that much closer to Sandy when they got to that board.

Bruce lit up suddenly.

"Say..."

Michael was sure Bruce had just figured the perfect way to snatch the board off the cliff. Instead, Bruce pointed back down the gully beside them.

"You know, the insulators are right down here. A whole telephone pole full of 'em."

Michael had forgotten all about the stupid insulators, he had a much grander quest now.

"We'll get those later. Somebody else is gonna grab the board if we don't get it first."

Bruce's hand dropped to his side, defeated. He glanced longingly back toward the wetlands – where he'd no doubt been headed to sing before he stumbled onto Michael's secret fort. Clearly, there was a decision to be made. Bruce could go back and sing alone, or maybe make a real friend. His shoulders lifted in resignation as he looked back at the surfboard on the hillside.

"All right," Bruce sighed. "But it's sort of a hike. We'll need fort' fication."

Bruce forced a couple wide fingers into his back pocket. He withdrew two crumpled Pixie Stix and handed one to Michael. They tore the straws and dumped the crystals over their tongues, reveling in the tasty burn as the sweet foam filled their mouths.

Michael stabbed the straw into the air, and Bruce immediately followed with his. The shadows over the badlands revealed their broken straws as mighty swords crossed over the heads of two great warriors.

"Both for one and one for both!" they pledged, although through the fizzing foam on their tongues it sounded more like, "Bo-fo-un-an-un-fo-bo!"

-=-=-=-=-

"Geez. I dunno."

Their trek had given them time to think it through at least a little bit. The hillside across the ravine wasn't that far away if you were a bird. But on legs, they had to cut inland quite a ways to get around what Michael had come to call *the wetlands* (Bruce said the little bay was really just called "the backwater," but he liked the sound of "the wetlands" now that he heard it).

There were deep gullies along the way, and they'd lost sight of the board every now and then. Still, the closer they got, the steeper the cliff looked. By the time they actually stood on the packed earth beneath the surfboard, their quest to retrieve it looked pretty dangerous.

The board's fin was stuck maybe three quarters of the way down the side of the cliff. That still put the tail a good twenty feet above them.

The ice plant shackling it ended in a twisted gray mat several feet over their heads, and holding the ice plant was the ugliest, most unstable looking soil Michael had ever seen – a thin crust of sandy, yellow, seashell-encrusted nastiness just waiting for a reason to crack off and fall.

Camelback Mountain back in Phoenix was mostly sandstone. Even *that* stuff crumbled in your hands and every kid in town knew you weren't supposed to climb it. That rarely stopped anyone from trying though. Some made it, but most were rescued halfway up. Just about every spring someone wouldn't be so lucky. There were half a dozen white crosses along the trail near its base to prove it.

Michael didn't even have to kick off a chunk of the hillside to know it was worse than the sandstone of Camelback Mountain, but he did anyway.

It powdered like a dirt clod.

Bruce found an old stump and sat.

"Well. We tried," he puffed, "I guess Sandy would be happy someone at least tried. I mean, you know – if you were to tell her that, or something." Michael felt spent, deflated. His new friend's resolve had failed.

Far above them, the still-shiny part of the board flamed in the sun, which was almost directly overhead now. Hi over the board, the top pickets of Sandy's redwood fence towered like the gates of Heaven.

Michael was inspired all over again.

"You know that *Jason and the Argonauts* movie?" He said.

"The one where they sword-fight skeletons? Sure, I *love* that movie."

"Jason had to grab some furry thing with *Golden Fleas* off the side of a hill to win the princess."

"Yeah..." Bruce said, uncertainly.

"Well, things never looked too good for Jason. 'Specially when he had to fight that dragon-dog thing with all the heads."

"No...*that* was bad. I thought he was a goner."

"But Jason got 'em. *He got the Fleas!*"

"Yeah..." He could see Bruce was with him now, "Yeah, he sure did."

"Well. This is kind of the same thing, I think."

Bruce nodded, but then he shook his head.

"But that was a movie."

"Yeah." But Michael wasn't listening, now he was deep in another movie, one he remembered where a sailor climbed up a cargo net and there were all sorts of sharks underneath him. Now that Michael thought of it, the dead ice plant looked like a cargo net.

"Hey, give me a boost up to the ice-plant!" Bruce squinted up at the flimsy overhang.

"Oh, man. It's too high."

"No, I think I can make it. Is that stuff strong?"

"Geez. Not very. And there's all sorts of squirrels and rats and things living in it."

That didn't faze Michael in the least, he was on a roll. He hopped onto the stump right next to Bruce.

"I can do it! Let me get on your shoulders."

"I don't think I can carry you."

"Only has to be for a second. Just get me close."

Bruce moved himself off the stump and, with a groan, bent down as low as he could.

"Well...okay. But I think you're gonna kill yourself. So don't blame me, okay?"

Michael got one leg over Bruce's shoulder, then the other. He settled on and found his balance.

"Okay."

Bruce rose up, staggered forward, adjusted, and then they were moving slowly forward again. Each step thundered. Michael thought about *Jason and the Argonauts* again, this time it was the scene where the Colossus waded through the ocean.

The ice plant cargo net was within his reach.

"Alright. Just a little closer."

Michael stretched his arms high up into the ice plant, burying his fingers deep into the knotted roots for a good hold. It was gritty, cold, and wet and sort of gross, but he gripped tighter and pulled, testing it. Bruce was huffing, shifting his weight to hold him, it was now or never. Michael put more weight onto the ice plant and began to draw himself up.

"Okay, let go."

"You sure?"

"Yeah, leggo."

"Okay."

There was a moment, right when Bruce stooped to back away, that Michael wasn't sure at all. For a split second he felt more like a condemned man right when the gallows door drops away – weightless and ready for that final *snap!* His legs swung hard against the packed earth and broken seashells. His scraped knees stung enough to made his eyes water, but he saw the top of Sandy's fence through the blur, and he put that sting away. *And then he was climbing.*

He climbed the way lizards do – flat to the wall, bending sideways hand and foot by hand and foot. The living ice plant snapped slime over his face and chest, the dead stuff and broken seashells scraped the living Jesus out of his skin.

Far above, the surfboard still pointed straight to Heaven.

It was tough work. Tougher than he'd imagined in his *Jason and the Golden Fleas* scenario. He liked climbing trees and ropes and things, but this was very different. The drier part of the ice plant was strong, but not *rope* strong. He had to make sure there was enough of it under his knees and elbows at all times, otherwise it stretched and snapped - and it was a long way down to the path now. His hands were plastered over with ice plant juice and sand; the further up he went, the harder it was to hold on.

And he was tired now. *Dead tired.* He dug his feet under the roots, found something solid and rested. It seemed like he'd been climbing forever, but when He looked up, the surfboard was still a long way off.

"Are you okay?" He heard Bruce ask.

"Yeah," He said, but it wasn't very convincing even to him.

He took a deep breath, and started again. His knees and calves were really raw now, a constant sting. His shirt was soaked through with pea green slime and mud.

But he was making headway. The board was in bad shape, he could see that now – deep gouges the entire length of it. His original jubilation tempered now, he really started to wonder how and why the board happened to be where it was. Up ahead was Sandy's fence without a gate or anything on this side – not that there should be, you could break your neck out here.

He tried not to think too hard about that last part.

Below the fence-with-no-gate, was a surfboard Sandy probably used a lot, a board that belonged to her friend's brother. Obviously it had been in her backyard before it found its way down here. Maybe it *hadn't* come to this end by mistake. Maybe she wanted it to stay exactly where it was. What then?

That thought stream broke when something snapped through the ice plant near his elbow. Suddenly his present situation was numbingly clear – hanging high above the hard-packed path, on a cliff that was completely unstable. Something Bruce had said finally sank in:

There's all sorts of squirrels and rats and things living in it.

The crackling began again, and Michael pulled his hand away, but quickly grabbed another handhold when he felt himself slip.

Then Bruce said something else, *"Oh no!"* and Michael's heart stopped cold.

Michael slowly turned his head, terrified to find the creature Bruce must have seen – the one that was about to have his arm for lunch. *It had to be big for Bruce to see it from down there.*

But Michael couldn't see anything moving near his elbow or anywhere else in the ice plant.

"Michael! I – uh. *We've gotta go!*"

"What!?"

He pushed back from the hillside enough to turn his head around.

Now he saw what Bruce saw: two kids running toward them along the path.

They were the guys he'd seen outside Big Jerry's. Sandy's friends had come for the board.

"Hey! Hey, kid! What're you doing?"

Far below, Bruce bounced in place on his toes, ready to run. Even from here Michael could see the fear in Bruce's eyes.

And now Michael saw just how far he'd actually climbed. The path below him was a mile away, maybe ten miles. *Suddenly, that path rushed straight toward his face.*

Then it backed off.

Michael's stomach seemed to fill with helium, his head quickly followed. He turned back to the ice plant, pressed himself to the cliff and closed his eyes until the feeling passed.

Bruce's plodding footfalls tore away down the path. The voices of the other boys, their footfalls, were closing in fast.

"Yeah, you better run, fat-face!"

"Touch that board and you're dead, you little freak!"

He couldn't stay where he was much longer. The plants under his elbows were making telltale *"pops,"* ready to give way. Michael shifted slowly, carefully to a new spot. If he moved too fast, the net of dead plants would rip away; he'd drop to the path and break every bone in his body.

The two boys circled below him like vultures.

"Climb down here you little creep!"

"But how are *we* gonna get it? Let's make *him* do it – he's up there!"

"Pete, you doofus, he's trying to steal it!"

"If it wasn't for you, it wouldn't even be there!" Pete whined.

That odd crackling sound rose up again and went silent, exactly as it had before. Now Michael realized what it was – it wasn't any rat – it was *static*. He stretched into the ice-plant beside him and yanked out a smashed-up transistor radio. It came to life long enough for a DJ to announce *The Turtles*, and then went silent forever.

"My radio! She threw my radio off the cliff!"

She threw his radio off the cliff?

If it wasn't for you, it wouldn't even be there?

Finally, it was clear. Not only was he scared to death – *he was an idiot!* He'd risked life and limb trying to rescue this stupid surfboard off a cliff for Sandy, and Sandy had thrown it there in the first place!

Something whipped through the air, struck the hillside and glanced off. He sucked himself tight to the cliff. The rock took forever to slap the ground below. *Now, he was terrified.* He was up too high, too tired to dodge the rocks, and there was nowhere to go but down.

Michael closed his eyes. He opened his mouth, took in silent breaths, and hid in his own darkness, waiting for the end to come. It was a place he'd been many times before.

"Here I come, Mikey…ready or not, Mikey…"

"Knock his head off – that'll get him down!"

Another rock slapped the hillside, this one stuck, buried itself beneath the ice-plant inches from his shoulder. Then another, *even closer.*

Thwack!

Thwack!

Mikey shivered in his shell of darkness. It was a thin shell, only a hiding place not a fortress and Mikey knew it. But it wasn't rocks he feared.

It wasn't even the height anymore. In his world the boys were already gone and so was the cliff. He was back in the basement now, back in the cupboard. A hiding place that wouldn't stand up to the Louisville Slugger in Nicky's hands.

Thwack!

"Ready or not...Mikey..."

Nicky knew that too. And worst of all – Nicky knew exactly where Michael was hiding. He always knew.

The basement floor was concrete. Michael could hear every footstep Nicky took. Overhead and all around, shifting uneasily in their cages, Mikey's pets heard them too. And every time Nicky swung the bat – *Thwack!*

The door flew open. Blinding light –

A rock bounced off his right shoulder. The pain shot through his neck a moment later.

"Got him!"

"Yeah! What a shot! Woo! Woo!"

Any other kid would have dropped to the ground, any other kid would have let go. And, in a way, Mikey had let go.

The air grew still and cold around him. Beneath his fingernails, a throbbing, then icy pinpricks ran up his fingers through the back of his hands. A grey lizard made its way through the ice plant forest, slithered over his hand unconcerned. High overhead, a seagull flapped its wings twice and soared toward the beach.

Michael turned enough to face his tormentors, oblivious now to the missiles they flung. Two boys. He saw them very clearly now. One tall and skinny with butch-waxed nubs of hair, the other small with a pinched face, and a galaxy of freckles. It seemed their faces were inches from his own, now and in their eyes he saw nothing but thin layers of soil, water, and air.

Things that could be twisted and molded, reordered, or simply dispersed.

He saw kids formed very much like himself, but a moment from now *he wouldn't see kids at all.* He would see torn flaps of pink skin, and yellow fat, he would see pink muscle and blue-gray nubs of bone – because the heat of fear and anger had left him, and now his blood ran cold, and when Mikey ran cold, *bad things happened.*

A whisper, then a blast of frigid wind, so cold and strong that Mikey felt himself lift, felt the hair pull back from his face. But the boys didn't feel any wind, or see its effect - no one ever felt the cold Mikey did until it was too late. And just when he was sure they were goners.

"Michael, leave it there!"

And for the first time ever...it all came to a stop!

His fingers tingled with warm blood, his chest ached. The cold had moved somehow; shrunk back into the shadows.

Sandy leaned out over her fence and relief rained down on Michael like a summer cloudburst.

The jerks on the path couldn't know how lucky they were.

"Hi, Sandy," He said, sheepishly.

"You know him?" One of her "friends" said from below.

Pete said, "He's that kid from Big Jerry's, remember?"

"I thought it was your board." Michael said to Sandy. That wasn't exactly true, but it was a lot simpler to explain. His arms were starting to fall asleep; he shifted his weight, pushed away from the cliff just a little. As soon as he did, his perch began to slide out from under him. He pulled himself close again, head spinning.

"Michael!"

He took another deep breath.

"Tip it over so it slides down here!" One of the kids said.

"Don't you dare!" Sandy said.

"If he doesn't we're gonna beat the holy shit out of him! *He's gotta come down sometime!*"

Sandy's face went so red, even from his perch it looked like the next thing he'd see would be steam coming from her ears. Then, just like that, the red disappeared, she looked calm.

"Michael, can you do that without falling? Flip it over?"

Michael squinted underneath the board. The fin had actually ripped up most of the plants around it. He had no idea what bizarre physics held it there in the first place.

"I think so."

She let out a breath even he could hear from where he was.

"Okay, go ahead."

He pushed himself up a couple more feet, reached out and touched it.

It was the first time he'd touched a real surfboard. It was waxy and strange.

A feeling of wonder and awe came over him. He imagined himself "*sittin' on top of the world*" like in the Beach Boys song, catching a wave and riding it right on into the shore with Sandy right next to him.

"Come on, numb-nuts. Do it!"

Now, he *really* hated these guys.

Michael slid a hand underneath the board and scrunched himself to one side. In the end, one shove was all it took. The board slid down three feet stopped and pivoted, it leaned out with the majesty of an Olympic platform diver. Then it heeled over and took off straight down like a wayward rocket.

Pete and the other kid stumbled two ill-advised steps right into its path, arms outstretched as if they actually expected to catch it. At the last second, self-preservation kicked in and they flopped to one side. It was a good thing too, because the board soared right through the space where their heads had been.

Its nose whacked the stump he'd used to climb onto Bruce's shoulders, and then split right down the middle with an angry screech. The splinters pin-wheeled into the gully below.

Pete went white. The other kid's mouth formed a large and perfect "O."

Sandy laughed – a belch of a *"guffaw"* that took Michael by surprise.

That made him start to laugh too – but then he started to slip so he shut up.

"Doofus! You cretin! You broke it! You broke Ray's board!"

"He did what you wanted, Tom," Sandy called down, *"You're the idiot!"*

Pete bounced in place the way Bruce had when the other kids had first appeared but his movement was even more frenetic and crazy – like a gazillion volts were running through him.

"What am I gonna do! What am I gonna do! *What am I gonna do!"*

Tom was livid, but more controlled. He bent suddenly, scooped up a rock and threw it so fast his arm was a blur.

A sprig of ice plant popped into the air not five inches from Michael's nose. He buried his face into his shoulder; sure the next one would kill him.

He popped his head up again when he heard a loud *"smack!"* and a scream that sounded like a girl's.

But it hadn't come from the one girl anywhere around them.

Down on the path, Tom was doubled over in pain, he clutched his right elbow. Tears streamed down his cheeks – enough to dot the path beneath him. The rock that got him was still spinning in the dirt.

"You fucking broke my arm!"

"Good! Now I'm gonna fucking break your skull!"

A shower of poolside landscaping pebbles filled the sky, whizzed over Michael's head. From that height, the sound they made hitting the ground was like machine-gun fire. The sound they made hitting Pete and Tom's flesh and bone made Michael's teeth rattle.

Bruce's face had joined Sandy's over the fence. His face was so flushed, Michael could barely tell where Bruce's scalp stopped and his red hair began. But he was smiling broadly.

Sandy held a small hill of bright blue stones in both hands. She didn't need to throw more rocks, Pete and Tom were already crying and hightailing it back down the path, but she tossed them anyway for good measure.

Michael pressed his head to the hillside, and waited for the last missile to thud to earth.

"W-wow!" Bruce said, staring at Sandy with unabashed awe.

Michael felt a warm flash of jealousy at that. It passed quickly. He had more urgent problems. His arms and legs were shaking now. Over his shoulder the ground loomed up again, his stomach rose into his throat.

"Can you get down?" Sandy said.

"No. I don't think I can."

"Face the wall and keep your head down."

He had no problem with that. He was practically kissing ice plant roots. But he couldn't hold on much longer. His arms and legs were killing him now.

Go ahead, let go…

He imagined himself slipping away. Releasing, and drifting down. His fall would be slow and strangely silent. The sky and the hillside would pull away. There would be a sharp stab of pain, *then darkness.*

Do it, you little weenie.

He heard Sandy say, "Help me with this." Then, "Michael, hold on. We're gonna drop a rope."

Do it. You're too tired to climb a stupid rope.

Michael shut his eyes. Nicky's voice was only in his head. It wasn't really Nicky. Nicky was gone, gone forever.

Something slid over the nearby sand, pushed through the growth beside him – the rope.

Michael opened his eyes to find it. The coiled rope was still in their hands, something *else* was moving toward him, shivering the ice plant in small bursts.

…all sorts of squirrels and rats and…things living in it…

The rope whacked Sandy's fence then thumped onto the cliff above him. Wet chunks of ice plant the size of French fries rained down the back of his neck.

"Try to grab it!"

He couldn't look up there, couldn't look away from the ice plant that seemed to crawl toward him. The earth moved slowly upward beneath it.

Sand sifted away at the edges.

"Michael!"

The rope snaked down five feet to his left, a thick hemp rope knotted at every yard. Sandy surprised and amazed him once again. She probably climbed up and down this cliff all the time – he wondered if her parents had any idea, and his respect for Sandy went up ten more notches.

The ground beneath him shifted up, a long, rectangular mound, and he quit thinking about Sandy.

He couldn't work his way to the rope. *He couldn't move at all.*

You're weak, Mikey. Just let go. It'll be easy. Easier for Mom, too.

Sandy scrambled over the side of the fence.

"Stay put!"

The mound pushed its way through the ice plant, the last grains of sand slipped away and then Nicky grinned up at him, his face muddy and blue, liquid oozed from his torn lips. Loops of broken thread waved like insect antennae from the corners of his eyes and mouth, Michael shoved himself back. His footholds gave. The hillside rushed away a*nd he closed his eyes for the last time.*

Nicky was right. He was too scared, too weak. He was falling to his death, and maybe the end would hurt... *but maybe it wouldn't.*

"Got you!"

A sun-sweet envelope of Coppertone and softness wrapped him in a sense of pleasure he couldn't even begin to describe. Michael's eyes opened on an angel crowned with sun rays.

-=-=-=-=-

The rest of that day was a blur, like a great dream that fades a little more every time you try to bring it back, but still makes you feel good. Michael did remember a sting of Bactine that Sandy's mom sprayed on his arms and legs. There was the super-sweet buzz of orange Tang sipped through straws as they dangled their feet in Sandy's pool.

One thing was very clear: from the moment Sandy threw that first stone, something had changed for all of them.

Chapter 8

The rest of that summer they hung together like Musketeers. Little by little the fort changed. First, the paint-buckets and driftwood seats disappeared and they dragged real chairs all the way from her parents' cabana. Soon after that, flowers began appearing, stuck right into the walls, or in pickle jars.

One day Sandy brought in a funny little clay pot, and plunked it down next to Michael's magic crystal. She pulled five long twiggy things out of her beach bag and poked them in.

"Sparklers!" Bruce said.

"These are *way* better than sparklers," she said, proudly.

Michael had no idea what they were. They really did look like sparklers – thin red sticks with a thicker, sparkly skin about three-quarters of the way up. When Sandy produced one of her dad's cigarette lighters and lit them, Michael and Bruce both stepped back.

But nothing happened – at least in the way of sparks. Each stick had one tiny tongue of flame at the top – but that was it, and then the flames died too.

"They must be duds," Bruce offered.

Thin gray ribbons of smoke twisted into the air.

"You smell something funny?" Bruce's nose looked like it was trying to tap dance across his face.

"It's *incense!*" Sandy said, "*Strawberry Fields*. Like the song."

The air grew super sweet and thick. To Michael, it was kind of like dumping red Kool-Aid powder into a dry pitcher and taking a deep breath, his eyes watered. At first, the three of them just stood there, breathing it in and then –

At once, Bruce and Michael ripped through the door, literally ripped through because it wasn't nearly wide enough for the both of them. Michael coughed but he was okay.

"My –" Bruce wheezed. "My – *asthma...*"

Bruce choked and wheezed and wheezed again, his red freckles popped out like fire ants against skin that had taken on a pale green hue.

Bruce fought something out of one of his pockets. A small silver pipe dropped to the sand, and Bruce flopped onto it, pulled it to his face and nearly swallowed it whole. He took a deep, reedy breath.

"Are you okay?"

He sat in the sand and nodded, then sort of crumpled slowly onto his back. Bruce looked like a hippo shot with one of those drugged rifle-darts on Wild Kingdom.

"Yeah...will be...in a minute." Little by little, the green faded and pink filled back in around his freckles.

Finally, Sandy emerged from the fort. She dropped the still smoking *sticks-of-death* on the ground and kicked sand over them with her bare feet.

She coughed once too.

"I guess one would've been enough," she said.

"Guess so."

The fort never did quit smelling like strawberries.

They met mostly at Sandy's house after that – sometimes Big Jerry's. Whenever a new movie came to The Cove Theater, they'd drop three quarters to see it, and then head back to Sandy's to swim.

Sandy's house was *boss,* even though their pool did make Michael miss his own pool back in Phoenix, but the Randall's cabana was the coolest.

The cabana was huge, and full of all sorts of furniture that had once resided in the Randall house itself – but only for a year or two. There were chairs made from inflatable plastic, or molded plywood, eve completely chrome ones. There was a ball light on a chrome stalk that stretched from one side of the recreation room to the other. Best of all there was a Ping-Pong table, and a big, mahogany console color TV with a record player.

Sandy's mom was great. She had shiny chestnut hair that was sort of "poofed-out" on top. She used a lot of make-up, bright pink lipstick, and blue eye-shadow that made her eyes look like they stretched halfway to her ears – that sort of made her look like a cat, but a really pretty one. To Michael that figured, you couldn't be *Sandy's* mom and *not* be pretty.

They never did go to Bruce's house and they hardly spent any time at all at Michael's – and then only when his mom was home.

The truth of it was, even though his mom was fine with Bruce, she always seemed to get one of her headaches when Sandy was around, or she'd get some notion that the room they were in had to be cleaned right that second, and they were all just in the way.

Then one afternoon, they came in to find three of Nicky's paintings had appeared in the den.

To Michael, it was like a fist right in the gut.

"Where did your mom get these?" Sandy exclaimed.

"Whaaaow!" Bruce said.

They were fantasy pictures. Dark forests peopled by winged deer-like creatures with long, graceful necks. The deer-birds peered from the shadows at flying owls with the bodies of lions, and huge dogs who were really bulls from the shoulders up, and bears with long, scaly crocodile heads; creatures Nicky called, *'Half-halfs'* – even though some of them had three or four different animal parts at least. One weird combination after another weird combination, each creature stranger than the last.

Things from other worlds; whatever worlds were trapped in Nicky's twisted brain. The weirdest thing was, as strange as the creatures were, every one of them seemed perfectly natural and alive in his paintings.

Sandy said the paintings were beautiful and should be in a museum or a studio somewhere. Bruce looked at them with the same sort of awe he normally reserved for Sandy.

But Michael knew Nicky and they didn't. And as great as those paintings were he couldn't look at them without seeing the artist. And he couldn't see Nicky and not feel ice sliding down his backbone.

For the first time in years, he actually stuttered.

"M-movies g-gonna start."

Sandy looked at him queerly, but let the stutter go without comment.

But that didn't make Michael feel any better. Had she really let that go, or just filed it away for later to hurt him like Mom said she would? Bruce had noticed the stutter all right – but he took his lead from Sandy, the way he always did, and kept his mouth shut.

A cold ball of nausea rose in Michael's throat. The day had been so great up to now– the way it always was when Sandy was around. Now he was in the Bizzarro world and nothing was right.

He had his mom to blame for that – for *all* of this. For filling his head with lies about girls, and for putting these stupid paintings up.

Anger rose; he took a quick step toward the front door that was more a reflex to hold himself in than anything else.

"Hey, hold your horses," Sandy said, "the box office doesn't even open for half an hour."

To his horror, she leaned in close to the paintings. Her fingers moved up to touch one, and he had to stop himself from ripping her hand away.

"They'd weird out my dad – but my mom would go *ape* over these!"

She stepped back to take all three paintings in, and Michael swallowed hard.

She wasn't going to let him off the hook.

"Come on – where did she get them?"

"My brother painted them. Nicky. But he's dead now."

Sandy and Bruce looked uncertain, not sure if they should be laughing at some sort of bad joke, or giving condolences.

All Michael could say was, "He died. It was an accident," he said way too quickly. Small furrows over Sandy's eyes now.

"I'm sorry," she said. "He was *so* good."

"A car crash?" Bruce offered.

Michael didn't want this. Didn't want any of it. Better if his friends didn't know he'd even had a brother.

His mom had gone so far out of her way to do this. She knew he'd be coming back to the house with Sandy and Bruce today, and she'd actually left work to do this – none of these were up this morning at breakfast.

He envisioned her yanking the paintings out of the attic, a stupid grin on her face, giggling as she tore his grandmother's old flower paintings off the wall and replaced them with Nicky's monstrosities.

This was exactly what she wanted. She wanted his friends to ask about Nicky. To ask what happened to him.

It was all going according to her plan.

His mom didn't want him to have a girlfriend; he knew that – now she didn't want him to have friends at all. The rage flared hot and white; a match head the size of the moon inches from his heart.

"He fell off a mountain. We used to live on one. *He fell.*"

He didn't know how he got that out, but it did come out. And he didn't care that it was a lie.

Sandy nodded, satisfied.

But Bruce needed more details.

"Did he break open his skull?"

"Bruce." Sandy only had to say his name and Bruce shut like a clam. Later they rode their bikes into town pretty much in silence.

At least Michael hardly said a thing, and if Sandy and Bruce were talking he didn't hear them. *Planet of the Apes* had just opened at The Cove. Word had spread like wildfire that the ape-people looked absolutely real. They'd been excited at the prospect as only kids can be. Any other day, they'd be hauling butt, racing their bikes to the theater, jabbering like wild monkeys all the way.

But now all Michael could think about was his mom, *and Nicky, and those stupid scary paintings.* He was still angry. But deep down below all of that, he was frightened.

This changed everything.

Sandy was watching him, her head slightly cocked. He didn't know how long she'd been looking his way.

"What?"

She shook her head, "Nothing."

Bruce was banking crazily in front of them, over-stretched jeans in a fierce battle with the tiny seat of his Huffy Impala – fighting to keep it from totally disappearing up his butt crack.

Any other time, Michael would have laughed like an idiot at the sight. Not today.

Sandy turned her focus to the road, and so did Michael, but it wasn't long before he felt her eyes on him again. When he looked up, she didn't turn away. She didn't say a word, but he had the weirdest feeling she was talking to him anyway.

She slid her sunglasses up and smiled. And suddenly all Michael saw were hazel-green eyes and pink lips. Something hot that wasn't quite anger stirred in him. It melted every other feeling away like so much wax.

At that moment, he wanted to kiss her so bad it made his heart hurt.

He didn't, of course. Not with Bruce there. But right then he knew that kissing Sandy wasn't beyond the realm of possibility any more.

And despite everything else, he smiled back. One thought ringing clearly now, as startling in its own way as laughter in an empty church:

His mom wasn't his whole world.

Chapter 9

The Bottle-rocket

Planet of the Apes was everything advertised and more. Usually, monster faces didn't move much when the actor growled or talked, so you had to work your imagination quite a bit to really get scared. The ape-men in *Planet of the Apes* were the real deal – you could see every scowl and grimace!

Michael and his friends were swept away – from the first gorilla on horseback, glowering right into the audience, all the way to the shock ending. When the lights came up, all three of them sat there slack-jawed.

Then they sat and watched it again.

It was just as great the second time around.

"Man those apes are *real!*" Michael said.

Bruce nodded, "You can see them sweat. I mean, wow!"

"Let's watch it again!"

"Enough!" Sandy laughed.

"Oh, geez, it's past four!" Bruce said. "My dad will kill me!"

Michael really wanted to watch it again, and the last place he wanted to go now was a house with Nicky's pictures on the wall. But it didn't look like he didn't hold much sway on this one.

"Alright, let's go," he sighed.

"Get your filthy hands off me you damn, dirty apes!" Bruce quoted.

"Did you get *Famous Monsters'* this month?"

"Not yet."

"I bet they have something on the makeup."

"Ugghh, that magazine's creepy." Sandy gave an exaggerated shiver.

Bruce and Michael just sort of looked at each other. No matter how much you liked them, girls were just different.

"Do you think the book's anything like the movie," Bruce wondered aloud as they made their way back through the lobby. Sandy had stopped to talk to her friends, Sue and Amy. They stood with a knot of kids near a big poster.

Michael had met Sue and Amy at The Cove a week before; Sue was tall and skinny with black, frizzy hair. Amy was another white-skinned redhead like Bruce; she was sort of cute though. He nodded when they waved.

A couple guys started to talk to Sandy, and that made Michael a little restless.

"Probably not," he answered finally, suddenly not caring much about *Planet of the Apes.*

"Look, you guys," Sandy said. "There's gonna be a talent show!"

The poster was for *Ed Sullivan's Search for Young Talent* – and that was a *very big deal.* It read they were looking for talented kids, third grade through eighth, and the La Vista school district was sponsoring a contest right here in town. If you won, you'd go up against other winners in California, and the top three would be on TV!

Nobody sang like Bruce. In one day Michael been humiliated and shocked by Nicky's paintings and thought he'd lost Sandy forever – only to find himself closer to her than ever, enjoyed the best movie ever with his best friends, and now – Bruce would be propelled to stardom. It had turned out to be the greatest day of his life.

"They're holding it here at the Cove instead of the auditorium" Sandy said, "– that's really cool!"

"Bruce – you're gonna be a star!"

Sandy gave him a sort of awkward grin, as if Michael had just told a joke she didn't get; one that might have been mean on top of it.

Bruce's eyes were like saucer plates.

"No way," Bruce said.

Michael was floored. It hadn't even occurred to him Bruce wouldn't want to.

"You gotta! Nobody sings like you."

"Bruce sings?" Sandy looked astonished. "You've heard him?"

Sue and Amy gave each other a look; but Michael wasn't sure if that was because they thought it was a joke Bruce might be talented, or because they were shocked Sandy actually hung out with someone like Bruce enough these days to care. He guessed it was a little of all those things.

"Yeah, and he's really good, too," Michael said, more defensively than he wanted to.

"Bruce –" Sandy, said, but he was already hefting it for the street.

"I'm not gonna do it!"

"Bruce, come on!"

But Bruce was on his bike and halfway down the street before Michael and Sandy even made it out of the lobby.

"What's his problem?" Michael asked.

Sandy didn't say anything.

-=.=.=.=.=-

Michael insisted they stop at the magazine rack in Big Jerry's on the way home – and, sure enough, *Famous Monsters of Filmland* magazine had a big article on *Planet of the Apes*. There was a whole thing on monster make-up, going all the way back to Jack Pierce who created the make-up for the Frankenstein monsters. It turned out a guy named Rick Baker had done the makeup on *Planet of the Apes*, and it was some sort of break-through for the industry. He used a new type of latex foam your skin could actually breathe through. How boss was that?

Michael tucked his brand new, but already dog-eared copy of the magazine under his arm. *Famous Monsters* had momentarily replaced all thoughts of Bruce in Michael's head. But even though he had a brand new treasure to read, he hadn't forgotten he was with Sandy. *And, for once, they were alone.*

That feeling of heat came back.

"I wish I could sing." Sandy said. "I wish I had some kind of talent."

That came like people said, "out-of-the-blue," and the last thing he wanted to do right now was bring Bruce back into the moment, but he nodded as they collected their bikes outside of Big Jerry's. He'd often felt that way – like he couldn't do anything cool – but Sandy was perfect. It was weird to think she'd have to wish for anything. She didn't *have* to do anything.

"You gotta hear Bruce – I'm not kidding, he's amazing."

"Doesn't sound like he wants me to."

"Yeah, he does." Michael said. The haze was gone, and the shadow of the bridge was stretched halfway across the badlands. He shook his head. "You can't keep something like that all bottled up. *It'll blow up on you.*"

Sandy frowned, and shook her head.

"You make talent sound like something bad."

"No, it's great. I guess. It's just, if you have something like that, you just have to use it right? I mean you *have* to. If you don't it'll just come out another way, right? It'll..." he shrugged, "blow up." Sandy gave him an odd, sideways glance.

They were just cutting circles in the sand with their tires, not really going anywhere. *Home* was in different directions for both of them; but neither seemed to want to get there very much.

The sun had finally tapped the horizon, and everything in the valley, even the backwater, was tinged red. It was later than Michael had ever been out without his Mom.

Sandy didn't say anything. She watched him, expecting Michael to do or say something else. So he did.

"You ever make a bottle-rocket?"

"No." She laughed, clearly on a different track.

"You fill a Coke bottle halfway up with vinegar. Then you dump a whole bunch of baking soda in, stuff the neck up, and turn it over." She shook her head.

"Well, that soda and vinegar turns into something else – *something that has to get out.* I don't know why. *It just has to.*"

"So it flies away?"

"Yeah – it flies away if that stuff can get through the neck in time. But if it can't – you just better watch out 'cause it blows up – a*nd if you're next to it, it blows you up too. You can't stop it.*"

Now she was looking at him the same way she had this morning - like the world had just stopped and waited, for another word, another action...from *him*...to get it moving again. It made Michael feel strange and oddly numb, but tall somehow; really tall. Like he could stand up on his tiptoes and float right up into the clouds. Or make a fist and crush a mountain.

But then he thought about his mom, and Nicky, and that deflated him.

It occurred to him that he was just about Nicky's age now, and getting close to Nicky's height. And that was weird to think about, because Nicky would always be the same, and in one way or another, he would *always* be with Michael.

"I guess we should go," he said, not wishing to go at all. He knew he was in trouble for being out this late, probably they both were. But going anywhere without Sandy was the last thing he wanted.

"Yeah," she sighed. "Mom's gonna have a cow." She made one more wide lazy circle in the sand with her bike and headed slowly down the road.

"See you, Michael," she said over her shoulder.

He nodded, "See you."

A slow, silent ache throbbed where his heart should have been beating. A terrible feeling that he'd just missed something, something very important.

But just up the hill, his mom would be mad at him for sure. She'd be waiting for him, waiting with a wall full of Nicky's scary paintings.

-=-=-=-=-

Michael pulled all the way around to the side of the house and leaned his bike against the wall. The pumpkin vines had snaked their way uphill over the last few weeks. They were practically in his room now. He moved carefully between them, ever mindful of Sandy's admonition about stepping on them.

He stopped dead in his tracks halfway to the window.

One of the leaves had broken off. It lay flat in the sand, stem crushed, the hollow tip of it glistening wet in the last light of day.

He'd been careful stepping out the window this morning. And if he had broken it then - would the wound still be wet? Wouldn't it have healed by now? He had no idea. Lots of tracks on the hill now – he'd been using his bedroom window as a door half of the summer.

A week ago, he'd seen a big yellow flower with a round bulb beneath it right next right under the sill. Sandy had said flowers like that were pregnant. He parted the leaves over it now. The flower had just about dropped off – just a nub of brown and yellow now, like an old used tissue.

But the bulb had already tripled in size. The baby pumpkin was safe.

Michael poked his head into his room. Two green riflemen still stood on lookout atop his pillow. If anybody had been up here, they hadn't come inside.

He climbed quietly through.

His door was still closed, and even with the open window, the smell of mildew was stronger than ever. He actually wished he had one of Sandy's strawberry sticks with him.

Not a sound from the rest of the house.

He could just read his monster magazine and fall asleep; Mom worked tomorrow, she'd be gone before he woke up. She wouldn't be so mad a day from now.

But his stomach groaned. There was nothing to eat in his room.

Popcorn & Milk Duds had kept it quiet for two showings of *Planet of the Apes* but that was it. Mister Ackerman's *Famous Monsters of Filmland* magazine had eaten the last of his allowance. After that, being alone with Sandy was all he'd needed to keep him going. But now he was on his own.

He slipped his shoes off, found the little key switch on his lamp and settled in to read.

He found the section on Jack Pierce, the makeup artist who created Frankenstein. But he couldn't concentrate even on that. He was *starving*.

And that wasn't the only thing.

Why couldn't he just be with Sandy? Why did he even have to come home anyway? Just because his mom wanted him to?

A stab of pain deep inside that rivaled his hunger: *Mom put those paintings up to drive Sandy away.* That was clear.

And they'd still be there in the den – right next to the kitchen.

His stomach growled again. Michael took a deep breath and slid quietly off his bed.

He didn't want to see the paintings – or his mom. If he was careful and didn't walk into anything on the way to the kitchen he'd be fine. She was probably completely out on her headache pills. He hadn't heard a peep from her.

Maybe she wasn't even here. Maybe she'd never come back from work. Maybe she wouldn't anymore. *Wouldn't it be great if she just went away and never came back?*

That tall feeling returned. The sense of awesome power he'd had when Sandy looked at him that certain way.

Yes. Mom tried to get rid of Sandy with Nicky's paintings. She tried, but it didn't work. Far from it. They'd blown Sandy and Bruce away, especially Sandy. She'd gotten so close to one of them she'd practically crawled inside it. And the way she'd looked at him had been different after that. He could see it. Like he really meant something to her.

But bad thoughts followed good ones, as they always seem to, and this one hammered him:

What if it's really *Nicky* she likes?

It was like someone had shot his head full of Novocain. When he had an image again, it was one of Sandy sitting in the den with his mom. *And his mom was telling Sandy everything...*

And waiting deep down, mixing and gurgling and ready to charge up like a rocket, or explode if it didn't was that thought again: *Wouldn't it be great if she just went away?*

In a moment the rage bubbled up and burst a balloon full of hot acid in his throat. His hands balled up tight. Every cord and fiber in his body twisted then pulled taut.

Michael's fingers tingled. The air cooled and pressed itself around him. The world was still. Just that quickly, he had gone cold.

And he saw his mom the way she'd been at the beach, her hair streaming back on the ocean breeze, her smiling face almost appearing to fly.

The thrumming of a hummingbird's wings in his ears, faint as an echo. And then it cut clean and turned fierce; part howl, part roar; the scream of something that wasn't part of this earth, of something that was never meant to be.

His mom's face began to change...

Nicky sat plain as day in his open window, a gleeful smirk on his lips.

"Yeah, Mikey. Go ahead and do it..."

Michael shut his eyes. The roar faded to a buzz then blipped out.

When he opened his eyes again, Nicky was gone.

The warmth bled back into his fingertips, back into the night. He sat up in his bed, feeling heavy and slow.

He would get rid of Nicky's paintings, of any trace of Nicky, once and for all.

Michael turned the crystal doorknob slowly, the hinge creaked when it popped open, but no sound answered it. A faint smell of rancid food bled into the mildew when he cracked open the door. He'd hauled the garbage out that morning, he was sure of that.

The odor grew worse in the narrow hallway between the bathroom and kitchen.

The bathroom door was partway open, a wedge of sickly, yellow light pooled in the hall.

"Mom?"

The spoiled smell was strong now, tinged with something sharp and medicinal. The bathroom couldn't have been more than five steps down the hall, it took forever to walk that short distance, but once he was close enough to see an open hand laying still as a mannequin on the linoleum, the lead left his feet and he leapt through the door.

"Mom!"

She sat wedged between the shower and the toilet her head cocked against the bowl, a yellow-green comet-trail of vomit painted the wall beneath the sink.

The flesh of her arm was cold when he grabbed her. Her head lolled back and struck the wall. She wasn't breathing.

"Mom! Get up! Please!"

Her hand released an empty pill bottle that clattered across the tile and glanced off the side of the tub.

The ugly yellow light over the mirror flooded the room, flared from the walls, tearing into his eyes until the light was all he could see. The room whirled.

The terrible shriek of Nicky's monstrosities rose up again, ricocheted against the wet walls inside his head.

"I'm sorry, Mom! I'm sorry!"

He slipped, cracked his knees against the floor, slid and fell out the doorway. The hallway was so small it seemed he couldn't get through it without scraping the walls, the floor rolled beneath him as he ran, knocking the phone off the kitchen counter when he reached it. He corralled its pieces between his forearms. Somehow he dialed Sandy's number.

"Randall residence, Sandy speaking."

"M-my mom's hurt!"

"Michael?"

"She fell down – she's not moving!"

"Daddy! It's Michael! His mom's had an accident! She's not moving!"

There was a commotion on the other end of the phone, and then

Doctor Randall's voice, deep and calm.

"Michael, is your mother near you?"

"She's in the bathroom."

"Take the phone with you as far as it will go and get back there."

He scooped it up and ran down the hall. The cord stopped just before the bathroom door. He heard his mom groan, she shifted, the pill-bottle rolled again.

"She moved!"

"Good. Good. Is she bleeding?"

"No!"

"Don't try to move her. I'll be right there.

-=-=-=-=-

Chapter 10

"She's gonna be okay now," Sandy said. "My dad's a really good doctor."

Michael nodded.

Guttural, awful sounds rattled from the hallway. His mom had been lucky, at least that's what Doctor Randall said, she'd already gotten rid of a lot of the bad stuff in her stomach on her own. He'd given her something to get rid of the rest of it, and apparently that was working too. Each terrible spasm sent shivers up and down Michael's spine.

Michael and Sandy sat together on the good sofa in the den. In the worst way, he'd nearly gotten exactly what he'd asked for.

Every light was on, but the bulbs were dingy and yellow and seemed to throw more shadows than light. There wasn't a lamp near the paintings on the far wall. But even in the shadows he could feel Nicky's creatures watching them. Michael couldn't make out their monstrous faces - but he knew they were grinning.

Sandy's mom carried a battered TV tray with two steaming mugs from the kitchen, and sat it down in front of them.

"Here, you two."

"Thanks, Mrs. Randall."

He could tell she'd made the cocoa with water, not milk. It tasted thin and strange, but the sweet liquid warmed him at least, made him feel alive.

Michael's call had caught the Randalls on their way to a party. Sandy's mom wore a tight silk shift the color of seawater at the very tip of a wave. As usual, her cat's eyes were painted with a shadow color that matched her dress, and her false lashes swept them practically to her ears. There was something about her nice clothes and makeup that made the night even worse.

Sandy's dad appeared in the hallway, dabbing sweat from his forehead with a washcloth. He was a tall, gaunt man with white hair, and much older than Sandy's mom. Michael had never met the man before tonight. It occurred to him that as pretty as Mrs. Randall was, it was actually the doctor who bore the blueprint for Sandy's features.

"Can I talk to you back here for a moment, Michael?"

"Sure."

"It'll be okay," Sandy said and he nodded, but all of a sudden Michael couldn't look at her.

His mom's bedroom door was half open. Doctor Randall turned out the light and closed it, but not before Michael caught a brief glimpse of his mom in bed, face pale and dingy as the wall behind her. There was a towel next to her pillow, a wash bucket beside the bed.

Doctor Randall motioned Michael toward his own room. It felt like the last walk of a condemned man.

Doctor Randall followed him in, shut the door behind them.

"Why don't you go ahead and sit down."

He cleared his throat, "She hasn't been able to tell me very much. I've asked her to come in for some tests."

"Tests for what?"

"I'd like to know what causes her headaches. She has bad ones, doesn't she? She takes medicine for them."

"Yes, sir."

"Does she seem...forgetful sometimes? Does she lose track of time?"

"Yes."

"Does she say she smells odd things at times?"

"This house sort of stinks."

He smiled. "The ocean does that. The price we pay for paradise."

Sandy's house never smelled of anything but flowers that Michael could remember.

"Does she ever smell things that aren't there? Fruit? Oranges maybe?"

"I don't know."

"Has anything happened lately? Anything that might have made her very upset?"

Yes, I went cold and nearly killed her.

He shook his head, "no."

"Your mom...well, she made a bad mistake tonight. Even the best people do that sometimes. She mixed some things she shouldn't have.

"She won't go to the hospital, and she may not come to my office – I can't make her do that. Whatever she decides to do, you to take care not to upset her for a while. *Be a good boy.* Can you handle that?"

Michael nodded.

Doctor Randall managed a smile.

"Thought you could."

The tall man clasped his knees and rose, but before he opened the door he gently squeezed Michael's shoulder. It was a small thing, but for just a second Michael saw his own dad standing next to him, *could feel his dad there,* and for a moment Michael was close to tears.

Doctor Randall hesitated at the door. Without knowing it, he echoed the words Michael had been repeating over and over to himself for months.

"It isn't your fault." the doctor said.

But this time, Michael knew he was wrong.

Chapter 11

"It's Mister Romani, from the diner."

Michael had been awake when the phone rang, but he'd barely slept all night. The need to rest, to sleep, was almost like hunger. The phone was all the way in the kitchen. By the time he had dug himself out of his sheets and made it through the doorway, a cough had rattled from Mom's room, her bedsprings creaked. Her first words that morning sounded more like a croak.

"I'll talk to him."

The morning had crawled in yellow and dingy as the night before. The house was still mostly dark and smelled of mildew and vomit. It was a brand new day, and nothing had changed.

The night had been an endless circle of guilt and anger, punctuated with images of his mom, her shoulders propped against the vomit-streaked wall between the toilet and tub, the pill bottle rolling across the dirty floor.

Now he waited by her door with the phone, trying not to get the cord tangled, feeling like no matter where he stood he'd be in the way.

More than anything, he wanted everything to be okay. He was scared, more scared even than he'd been with Nicky. Scared of what he'd done – and scared of exactly what would come out when that door opened.

He wasn't prepared for what did.

Overnight his mom's skin had gone from sickly yellow to gray. Thick pouches had swelled beneath the thin flesh of her face, giving her a lumpy, misshapen look. Her golden hair had straggled into coppery knots. Fire-red eyes burned their fever into him before settling on the phone in his hands.

She knows. She knows I went cold on her.

Her fingers left sweat cooling on his hand, and he shrank from her touch as she took the phone. She disappeared behind her door, leaving a fetid draft of tears and sickness in the air.

In the kitchen, Michael pulled a Rice Krispies box from a Variety Pack, pushed in the perforations and poured in some milk. He liked the packs because you could eat the cereal right out of the little boxes and have a different cereal every day if you wanted; but today they were simply quick and mobile. He didn't want to be stuck in one place when Mom came back out.

So he took his breakfast back to his bedroom, past his mom's muffled explanations to her boss, and awaited damnation. He ate quietly, trying to shrink into the background, become invisible.

Rat Fink grinned from his closet. He couldn't help thinking that Rat Fink's eyes looked a little like Mom's did this morning.

The sun had risen enough now to shine some warmth into his room, and that made him feel a little better. And the open window made him feel like maybe he could get out fast if he had to.

The cereal could have used more sugar. He stared blankly at the door, calculated his chances of getting to the kitchen and back without running into his Mom. It wasn't worth the risk.

Rat Fink grinned at him. And Michael noticed something that shifted the sand of his world even further; Rat Fink's eyes were even more bloodshot than before. But they hadn't changed on their own.

The surface of the poster was mostly shiny. But even from Michael's bed he saw dull patches all over those bulbous eyeballs, faint, oily rings spreading outward from them; *oil paint.* He even knew the color - Grumbacher Red. There was no mistaking it. Shadows of linseed oil had bled out through the paper beneath the pigment.

And it wasn't just on Rat Fink's eyes. Now he saw splotches on the closet door, streaks of a bright crimson, on the carpet – even on his bedspread. *Nicky said that all you had to do was open a tube of oil paint and it was magically everywhere.* It spread like hot butter and took weeks to dry. That's why Nicky had to paint in one small corner of the garage. Mom wouldn't let Nicky paint in the house.

Michael's door cracked open and he nearly threw his cereal.

Incredibly, his mom was dressed for work. Her puffy eyes blinked painfully against the light from his open window.

"We'll talk when I get home," she rasped.

He sat very still as she walked back through the house; waited for the scrape and rattle of the front door slamming shut.

When he knew she was gone, he ripped Rat Fink off his closet door and stuffed him in the trash outside. And then Michael did something he rarely did - he cleaned. Not just picking up toys, or hanging clothes, or wiping up crumbs. He pulled on his Mom's Playtex gloves and scoured the house with Mr. Clean and Comet. He scrubbed the black mold off the closet walls with bleach. He mopped the bathroom and kitchen. And all the while he worked, he thought of nothing but the cleaning, was very careful to see only the gloves on his hand, and the dirt in front of him. He wrung out rags, sponged tiles and watched his hands doing these things as if they were attached to someone else.

The truth was, if he thought of *anything* else he'd eventually make sense of things. He'd understand what happened to his mom last night, and he'd know exactly how his poster came to be painted over. And the truth was more than Michael could bear.

So he kept cleaning, and hours later the house smelled good and the paint he couldn't completely erase was hidden.

Chapter 12

Jumping the Fence

She was blond and buxom. She had a pretty smile, and little teeth that flashed like pearls when she wasn't acting too shy to let them show.

Billy didn't notice how she stuttered a little when she talked, or that she was a little slow in general. He didn't know that her favorite books were the ones with short words and pictures of dads who wore brown hats and suits, who's wives pecked them on the cheek as they tucked a newspaper under their arm each morning, freshly rested, breakfasted, and on their way to some important job the books never did get around to explaining.

There was a lot Billy didn't know about the girl. But what he did know, he kept like a precious treasure. It filled the dream he was having when the boxcar lurched and slowed, telling him to *get the Hell out* of his dream and *get moving.* That pissed him off – the random nature of things when it came to time. So many ill-timed...*interruptions* in his life. So much frustration.

A lot of things pissed Billy off. That was a problem he'd been told he had. He knew the real problem, though, was just timing. Like trains getting into town before a dream got good and wet. Or the way people happened to show up when they shouldn't - even when he'd planned carefully, watched things, and really knew what the situation was...once in a while, the timing of things just got messed up.

Now, as the Santa Fe began its lurching approach to the freight yard, it was time to leave the shelter of his boxcar and get moving again. He rolled the door open a few inches; just enough to slip his lanky frame through it, and the smell of dust and sweat gave way to sweet desert blossoms, and the ocean beyond. He braced himself, timing his jump to the gravel passing quickly beneath him. Moonlight filtering through the fog threw ghostly images of the perils around him. He knew this place well. Tall stands of prickly pear, a few barrel cacti, and that was the worst of it here. Just a matter of pitching out far enough, bend your knees, and keep moving forward; don't get sucked back under the wheels. He'd seen that happen to a hobo riding the line just outside of Tucson. Young kid, first time on the cars. Tried to push off with his hands on the floor and wound up swinging himself under the carriage. Those big iron wheels sucked him right across the track. Barely had time to scream. Hefty kid. Left a trail of himself nearly a mile long. Billy still laughed his ass off about it sometimes.

But seeing that mess had taught him to be careful. Momma always said he was a *learner*. He picked a spot ahead where the cactus hadn't taken over, and then Billy bounced twice, pumped his ropy arms, and leapt.

He hit the bank running, but the force of it swept him down and rolled him into the dirt and gravel. Then he was up, slapping the sand and dust off his pants, and laughing again about the kid in Tucson, and about the way he himself wasn't stupid enough to swing under a train. He hadn't gotten off Scott free as far as the cactus and scrapes went though. He yanked a slimy green paddle of prickly pear off his shoulder and winged it up the bank. It shattered against a tie as the last of the boxcars passed him. The needles stung like a fresh tattoo. Billy pinched two furry patches out of his filthy skin, and flicked them into the sand. A shiny raw hole in his elbow dripped fresh blood.

He dug a crooked match and a mostly crushed Lucky Strike from his shirt pocket, licked the paper sticky enough to hold the tobacco in, and lit up.

It was mostly flat desert here, with a few low hills rolling off to the west. The power poles broke toward those hills half a mile ahead. Yeah, he knew *right* where he was. He'd follow the track until the poles split off, then follow that line straight to the ocean. *Straight to her.*

She'd be different than that buxom little blond girl in Williams, Arizona. That was a long time ago. His first, but he still remembered the details of her very well – especially the ones even her young boyfriend didn't know and never would. He'd learned to be patient, from that one.

He'd had plenty of time rotting in that stinking cell in Florence to figure things out. *He was a learner, after all.*

And today, he knew his timing couldn't be better.

-=-=-=-=-

"What are you doing comin' in? I was gonna drop this by."

She'd actually startled Joe; even through the thick haze of her pain Brit could see that. Here she was, raising her one surviving son on the only job her hard-won degree could get her in La Vista. In no time at all she'd gone from being served at country club socials, to slinging hash and eggs for a crotchety group of regulars six days a week; she'd gone from Phoenix, where summers could be hot as Hell, to actually *being* in Hell.

But hey, her boss cared. It gave her an odd little lift.

And here he was now, stuffing food in a wicker basket lined with a red and white checked tablecloth, her month's pay tucked neatly under one fold. Maybe it was the concrete hat she'd worn since the phone rang this morning – or maybe her brain had finally popped, spluttered, and dropped flat to the floor of her skull the way she'd imagined it would one day, but she felt *tears* forming.

"You're a good man, Joe."

"Hey. Hey, now, what's that for?"

His hand stopped the tears halfway to her chin, before her own hand could; a warm touch that carried with it just a trace of pumice soap and hair cream. Even with his advanced years, Joe was a handsome man, and despite everything, Brit wished she had tried a little harder this morning, that she didn't look the way she felt.

But, "you haven't started the coffee," was all she could say.

"Geezus. I'm forgettin' how to run this place."

"I'll get it," she actually smiled, even though the corners of her mouth seemed to slice painfully into her temples with the attempt, "I *know* you haven't finished the books yet."

"All right, just until I get to the books. After that, you're home sleepin' today."

Even as she collected the stainless (but stained just the same) filter from the wash basin and measured out the crushed beans and cinnamon, the regulars had begun to assemble.

There were different *regulars* on some very specific days and times, and three that came most days. She knew them all now, knew their quirks and habits, the one or two (at most) menu choices they were likely to make and often had the tickets drawn by the time they'd reached the counter. She knew who had a wife, and who didn't. Who had kids, and who never would.

All but two, were men – and those other two, Gert and Sal, may as well have been. They all knew Brit now, at least to the degree she'd let them. *In an odd way they were her fans.* It wasn't the doughy pancakes and fresh-from-the-can hash that kept them coming. For whatever reason her continued presence at that counter made them comfortable now, and yes, she knew she looked pretty damn good for a 32-year old mom and that didn't hurt. Whatever she was to them, confidant or psychiatrist, mother, daughter, or the never-to-be girlfriend they'd been too timid to talk to back when they should have, they were here to visit with Brit as much as to eat and muse over yesterday's news and sports with the others. In a weird way, she realized, this *pointless* job had a certain amount of satisfaction attached. And she tried not to think, at least not for now, what that moment with Joe had meant. But it did make her smile, if painfully.

For the first time since she and Michael had rolled onto Route 66, *she was actually thinking of herself.*

And she didn't feel the least bit guilty in doing so.

Had it taken nearly killing herself on pills and booze last night to do it? Had she really undergone a fundamental change here, or would the Hell of her situation with Michael come roaring back when the medication hangover wore off?

She waved as a foggy silhouette approached the window. That would likely be Ollie. She waved him in as she checked the coffee.

The water percolated, sending the first pungent stream of molasses-colored heaven splashing into the pot. She'd pretty much avoided the stuff before this job – and then had fought the urge for weeks before giving in.

Now Joe's harsh brew was a tonic. She slipped her mug beneath the spout for a few sips of the really strong stuff, swirled it twice to cool, and downed it on her way to the front door. Immediately her heart started pumping again, and the concrete hat began to loosen.

The silhouette was gone.

Ollie worked construction in La Jolla, a couple towns south. On Wednesdays he was usually the first to arrive, sometimes earlier than *Joe's* happened to open. If Ollie found the front door locked, he would eventually amble around back.

She unlocked the door, just in time to see Bob, an artist living mostly off his pension, trudging toward her up the hill. By the time he'd plopped himself into his seat at the counter, three others had appeared. Before she knew it the counter and two tables were filled, and all she could think about was how Joe could never have managed that day without her.

-=-=-=-=-

It was late in the morning when Michael reached the fort. The scent of strawberries had faded to barely more than a hint, but would likely always be there. For a long while he sat and stared through his makeshift window at Sandy's house.

When he tired of that and made his way up to Big Jerry's, it was past noon and Jerry was the only one there.

"How're the vines, big *kahuna?*"

"All the way to my house. There's a pumpkin growing right next to my window."

"That's good luck. That means the vines like you."

"I sort of have to step around 'em to get out."

"Good man. Keep steppin' around 'em. Breaking a stem – that's very bad luck."

Michael wasn't sure if the pumpkins had brought him any good luck lately, but he sure didn't want more bad.

He bought a packet of root beer flavored Fizzies and a Dr. Pepper, and Big Jerry told him Sandy had come by on her way to the beach and that Bruce hadn't come by at all. He was sort of surprised that Bruce hadn't been with her, but even more surprised that Sandy had gone to the beach.

She hadn't been there since the day of the messed-up surfboard rescue.

Michael had a pretty good idea where he'd find Bruce, though. He thanked Big Jerry and headed for the wetlands.

He heard Bruce long before he saw him. *There's something about a really great voice*, he thought, how it can fly and take you right along with it, let go and drop you a million miles down, and even though you know it's gonna hurt, you still go with it. As if you need to fall just as much as you want to fly. Bruce had a voice like that.

Michael knew the song, *Once Upon a Time;* it was on one of his mom's John Gary albums. The song told of young love long gone, and even though Michael hadn't even kissed Sandy yet, or *any* girl for that matter, Michael saw himself as an old man looking back on this summer with Sandy, and a horrible emptiness swept through him, dropped him a million miles down. Was it possible he wouldn't know Sandy one day? Could this time end like his life in Phoenix had?

He waited until Bruce finished the song before leaving the cover of the reeds. Friends or not, he wasn't totally sure Bruce wouldn't run again – he'd acted so weird about singing yesterday. Michael wasn't sure *what* he'd do.

"Hey Bruce."

There was a slight hitch in Bruce's shoulders before he turned, but one look and it was clear this was a different Bruce. He looked calm and confident, in a different world. Sort of like one of those statue Buddhas.

"I was just practicing. You know, for the show."

"You're gonna do it!"

He nodded slowly.

"Yeah. I did a lot of thinking. You're right. I should sing. I mean, I'm not even gonna think about winning or anything. But I should sing. *I'm good at it.*"

"Sure, you're gonna win. Who else can sing like you?"

Bruce turned pink. Not totally red this time, just pink.

"Well..." he said. "I'm sorry I didn't meet you guys at Big Jerry's today. I just sort of had to come down here..."

Michael told Bruce he hadn't been there anyway first thing this morning, but that Sandy had gone to the beach. He told him about his mom and how Sandy and her folks had rushed over to help. He could tell that, as awful as the whole thing had been, Bruce was a little jealous that Sandy had been over. Michael didn't say anything about his Rat Fink poster.

"I hope your mom's okay."

"She slept in – but she went to work anyway." Bruce nodded.

It was turning into a hot, blue day. A lazy breeze waved through the reeds and died quickly.

"You say Sandy's at the beach?" Bruce looked out at the patch of ocean beyond the bridge.

"Yeah." Michael felt a sense of something powerful in the air – like the welling static just before lightning strikes. He felt himself rise high, all the way up to that big yellow ball in the sky, and suddenly that fence his mom had built began to look small and insignificant below him.

Bruce nodded with a sort of sad resignation, the way he had when Michael had pleaded his case for rescuing the surfboard and Bruce had finally given in. But then his shoulders flew back and he smiled. The decision to sing in the competition had been a big one for him, and just maybe it had pumped him up enough to make another one. He shrugged away years of being teased and jumped a fence of his own.

"I think I've practiced enough today."

-=-=-=-=-

On this hot, summer afternoon, La Vista beach was nothing like it had been that night with his mom. Today it was super-charged and wild with kids. La Vista was a small town, but there were other towns around it with no good stretch of sand of their own, and it seemed like every kid from every one of them was here – laughing and screaming as if they were riding the biggest roller-coaster in the world.

Sails cut the smooth water out past the breakers like white-finned sharks. Heads bobbed in the swells. In a whole section of their own, older boys dipped and skimmed their boards through the cool blue skin of the curls.

A breeze came with a rush of salt and electricity and the sweet stink of the sea. Michael, dressed in shorts for the badlands, not for the beach, and Bruce with his enormous white body, stumbled like slack-jawed rubes between the towels of bronze-skinned bikini-clad girls.

"How're we gonna find Sandy in this crowd?"

Michael shook his head, dazed with the sensory overload. He couldn't believe he'd let his mom keep him away.

When it came down to it, finding Sandy was easy. You just took a bead on the "older boy" surfing section and drew a line straight up the beach from there.

Sandy sat alone, far up on the dry sand, conspicuously away from all the action, her head hanging over her knees like she didn't have a friend in the world.

Michael thought of his mom that night she'd brought him down here, the emptiness in her eyes, and the scary, off-balance feeling of that awful day began to shiver up his spine once again.

An older guy walked over and tried to chat her up, but she ignored him and he walked away.

"What's wrong with her?" Bruce asked.

But before he'd even finished asking, Michael followed Sandy's eyes as she looked up at the water where Tom, decked in blue trunks with a waistband so white it glowed, rode a long, white board with little yellow stripes. He skimmed along beneath a big wave easy as slipping down a water-slide. A small crowd of kids cheered him on from the beach, Pete right with them.

Sandy hadn't told him what Tom had done before she'd pitched that surfboard over her fence. It had to be something bad - they'd grown up together. But there she was, staring at the jerk like a puppy that just had its nose slapped.

It was a mistake coming here. A big mistake.

"What's she doing?" Bruce asked again.

"Hey, fat-butt!" A little kid with a group of big ones. *Bully-to-be and his trainers.* Michael had seen that group on every playground or public swimming pool he'd ever been to. The bully-to-be hasn't ever had his butt kicked and he'll say anything to get attention; the big ones are looking for a mark. The little one sparks off, starts a fight, and once again the big, bad, bully engine turns over.

Sure enough, his dimwitted big friends picked up their cue.

"Yeah, fat boy, quit blocking the sun."

"Blockin' it? Heck, put your shirt on. You're so white you're blinding me!"

Three big ones in this group, all crew-cut, butch-waxed, and tan. *High School.*

"Just keep walking," Bruce's eyes were wide. "It's all right."

Bruce moved forward, so big there wasn't much Michael could do but go with him. But Michael was starting to see red. He spun away.

"No it isn't!"

"Is that your friend, fat boy, *or your lunch?*"

The big boys laughed, the little one giggled like a girl.

Yeah, coming to the beach was a bad idea. *A very bad idea.*

"Hey!"

Sandy touched Michael's shoulder, and it was like a cool wave had washed over him. His anger disappeared. The same wave must have hit the jerks following them too, because they stopped in their tracks, their faces stuck hard between the stupid and dullard settings.

"Uh, hi, Sandy," the tallest one said, finally.

"These are my friends, Bruce and Michael." She looked at each of the bullies in turn, "Robin, Terry, Scott...and Kevin," Kevin was the little one; he looked wide-eyed at Sandy like God had just wrapped a lightning bolt around his throat.

"Uh, hi," Robin said. The others nodded, finally. She turned away from them.

"How's your mom, Michael?"

"She's okay, thanks."

"Uh, Sandy, do you wanna use my board?" Robin offered, meekly.

"Sure. You guys want to learn how to surf?" Sandy was suddenly animated.

"Geez, oh no." Bruce said. "I'll watch though."

"Michael?"

"Uh, yeah. I guess."

"Boss! Come on!"

Well, here it was. He'd wanted to *'catch a wave'* ever he'd first heard The Beach Boys utter that phrase, and now he had the chance. And it was Sandy who was going to teach him! Did it get any better than that? At the same time, he was about to look like a queer-bait dumb-ass. No chance to renege – the next thing he knew they were running full-tilt for the water, squeezing a huge, snow-white board under their armpits.

They attacked the cool water and high-stepped the foamy backwash, exhilarated beyond belief. For the moment he'd forgotten how lost Sandy had just looked watching her *old friends*, friends who'd called them names and wanted to beat them up a few short weeks ago, friends she'd actually stoned.

"Okay, we're gonna drop it over the crest."

Whatever that meant, he'd do it with her – she nosed the board over a small swell just as it broke; salt spray peppered his face. The sea roared past them.

"Climb on and paddle!"

Alive with the rolling surf, the board rolled beneath him like an angry gator. He scrambled on and a whitecap slammed the board right into his chest, nearly knocking him off. Sandy pedal-kicked alongside, steadying it.

"It's a little hairy out here so lay flat until you get it wired. OK?"

He caught about half of that; pressed himself tight to the board this time.

"See that swell out there?"

"Yeah."

"It's gonna curl right to left. I'll angle you back in. Hold on tight and just pull out before you eat sand. Okay?"

"Sure."

He'd caught the *"hold on"* and *"pull out before you eat sand"* parts. None of it sounded good. His heart was already pounding so hard his ribcage was slapping the board. Sandy turned him around over the water until he saw the pink bulk of Bruce a ways up the beach. He let go with one hand long enough to wave. There was a moment of incredible peace as the water beneath him turned to green glass. A breeze raised goose bumps across his back and arms, his ears sang with the cries of seagulls rang with the happy shouts of kids playing along the beach.

A terrific roar took all that away. *He braced himself.*
"Here goes! Hang tight!"

The wave struck and it was like being fired out a torpedo tube. He nearly lost the board the instant the wave hammered him. Over the pounding surf he heard Sandy scream, "Yeah!"

I'm flying!

He rocketed toward the shore, zooming! The nose of the board skimmed pure air.

However long the ride had lasted, *it wasn't long enough.* He almost forgot to roll off the board before it stuffed itself into the sand and him along with it – Sandy's *"pull out before you eat sand,"* admonition.

"Wow!"

"All right!" Sandy had body-surfed in, now she splashed up behind him, laughing. They chased the board down together.

"Good ride! Watch me take one!"

Half-reluctantly, he gave the board up. He strutted back to Bruce.

"Man that looked like fun!" Bruce said.

"That was boss! You gonna try it?"

"Naw. Well, maybe later. I don't know."

Sandy was already way past the spot where he'd been. There were a lot of surfers in the water, but only a handful that far out. She didn't take the first wave, even though some of the others did.

"What's she waitin' for?" He asked.

"I don't know. A good one, I guess."

"What's a good one?" Bruce shrugged.

They counted seven waves before Sandy made a move, and when she did, finally, Michael didn't even see what she had noticed at first. Then he saw a swell that was starting a heck of a lot further out than he'd been looking. When it grew, *it grew fast.*

There were only two other surfers with her now; they began their turns and Michael's heart sank. One of them was Tom.

"Maybe she doesn't see him." Bruce offered, hopefully.

"Yeah," Michael said, but he couldn't make himself believe that. Just the opposite, he was sure she was out there now *because* Tom was. Even worse, Michael thought, it was probably the only reason she'd taken him out there to try it. He put the thought away.

The wave curled and they all took it. The other guy wiped out immediately. But Sandy and Tom hopped up like it was nothing. It wasn't like Michael needed anything else to prove Sandy was cool, but she made it look *so easy*, he was dumbfounded and not just a little torn up inside.

Tom was good too. *Really good;* he walked the board confidently, without a care in the world. Worst of all, *he was really good at something Sandy really liked to do.* And even though they acted like they didn't even see each other, Michael knew it just wasn't that way.

Like that moment alone with Sandy after the movie, he sensed he was near some great sort of understanding here. At the same time, it was like he didn't understand anything at all. Whatever was going on, he could have been watching it from another galaxy.

The closer Sandy and Tom got to shore the heavier the traffic. They zigged in and out of the bobbing heads and belly-boards like it was a game. Robin, of the borrowed surfboard, and his bully friends had melded in with a big group on the wet sand, they were shouting, cheering with a big knot of kids.

And just when Michael thought he'd seen everything, Sandy turned right around on the board - actually walked a little circle! Michael couldn't tell if Tom actually heard the commotion her move had stirred on the beach over the roar of the waves – he just saw everyone cheering. He had a big smile on his face when he hopped off his board in the shallows. He thought the cheers were for him.

"San – dee – rules the waves!" they shouted.

"Yeah! *Sandy rules the waves!*" Bruce repeated and then looked quickly around like he'd surprised himself.

The other surfers slapped her outstretched hand, nodding their approval.

"Nice spinner, wahini," One of them said.

Tom's smile faded fast. Michael saw red in his face. Suddenly Michael felt better about things.

"*Come on you guys!*" She shouted. She was looking at the two of them.

"Wanna try it?"

Bruce shook his head. "Maybe a few waves later..."

Robin had to go, and with him went his board, so Terry, another one of the former bullies (who all suddenly seemed to be Michael's best pals now), offered his.

What had turned out to be *many* waves later, Bruce seemed happy enough to sit on the shore and watch. But Michael was having the time of his life with Sandy; he came close to standing up once, but wiped out immediately.

Sandy laughed at him a lot, but Michael didn't mind.

It seemed like no time at all had passed when the sun began to slide beneath a rusty horizon, and the breakers took on a rosy glow. On the beach, the barbecue pits were lighting up for weenies and burgers. The Beach Boys sang *Don't Worry Baby* from dozens of transistor radios.

Michael took one more wave, got one foot beneath him – and then wiped out again. They caught the board in waist-deep surf and spun it back out.

This time they paddled way past the breakers, where the ocean swelled and fell in a soft rhythm like the chest of a dreaming child. Michael and Sandy stretched over the board, letting the water lap over their shoulders and backs.

He was going to be sore tomorrow, he was sure of that. All afternoon he'd barely gotten past kneeling, but his legs, back and arms felt spent and leaden from paddling. Sandy had thrown sand on the board and roughed up the wax. She said it kept your feet from slipping off, but it had probably taken two or three layers of skin off his chest and shoulders, and the hide that was still on him was deeply sunburned.

But none of that mattered; he wouldn't have changed a thing.

Beads of water gleamed gem-like from Sandy's skin. She rested her cheek on one tanned arm, her eyes closed.

Suddenly, she pulled herself onto the front of the board and tucked her knees under her.

"Hop on. Let's take one in together."

He drew himself on with proud ease; it had taken him half the day, but he was getting it now. Once the board steadied he slid up behind her. A big swell rolled beneath them, and he quickly grabbed the sides for balance.

Sandy moved as one with the board and the wave below.

"You just have to find your center," she said. "It's right *here* for me."

What she did then surprised and scared the heck out of him. She took his hands and placed them on her stomach. Her stomach was warm, tight, and somehow incredibly soft at the same time. His chin rested atop her right shoulder and Michael couldn't help seeing the reddish line above her suit top, the mounds of white curving gently below. He swallowed hard.

She effortlessly unfolded herself till she sat; knees hugging the sides of the board. The movement seemed to weld her to the raw skin of his chest. His head felt like it was a good three feet above his shoulders. He had never been this close to *any* girl, and this was *Sandy*.

Suddenly his face burned hotter than the sunburn, He tried to inch back a little bit, but the roughed-up wax caught him; Sandy slid right back until they were touching again.

"We can stay out here *if you want*," she said. He wasn't going anywhere.

"See those clouds way out in the northwest?"

"Ye – yeah."

"Somewhere past 'em's Catalina Island. There's a little town called Avalon right on the edge of the Island. Avalon's named after a magic island that disappears in the mist if you get too close."

The ocean rocked them and settled. They were out pretty far now, but at this point Michael wouldn't have cared if they floated all the way out to Avalon and disappeared in the mist.

"You okay?" She asked.

He nodded.

"Me too." She looked back to the rusty clouds on the horizon.

"There's a sea lion that swims around the boats that tie down in the Avalon cove."

"Sea lion?" He liked the name, tried to imagine what that might look like.

"Yeah. It's like a seal. This one at Avalon is real friendly. Not afraid of you at all. He's sort of like a puppy, you know? You can pet him, and he's so smooth and soft."

Through all their maneuvering, he still hadn't taken his hands from her stomach. *He was afraid to.* She felt smooth and soft, sleek, probably the way the sea lion on Avalon did; not like *anything* he'd ever felt before.

And then he did something braver than standing up on the surfboard, braver than facing the biggest bully in the worst school he'd ever gone to.

He spread his fingers out until they touched her suit top.

And when she didn't knock him off the board or scream bloody murder or anything, he got bolder, moved his fingers higher. He'd thought about breasts a lot, but he really had no reference for what they'd actually be like, or what would happen when you touched them, he'd only known he wanted to. When it came down to it, he found it was sort of like what you'd think clouds would be like when you touched them.

He and Sandy sat that way for a long time, neither one saying a word, rocking slowly, out there where there didn't seem to be any time to take account of anyway, and the swells were gentle. In the rosy distance, he thought he saw the misty ghost of Avalon – a place he had never even known existed until today. The setting sun warmed them, the sea rolled beneath. He heard seagulls cry and somewhere, far away, kids laughing. The Beach Boys were still playing, but it was a song Michael didn't know, and could barely hear. His entire world had become wrapped in some sort of timeless, magic cocoon.

He felt Sandy's hand on his; sure she meant to rip his hands away.

Instead, she squeezed them.

That was all it took.

"Oh, man!"

"What's wrong?"

"Nothing!"

She turned back to see what was wrong.

Michael immediately belly-flopped onto the board, his face so hot he was sure it was steaming.

"We should paddle in," he said.

She grinned. It was sort of a half-grin, really. He couldn't read it.

"Well...okay," she said, finally.

They had drifted far, and a good ways south – close to the point where the hill Sandy's house was on made its way down to the ocean and there were a lot of rocks. Bruce had trotted down the shore, following them; he waved his arms and pointed at the hazard.

"Okay, this can get hairy with two of us." Sandy said. "If you start to fall just dive deep okay? Better to eat sand than get conked by the board okay?"

"Okay."

They paddled into the rougher stuff.

A decent swell was already coming up.

"We should get a good ride from out here."

"This one?"

"Not yet."

They rode out three more. The fourth looked just like the last three to Michael, but suddenly Sandy swung the board into position.

"This is the one – and we're taking it standing!"

Beneath them, the ocean sucked in a huge breath of foam, hissed a final warning, and then dropped away into a brilliant silence. Sandy smiled over her shoulder. To their left, the swell peaked into a long runner of whitewater.

It hit him then that Sandy might just be crazy. But just maybe he was too – there was no way he could stand up on this thing. Especially no way they *both* could. He was gonna look like an idiot in front of Sandy and her friends, and then they were both gonna get their brains dashed out on the rocks.

The crest sizzled, then *roared*; it slammed into them and the next thing he knew they were slicing toward shore. Sandy leapt to her feet. And Michael went for it. He actually stood up.

For a moment.

He hardly felt his feet leaving the board. And when they did, he flew quietly for what seemed like miles. He saw the coastline, the towns beyond, the mountains and deserts beyond. *He saw the sand dunes, Yuma, and then Phoenix far below, all the way to Arcadia and his brother's grave. And all the while, the catbird bones flew beside him.*

And then all of that went away.

Sandy smiled, her smile pursed into a kiss.

Michael cannonballed into the cool water, and it was like falling through the clouds into heaven. It was all bubbles and blue green water streaked with red sunset. He rolled along the sandy bottom and rolled right back up and when he exploded through the surface, fists in the air, so happy he wanted to cry but he laughed instead.

"Yeah!" He screamed.

Sandy hadn't made it much further than he had. She whipped the water out of her eyes, laughing; her hair flung sunset rubies into the sky. The board, however, had ridden pretty well on its own. Her friend Terry was already chasing it down in the shallows, trying to save it from the rocks. Sandy and Michael skimmed over the bottom on swells, dodging seaweed and boulders. Terry corralled the board; waved at Sandy - *did she want another ride?* She shook her head and waved him off.

Michael half-stumbled, half-swam over to her. A small wave broke around them and the next thing Michael knew they were facing each other, chest-deep, in the lapping surf. *It was his day today.* He had jumped a fence his mom had built, surfed, and even touched a girl for the first time. He'd been afraid of getting hurt at every turn – and he'd gone ahead anyway. *It* was his day to be brave.

He kissed Sandy for real this time.

The actual kiss happened so quickly he barely felt her on his lips. But his heart felt her, thrilling as his first ride on the surfboard, like his heart might beat right through his ribs. A moment when that heartbeat filled his ears and everything else fell away. Sandy blinked, and there was no sound at all; everything, even his heart, had stopped. Without knowing it, he'd asked *the* cosmic question, and in a very big way, now he needed a cosmic answer.

He caught a glimpse of Bruce on the shore, waving his arms, shouting something Michael couldn't hear, then Sandy's eyes flew wide open and the world rushed back in.

"Dive!" She screamed.

But he didn't. He turned just in time to see the nose of the white board with colorful pinstripes skimming straight for him, and that was all he saw.

-=-=-=-=-

"You did that on purpose!"

Sandy was raging mad. And that was just fine with Tom. *The beach was his. Sandy was his.* If she was going to bring some twerp onto *his* beach, she could deal with it. Accidents happened.

"I didn't even see you're little friend out there."

"Be cool, people." Lifeguard Pat defined cool. He was a UCLA student who never left the beach in the summer and in the winter majored in boondockers and surfing as far as Tom knew. No way he'd make a scene.

"Every surfer gets conked once in a while. What's his name?"

"Michael. Michael Helm."

Sandy's *little friend* had a little *"boo-boo"* on his forehead, that was all. Pat took a knee, held a bag of ice to the little snot's head, and the stupid kid just looked off into the ozone, making it all look worse. Yeah, it had bled pretty good, scalp cuts always did. That happened all the time out here. *But the twerp would think twice about going anywhere near his girl again.*

And Sandy would think twice about a lot of things now too.

Pig-boy, Bruce Stubik, shot Tom glance, *but so what?* Not like he'd stand up for anything. It weirded Tom out that Sandy had anything to do with Pig-boy. *It had weirded everybody out this summer.* But if that's how she wanted to waste her time, so be it.

Tom lifted his chin at the fat doofus, "You wanna say something to me?"

Bruce shook his head. Course not. He was such a big, fat, wuss.

All the other guys were cool. But now even Pete was tossing Tom a look. And that made Tom lose it just a little bit. *Because he knew that look.* It was the same rabbit-in-the-headlights stupid face Pete had that day at the pool when Sandy was too chicken to *put-out.* Like Sandy was some holy thing that couldn't be touched. But plenty of guys had, and Tom knew it. She'd been playing them *both* for suckers since last summer. Now this new kid was in the picture, this pint-sized *Mikey* twerp. Sandy was messing with Mikey now and Tom *still* hadn't gotten any. He bit his lip. His *cool* was slipping fast.

Pete was still staring at him, wide-eyed.

"What?"

"Nothin'," Pete looked down at his sand-encrusted feet. Finally, he trotted back into the surf.

The knot of kids that had gathered to see the bleeding kid started to break up. The real surfers were already paddling out to the breakers. Like Pat said, "surfers got conked every day." Mikey thought he was a surfer, now did he? Well he could pay for that label. *Lucky his head was still on at all.*

Little Mikey was just still too stunned to cry. But he would. He'd start balling any second and Sandy would see just what kind of little wuss she'd brought to his beach.

"How you doin,' little man?" Pat was doing *the finger thing.* Running one back and forth in front of the kid's face, waiting for Mikey's eyes to follow. But his eyes weren't going for it. For just a second, Tom felt unsure.

A tiny glint of fear that maybe, just maybe he'd gone too far this time.

Sandy took the kid's hand and held it. *That was a burn alright.*

"Michael, come on. Are you okay?

The kid took a quick breath, his head kicked back like someone had just stuck smelling salts in face. But nobody had.

And despite himself, Tom felt relieved. He pulled the surfboard out of the sand, tucked it under his arm. No sense hanging here.

But he didn't go back to the water, not right away.

There was something weird going on. Something odd Tom couldn't quite place. A crosswind? He looked down at his arms, surprised to see them covered with goose bumps.

Pete had body-surfed a couple waves. Now he ran up to them, dripping, smiling like nothing had happened.

"Hi, Sandy," he said, like a total dweeb. Sandy ignored him.

"Let me have a ride." Pete tugged at his brother's brand new board and Tom yanked it back.

"I get one more on it, dipshit, *the last one didn't count."* He tramped toward the water.

"Pat, Michael's hands are really cold."

The alarm in Sandy's voice made Tom turn back.

Now Michael was looking right back at him. But not just looking – *he was grinning!* It should have pissed Tom off.

It wasn't the same kid.

Tom took a step back.

Pat and Sandy were still working with Mikey like nothing was wrong – like it still was Mikey.

Pete yanked the board again, and Tom let go this time; Pete fell on his butt and the board fell on top of him.

The kid who wasn't Mikey seemed more interested in Pete now. He glanced back at Tom – just enough to catch Tom's eye – then tilted his head toward Pete again. Tom couldn't help but follow his gaze.

"Wha'd ya' do that for!" Pete whined.

"Yuh –" Tom's tongue stuck dryly to the roof of his mouth. Pete had extricated himself from the board. But he was on one knee now. *On one knee because the other was gone; only a blue-gray ham bone streaked with gore protruded from his Jams. Pete shivered, cheeks puffing like the gills of a dying fish. Blood gushed from Pete's mouth, from his nose and eyes –*

Pete threw the board down, pulled himself up, and smacked the sand off his Jams. Completely intact now.

"You're a real jerk sometimes. You know that?"

"Duh-" was all Tom could manage, just air passing uselessly between his lips.

"Go away – both of you!" Sandy hissed.

Pat pinched Mike's fingers.

"Talk to me little man. Do you know where you are?"

"The beach..."

"Good. Can you tell me your name?"

"Nick Helm."

Pat Farrell glanced over at Sandy, "Didn't you say..."

"That's not his name, Nicky's his brother. His name's *Michael.* He's completely out of it. *He's so cold! His lips are blue.*"

"What the heck?" Bruce rocked back on his palms, shocked. He stared, slack-jawed, at Tom whose mouth was open so wide now his jaw seemed glued to his chest. A slurp of white spit foamed over the corners.

Tom's lips quivered then shook, *"Duhn't guh..."*

When real words finally came out they were raspy ghost words, spilling from him all at once.

"Don't go in the water." He said, "Don't go in the water. Don't go in the water. *Don't go in the water!*"

Sandy spun to face him – realized it wasn't some lame-ass joke he was pulling – and then *nothing* made sense anymore.

The noise of the beach, of all the kids playing on it, blipped out she saw only a dim tunnel focused on the shape of Tom's mouth as he chanted his weird mantra, spit streaming from his lips.

The crotch of Tom's Baggies turned bright yellow, the yellow fanned out, a stream of pee coursed down his leg and foamed into the sand.

Pat the lifeguard, still working with Michael, had seemed oblivious to it all, but now he looked up too.

"Jeezuz!"

Tom bolted then – not toward the surf, but directly away from it.

And when the cry sounded, it came from everywhere at once.

"SHARK!"

"God! Look at the water!" Bruce screamed.

Tan streaks ripped the swells beyond the breakers; they slid below the surface.

The swells boiled, shattered. Boards rocketed into the air, their unhorsed riders crashed into the surf, into each other, and disappeared beneath the foam.

Tan streaks shot between the boards, dove deep.

"Stay with him!" Pat ran for the water. Bruce pounded down the sandy hill, but he fell to all fours at the foam line.

Megaphones blared, "GET OUT OF THE WATER, NOW!"

The entire length of the beach, lifeguards streaked toward the surf; surfers and swimmers streamed back to the sand like fleas from a dead rat.

But by the time Pat's feet were wet it was over; the swells rolled easy.

Nothing but glass beyond the breakers, the telltale streaks were gone.

Bruce knelt at the foam line, gasping, heart still thudding.

The last of the surfers splashed out, coughing, and winded. Empty boards beached themselves in the shallows.

"Everything's okay, now" Michael said, calmly.

Sandy blinked.

The cut had stopped bleeding, he had a gnarly blue lump on his forehead, but he was back.

"You're all right?" She said. And when he nodded, she heard herself ask the stupid question: "Did you see that?" *But maybe it wasn't such a stupid question.* Sandy wasn't sure she had seen it herself. She wasn't even sure exactly *what* she'd seen. Give or take a couple storms, a few broken bones, the ocean had been a pretty safe playground her entire life. *What had just happened?*

"I'm sort'a sick to my stomach. My head hurts."

"You took a surfboard in the face."

Pat Farrell had raced up to his tower and retrieved his megaphone.

"Do not go near the water! Leave your boards where they are."

But no one was going anywhere near the water to retrieve anything.

Sandy's friend Terry bent over his knees, coughing. He'd been out there, right in the middle of it – and he'd practically run back to dry sand on the tips of the waves.

"Man, did you see those sharks!" He started to retch, and shook it off. "So many – Jesus - they made their own damn waves!"

"Sharks – *hell no!*" Kevin had been there too, even with all the commotion, he'd nearly made it all the way in standing on his board – then wiped out in two feet of water. One side of his face looked like a bloody sand sculpture. He bent at the waist too, coughed a half-lung of seawater into a clump of brown kelp. That set off a wild circus of flies and sand fleas. His board had beached itself nearby, now it rolled back into the surf. Kevin simply watched it go, he shook his head. Then he dropped to his knees beside them.

"I've seen sharks, man. Up real close. *Those weren't sharks.*"

"They didn't swim like sharks," Sandy said. "I could see them in the swells. They didn't tack like sharks do – but they didn't bounce like porpoise either. They sort of...*lunged.*"

"*They pounced.*" Bruce's red eyebrows were squeezed tightly together over his nose, and had been ever since he'd come back from the water's edge. "*They pounced like cats. I saw them.*

"It was hard to see anything at first," he said. "There was so much splashing – and with the sunset in my eyes and everything. But then one came in close – real close and I swear –" He shook his head as if he wasn't trying to remember as much as dislodge the image, "I saw - *I swear I saw claws.*"

And even as they all shook their heads and some of them said flat out that was stupid - that Bruce hadn't been close enough to see *anything* – even with all that Sandy felt something deep inside her, like the sudden click of a switch.

Kevin grimaced, and spat, "Scary as freakin' shit – *whatever they were.*"

Terry crossed himself. "We got out. Lucky as hell."

"I've gotta go home," Michael stood, woozily; his fingertips probed the fiery red line over his temple, the blood crusting in his hair. A purple shiner was beginning to swell under his right eye.

"You shouldn't walk that far." Sandy said, "You were knocked clean out."

"What happened to Tom?" Terry asked.

Sandy shook her head at the image of spit at the corners of Tom's mouth, his pee streaming into the sand.

"I think he must have seen them coming and just wigged. He ran away."

Michael took a couple wobbly steps toward the bridge, and Sandy, still holding his hand, started that way too. She dropped his hand when Kevin quit trying to hawk up whatever portion of the Pacific Ocean was still inside him and asked,

"Did Pete go with him?"

Pete. He'd been in the water.

Sandy looked quickly up and down the beach, nearly duplicating the spinner she'd done in the surf. She couldn't see Pete. Didn't see his brother's new board anywhere.

"Look at that!" someone shouted.

A new crowd was forming at the south end of the beach, and Sandy ran to it, suddenly out of breath, her heart seeming not to beat, but to crash, bounce, and skid inside her chest.

A chunk of pin-striped surfboard heeled side over side in the shallows.

The torn flotsam rolled up not five steps away. Another wave belched a gout of sand and foam, and two more chunks rolled up behind the first just as Sandy's knees gave out and her heart with them.

Up and down the beach there was no one left in the water. As far as Sandy could see the waves rolled in alone, only foam and diamonds of red sunset riding them now.

Chapter 13

Michael barely felt the sand beneath his feet. He knew only that he was walking. His knees lifted and dropped rhythmically on autopilot, somehow his soles found the earth. He was moving forward. He was going home.

Above him, between the beach and wetlands was a bridge. Beneath it lay a trail of packed sand beside a dead river of green water. Big chunks of rust-streaked concrete were stacked at the base of the pillars, decaying rebar extended from them, bent like broken insect antennae.

Michael looked back toward the ocean, saw only bright halos and red diamonds, and had to look away. He lost his balance, but didn't fall; a dull throb of heat and pain behind his right eye. For just a moment, it seemed tiny flying saucers were circling around him.

How could he be at the beach? How long would it take to get back to Phoenix? To his house on Camelback Mountain? He couldn't even see the hump-backed mountain from here, and that was odd, because you could see it from everywhere in Phoenix. Vaguely, he wondered if he was dying.

A cool breeze whistled through the arches. In the wetlands beyond, tall reeds waved over the backwater like wheat. Now and then, a soft swell rolled the surface of the river beside him, lapped at the concrete pilings. Except for the surf, the beach sounds had faded away. It was peaceful beneath the bridge.

But the shadows there were black and deep. One long shadow broke from the rest. It walked toward him.

"Might be trolls in here, Mikey."

Nicky's face was a pale blue oval in the darkness. His scalp shined through butch-waxed nubs of hair.

"Boy, you really did it this time."

"I didn't do anything!"

But Nicky wasn't there anymore.

"Wanna play hide and seek?"

Nicky was all the way on the other side of the bridge now.

"Just walk on through, you little baby –"

But now the opening under the bridge looked way too small. Michael would have to crawl through, and even then it would be tight.

But he didn't have to go in there. Didn't have to go anywhere he didn't want to. He didn't have to do what Nicky said; his Mom always told him that. But Mom wasn't here.

But Mom and Dad were playing golf, weren't they? Nine holes of golf take one hour and forty minutes if they don't play behind slowpokes. It takes another twenty minutes to drive from the Phoenix Country Club back to the house. Twenty minutes if they start on time, that's if they don't stop and have coffee on the way back. But they never start on time, and they often stop for coffee, and that's time you can't figure.

And that's when Nicky starts his game.

Mom and Dad could be home any minute - or they could get home an hour from now. When they get home, Nicky's game ends. *But if they take too long...*

"You can't hide from me, Mikey. I know all the places."

And upstairs, Nicky was going through every one of those places, methodically opening each door, lifting the dust ruffle beneath each bed, sofa, and chair, punching every pillow; savoring an anger that grew more potent with each failure.

But one floor down in the basement, in the workroom where their father never has time to work, Michael has a chance.

There are tool cabinets filled with dusty tools. There are saw horses, and a long, sturdy counter with a built in circular saw that's never spun as far as Michael knows. And there are cages everywhere. There had just been a few in Michael's bedroom at first. But Mom didn't like them there. Didn't like the mess – didn't like the odor. So Dad's workroom became Michael's private zoo, the sleeping quarters of Long John the parrot; the hamster twins, Barry and Larry; and Rafael the iguana. Dozens of yet-to-be-named pets; painted turtles, chameleons, and horned toads.

And paintings, incredibly detailed and beautiful, some on canvas, others on Masonite boards, propped on or against every available piece of real estate. Despite the animals, the warm, sweet aroma of linseed oil pervades.

But the acrid, yellow smell of fear cuts through everything.

It comes from a metal storage cabinet beneath the saw-table. That's where Michael huddles in cramped, black, silence. There is no lock on the door, but there are small holes beside the catch, and he's tied the doors together with a shoelace. Nicky will find him, he always does, but he'll have to break the doors to get him.

A *"click- click, click-click"* above Michael, as Long John sidles from one end of his perch to the other, long nails tapping the dowel, a metallic scrape as he bites the bars with his sharp beak. A rustling of straw and paper from the hamster cage. A hiss from Rafael. The animals do not fear Michael. But they do fear.

"It's okay, you guys," Michael whispers.

But it isn't.

A break in the mayhem. And then a ticking sound over their heads that nearly matches the rhythm of Long John's nervous walk. Nicky's finished with the upstairs now. He's crossing the kitchen floor, deliberately tapping each kiln-fired Mexican tile as he goes, knowing Mikey will hear.

Michael had run before, but Nicky is two years older, bigger and faster. He'd tackled Michael halfway down their street and dragged him, screaming and crying, all the way back.

The neighbors knew. Michael saw their faces in the windows. But the houses were expensive and immaculately kept where the Helms lived, not meant for kids, and the few who lived in the neighborhood were taught to be seen but not heard. The faces he saw expressed not alarm but annoyance.

And the following Monday, word had spread through the school like a wildfire through dry chaparral, confirmed and embellished by Nicky and his friends two grades above.

School became, in its own way, nearly as hellish as home. At home, there were beatings when he was found, beatings and shame when he ran away. At school, the few Michael had let close enough to call his friends, eventually joined those who smirked and talked. The school bullies had found a new target culled from the herd.

So Michael played the game and hid.

Michael tugged the shoelace tighter. It was down near his bellybutton. With little room to maneuver, and total darkness, it had been nearly impossible to tie. It held fast. *But it wouldn't hold Nicky long.*

Mom and Dad would have finished their game by now. Michael imagined Dad walking down the path from the clubhouse in his red Cardigan, carefully tallying up the scores; the caddies unloading their bags, Dad's big forest green one, and Mom's smaller, robin's egg blue one; the attendants pull each club, wipe each head clean…

The basement door creaked open.

"Hey, Mikey, you're *not* in the basement. *Are you?*"

Michael's pets are fully awake, alert, their fear tuned to his own. Now the scent of their urine overwhelms that of linseed oil and paint.

Stupid thoughts zip through his mind now: Nicky will spend too much time looking through the tool cabinets and storage room, Nicky won't look under the saw table, Mom and Dad are already pulling into the driveway, Nicky will give up. The thoughts themselves offer little comfort since Michael doesn't believe any of them. But they do fill his head, they do keep his mind occupied, hold the worst of his imaginations at bay.

Still his imagination shows him things, terrible things. Things Nicky might do *(will do)*. He has a good deal of experience to draw from chokings, wet towels pulled over his head and tied around his neck, his arms being pounded, joints twisted to their limits, the fists in the stomach – but the worst was never what happened *to* Michael. *The worst was what Nicky forced him to watch.*

The door at the top of the stairs clicks shut. Nicky's steps are even, controlled. He doesn't need to creep, but he does. He could pull the cord over the staircase, snap on the light. But he doesn't. The rest of the house is carefully finished and furnished, but the narrow stairway to the basement is little more than a pile of wooden boxes. Each step thumps loud and empty, a fist against a coffin lid.

It had begun with birds. Traps made from overturned pails; tripwires of sticks and string.

Michael wraps the end of the shoestring around his hand and holds it tight. He hates being in the dark. He hates the small place he's in for everything but the *illusion* of protection it provides. It's hot; the air is thick with the smells of the paint and the animals. It's hard to breathe. So hard, *the way it is when a greasy palm is pressed over your nose and mouth, when a wet towel is pulled tight across your face.*

Michael's imagination is powerful. He can feel the wet rasp of the towel against his face, the tightness, the rankness of Nicky's breath –

His pets are moving faster in their cages. *They hate Nicky.* Rafael hisses even louder. Long John's beak cracks against the bars, he squawks.

The hot, pungent stink of decay is heavy in that place near the North wall, that place where the jasmine and the cats-claw grow at the far side of the house. That's where Nicky keeps *his* pets buried under handfuls of sand and gravel, barely covered by vines.

Even in the blackness, huddled in a tight cell, *Michael can smell that place*, can feel the tiny fingers of the vines tug against his, and then lose their grip as he pulls them away. *He can see the small feathers, down floating upwards on a swirl of stinking heat; gray wings stretched up between the pebbles as if in flight. Rows and rows of wings* –

"Guess what, Mikey." Nicky calls from somewhere in the basement.

"Mom and Dad are playing the whole eighteen today! *You're fucked.*"

Nicky rattles the cabinets. A roll of canvas topples, stretcher bars fall with it clattering to the concrete floor with the sound of machine gun fire.

One smacks the thin tin door between Michael and *Hell.*

His fingers shaking, Michael pulls the shoestring tighter, it cuts into his hands.

"We've got lots of time to play today."

Long John screeches, beats his powerful wings against the bars. That's why Nicky shut the basement door behind him. No one outside will hear Long John. No one will hear any of this.

"You think you're cool, don't you?"

A wooden stretcher bar drags, screeching, along the floor. Nicky whacks it against the concrete, it rings and echoes.

"You think Mom and Dad like you. Like they think the stuff you do is cool? You know what they really think? *They think you're a freak!"*

Whack!

"You're nothing but a FREAK!" *Whack!*

Closer now, so close.

"You don't have any friends. You don't play baseball. You don't play football, or nothing 'cause you're a wimp. Nobody likes you! *Everybody wishes you were dead!"*

He's standing right next to the cabinet.

Wham!

The percussion hits Michael like a trashcan lid slammed against his ear.

"Oww!"

Michael sucked back the sound so hard and fast it made his heart skip, *but it wasn't fast enough.*

"Is that you, freak?"

Nicky kicks the tin door. The string jumps from Michael's fingers; he struggles and finds it again, pulls it tight.

"What the hell is this?"

The shoestring pins Michael's fingers to sharp metal as Nicky yanks it, but Michael doesn't make a sound this time. Nicky yanks it again, and again.

Michael slips his fingers out, but the shoestring holds fast.

"The game's over, freak. I found you! Game's over." For once, Michael finds his voice.

"You can't get to me. Why can't you just go away?"

"Hah, you freak! I know where you are. I found you! The game's over! Now you have to come out and get what's coming!"

Wham! Wham! Wham!

But Michael wasn't giving up this time, even though he believed what Nicky said now, believed that Mom and Dad would never get back in time to stop this, and the pounding he'd take would be far worse the longer he hid.

Today, was different. He'd won. Today he'd found a place not even Nicky could reach. That realization struck harder and deeper than any mayhem Nicky had ever unleashed on him.

Wham!

"Get out here! Now!"

Yes. This was different. Nicky's voice was high, *shrill even,* and so brittle that the last word cracked and came out "N–aow!"

Nicky swung at the door again. He connected, but barely this time.

Michael was still shaking, but even *that* felt different. The fear was fading, just as Nicky's strength had seemed to. In its place, something new, something he'd never let himself feel before: *raw anger.*

This game of Nicky's. This stupid, mean game of Nicky's had gone on for as long as Michael could remember. And Michael had just taken it.

Had just *let* him do it. Because Michael never did anything without a reason to do it, and deep down Michael always thought there *had* to be a reason for Nicky - that somehow, somewhere, he had done something that *made* Nicky this way.

Today, at ten years of age, he had come to realize that Nicky wasn't like him at all. Nicky didn't need a reason.

It wasn't Michael's fault.

The stupid guilt was gone. *There was only anger now.*

It welled in his gut, a steaming hot geyser of it, blasted out through every fiber of him to his fingers and toes.

"I beat you, Nicky. *I win.*"

"No you didn't! You didn't beat me. I found you! I f-fucking found you, Mi-chael…"

Nicky had called him by his actual name, *Michael. Another first!*

"I – I found you. *Cuh, c-come out.*"

Nicky's voice was younger, smaller than Michael's now, filled with something Michael had come to know very well: *desperation.*

And all this fanned the furnace already blazing inside Michael. How had he *let* himself be tortured horribly by something small and pathetic as that thing beyond the door? The idea of it made Michael knot and twist inside, turned his entire body into a tight fist.

The stretcher bar swung again – and *shattered.* Michael imagined the pieces whickering into the darkness; saw the kindling float away like feathers. He saw Nicky, staring at the broken pine stump in his hands, the surprise, even horror, on Nicky's face. For a moment, Nicky's eyes seemed to roll up into his head.

And then Nicky's eyes narrowed.

"You didn't win nothing!"

Just like that, the old Nicky was back.

And Michael was back in pitch-black darkness, clutching a shoelace to his belly.

"You got me for a second, Mikey. You deserve something special for that."

Terrified commotion in all the cages now. The sudden *zip-zap* of rough cloth and leather over skin. Without seeing anything, Michael knew exactly what that was. Nicky was pulling on the *handling gloves* – the ones Michael never needed for Long John, but Mom had insisted they have.

Because the guy at the pet shop had convinced her that parrots were dangerous, that their beaks were, "*just like a vise made out of straight-edge razors.*"

"What are you doing!?" It was Michael's voice that was small and shaky now.

"I'm gonna do something special. I'm gonna make you a trophy.

"Wanna come out and see?"

Michael held the shoelace, fingered the knot that had kept him safe.

"Didn't think so, you little sissy."

The scrape of metal on metal, directly over Michael's head. The cages were being shoved aside, *his pets –*

"Leave them alone – I'll come out!"

Lights now, beaming down from the worktable over his fortress. The buzz of a transformer switched on, and the smell of ozone. An uncertain thump as the motor kicked in, and then the steady whir of the table saw Dad had never used.

Michael pulled the string on his knot. It held fast – he'd yanked out the loop by mistake! He tugged with all his might. *No good.* Tried to force his nails between the tiny coils. *Couldn't.* He shoved his knees against the doors, and only managed to wedge himself in more tightly. Just like that, his fortress had become a prison. *Worse – this was a grave. He was buried alive.*

"Leave them alone! I'll come out!

But he couldn't come out, could barely move.

"You shouldn't bring these dirty things inside the house anyway. They're stupid animals. They're worthless, like you. And they're weak like you are. They can't help themselves at all."

Over the whir of the saw – the squeal of Long John's cage door being wrenched open. A squawk, a shriek, the powerful but useless flutter of clipped wings, Mom had insisted on that because the last thing she wanted loose in the house was a *flying vise made out of straight-edge razors –*

"I make art, Mikey. I make it all the time! You've seen it – you know how good it is! I'm gonna make something really special for you!"

Michael cried, squealed like a baby at the top of his lungs, screaming for his Mommy and Daddy, for the neighbors, for anyone to help.

Over his head, the horrible, desperate flap of impotent wings, the whir of the saw, and a screech so sickeningly visceral that Michael *felt* the exact point where metal hit bone, then a drumming of wings at once more powerful, and more utterly useless, than any he'd ever heard in flight.

That pathetic drumming cut Michael's own screams down to nothing.

But Nicky's game had only begun...

Michael sat bolt upright in his fort, somewhere between twilight and dreams, the cold, wet tap of raindrops on his neck.

"Art." Nicky hissed once he'd pried Michael from his hiding place, "Better than anything you make!"

Lightning flashed the grass walls into long, feathered shadows that drifted with Michael's eyes and faded. He felt slow and impossibly heavy.

Feathers, scales, and blood.

See-sawing in his head like a line from a half-forgotten nursery rhyme, or the recipe of a witches brew.

Feathers and scales. Wings and tails.
Feathers and scales. Wings and tails.

-=.-=.-=.=.-

"The contest is next week," Bruce said way too brightly, as they stood in Sandy's den.

She knew he was just trying to cheer her up. He'd walked her home and she was grateful for his gallantry. Despite her certainty she was tough enough to handle anything on God's green earth, she wasn't sure God had anything to do with what had happened this afternoon.

But the truth was now she just wanted to be alone.

She'd broken her Dad's rule about calling boys the second she'd made it through their front door. She'd called Michael's house twice with no answer. Had he made it home? *Had he fallen into a coma halfway there?* She should never have let him walk all that way alone.

But seeing that crushed board and knowing Pete was gone forever; that in a matter of moments everything had changed, she'd gone into some sort of fugue. She'd actually cried, and Sandy *never* cried.

And though she didn't want to admit it, she'd been relieved when Michael hadn't answered the phone.

"Sandra, have you asked your guest if he'd like something...to...*drink?*"

Why is Mom being so weird? She thought, before answering that, yes, she had in fact asked Bruce if he wanted anything. Oddly, even her Mom seemed different now. Or maybe not. Maybe she wasn't different at all. It occurred to Sandy then that maybe she was just seeing her mother as she really was for the first time, and that idea was nearly scary as anything she'd seen today. She looked closely at the details of her mother's face, the way the thick creamy mask blended not so neatly into her neck, leaving the barest pink traces beneath her ears. The aqua shadow over her eyes was meant to be dramatic, but it made her look like some sort of Egyptian cat. Mom didn't need to wear makeup, she was pretty enough without it, but she did wear it, way too much of it. And what would she look like with her hair down? Had Sandy ever seen Mom's hair down? No. It was always teased up into a bouffant and sprayed stiff as a football helmet, or covered with a cap when she swam her perfect Freestyle in their pool.

Sandy hadn't missed her Mom's reference to Bruce as *"your guest."*

Mom never referred to Sandy's other friends that way. Of course, Mom had never been totally comfortable with Bruce visiting her one-and-only daughter in the first place. And she didn't want to say, *"eat"* in front of Bruce because he was fat. Worse yet, maybe she was making a *point* of not saying it. Maybe she actually wanted Bruce to feel bad.

Her Mom remained in the den just long enough to flash a perfect smile.

Mom's a phony...*and she's mean.*

And now Sandy looked closely at Bruce. He was so badly sunburned you could barely tell where his red hair began. His face was swollen to the point he had almost no features at all. He was a nice boy, *but he truly was ugly.*

She wondered if she was going a crazy. Maybe the awful events of the day had snapped her brain apart, and now she was looking at the world ass-backwards and skewed through a fun-house mirror.

Her mom was mean but pretty. Bruce was nice but ugly.

No, she wasn't seeing the world through a fun-house mirror. Her view wasn't distorted or backwards at all. It was clearer than ever. Her brain was working just fine.

So where did that put her?

She hadn't acknowledged Bruce's remark about the talent contest. He was trying to take her mind off the day. Over all, he was being just what he always was – nice.

His fat face waited patiently in front of her, supremely tolerant of her mother's bad behavior, of Sandy's own sullen mood. *Bruce is used to being treated badly.*

She stopped herself right there, not sure, and not wanting to be sure, where that track might lead.

And just as she opened her mouth to tell Bruce to go home, she heard a weak knock at the front door and her heart jumped right up her throat.

Michael. Who else wouldn't just ring the doorbell?

Sandy listened to her mom invite someone inside, asking twice before closing the door.

Then Mom was back in the den, a puzzled look on her makeup mask, a sad little bouquet of daisies and yellow carnations in her hands.

"These are from Tom. He wouldn't come in. I don't know why you quit playing together. He's such a nice boy."

Translation: He's so much better than Michael - his dad's rich, and his mom's not a suicidal drunk...

Sandy understood now, that after last night her mom would be even less comfortable with Michael's visits than Bruce's. She watched the puzzled expression revert to a vapid smile before her mom left the room, compared that with the image of Florence Nightingale her mom had projected last night - soothing Michael and his stricken mom, brewing hot chocolate from scratch. *How she must have hated touching the cabinets in that broken-down little kitchen. She'd probably stirred the cocoa with napkins wrapped around the spoon and pot handles.*

In her mother's eyes, Michael was now the unfortunate spawn of damaged parents.

Tom, meanwhile, was still the perfect son of *the Easton's. His* dad was a lawyer. Sandy had never breathed a word about what Tom had tried to do to her. In that respect, she realized she was to blame for Tom's untarnished image. And Mom would never know. No one would.

The flowers had a fresh, earthy aroma as she took them. Their stems were wet and springy in her hands, warm where Tom had just been holding them, cool everywhere else.

Despite everything, it touched her somehow.

But what did *that* mean?

Why was she picking at everything now? It was way too much at once.

She'd begun the summer as she always had, surfing with her two best friends in the world. As much as she loved them, *she'd wanted something new and exciting.* Now both her friends were gone, one forever, and the other…was *sorry.* And her parents – she'd been their daughter for thirteen years and she didn't really know them at all. Until now.

Everything had changed – and somehow, at the root of every last bit of that change, was Michael.

Sandy closed her eyes; took a deep breath that was steeped in sorrow, and the scent of Tom's flowers.

-=.=.=.=.=.-

Half a block from Big Jerry's Market, Brit washed down two more pills with an entire bottle of Dr. Pepper.

All day locked in his office and Joe hadn't finished balancing his books. At the worst possible time, he'd finally asked for her help. Like an idiot, Brit had stayed. She smiled through the pain now as she dropped the empty bottle next to the box of dried pasta and the sealed jar of Joe's homemade marinara.

It was just past mid-way of a pretty decent afternoon. A few puffy clouds overhead, with a dark mass up north. A little rain wouldn't be bad, she thought, if things happened to turn that way. Actually, anything would probably be okay. Despite the tom-tom pounding between her temples, *Brit was flying.*

She'd taken the first two pills in the bathroom an hour before she'd left. Even over the sweet, cherry-prune taste of the soda, she could still taste the two she'd swallowed dry shortly after she'd left – a very, very bad idea given the raw state of her throat from last night. Those two had nearly come right back out.

But that was all behind her now. The aches were still there, but oddly detached now, as if her limbs that had just fallen asleep.

The shame of letting Michael see her blotto, of letting Michael's friends see her –

Now she wanted to throw up.

Vaguely, she knew she was setting herself up for a replay of last night. Luckily, as bad as that night must have been, most of it had gone the way of so many of her dreams.

Morning had been Hell though. She remembered that clearly enough.

Still, she'd done her duty, forced herself to work, and work had made things better – for a time.

Now she had to face Michael, and she didn't have the strength.

As she turned up the street and their sad house appeared in worn stucco patches between the jacarandas and yellow-green snarl of pumpkin leaves, the small windows stared back at her, and a cold shower of dread washed the last of her strength away.

She couldn't go in there.

She'd already given up, there was no use going back. That's why the pills. That's why the booze last night. She couldn't do it anymore. She was spent, finished. The little bit of good she'd felt today with Joe, with doing her work, *with being needed* – all that was a sham.

Last night wasn't the only part of her that had faded. Her past had become a frustrating jigsaw. She was forgetting a lot of things these days.

The truth of it was, she didn't know how much longer she actually had.

One thing she did know - Michael was a dam with no spillways, no release at all. She'd done her best to hold him in, to make him feel like any other boy, but it was time to run now. *Just get the Hell out of his way and run.*

She looked back toward the beach, where the sun had already lowered itself past the hilltops on the way to its great escape.

The sea is always there for you...

Brit shut her eyes, squeezed her lids tight enough to bring tears and make the flying saucers orbit. But the ships didn't come this time.

She took a long, deep breath of salt air. Her one surviving son would be coming home soon. It was time to make dinner. To be normal again.

Dinner would be a challenge. Walking was a challenge. She dropped her keys at the front door, and the Dr. Pepper bottle wobbled overboard as she stooped for them. She watched, disconnected, as the bottle performed a neat little end-over-end in mid-air; and by the time her hand found its way to it the bottle had already nailed the landing, sticking nearly upright in the sand near her foot.

Her hand hovered in mid-flight for a moment, seemed to forget why it had been summoned there in the first place, and then simply waved.

Once inside, Brit set the basket on the kitchen table, pulled a glass from the cupboard, and cracked open the heavy refrigerator door, a fetid, sour smell in the air. She checked the milk. It was nearly empty, but fine. She pulled out the pitcher of sun tea, also nearly empty, and poured herself the rest of it, sipping as she took inventory.

The half-roast they'd had two nights ago, was gone, so was the block of cheddar.

Had Michael brought his friends over for lunch? *Not...that...girl.* The gears spun toothlessly in her head, trying to find purchase, to move forward and find the name she was looking for. The name didn't come, but the house rules *did* – and having friends over while Mom was away at work – *that* was clearly against them. *Especially not girls. No sluts in the house while Mom was away.*

Even with the fading vapors of Mr. Clean and Comet Cleanser in the air, the stench remained as she shut the refrigerator. *He'd brought his friends in and God knows what they did.*

"Michael?"

At the end of their narrow hallway, Michael's door stood partway open. She sipped the tea as she passed her bedroom on the way to his.

His window was wide open. *Why did she even bother locking the doors?* There was no reason to shut it now, she realized, and then everything came clear in one lucid moment.

Billy's body odor hit her before his fist did. Just before her face struck the plaster, she saw his silhouette just as she had in the foggy diner window this morning. There were ragged blue tattoos on his biceps – three crosses, just like Calvary. Just like her very own, personal, Crucifixion.

The word *"Bitch!"* blared and echoed through the shattered wetness inside her head. She vaguely connected it with herself as the flying saucers let loose a merciless barrage of white flame.

-=-=-=-=-

It was dark in the badlands. Clouds and fog had become one, and Michael was walking miles above the earth, high in the womb of heaven. The cool water caressing his skin wasn't yet rain, only the growing promise of it. Lightning ripped past with the scent and crackle of ozone, wrapped him in a high-voltage net of creation and awe. He was part of it all now, part of creation itself. The bottle-rocket of his soul had lifted away at last, soared high into space.

Michael had finally let himself go…

He dabbed the rain from his forehead, each touch hurling a spear of hot pain into his temples from the swollen knot there. He wasn't in heaven, or space, or anywhere but the sandy, ice plant-strewn desert of the badlands, *and it was late*.

He was woozy, sick to his stomach, but his feet were beneath him again, finding purchase where they could in the wet sand and mud, as he slogged his way up to the road.

Lightning flashed the fog, thunder blasting at its heels. What time was it anyway?

He couldn't tell from a moon he couldn't see. But he knew it was very late. He was in trouble, *big trouble*.

A few steps up the road and the real rain hit. Big drops, big as he'd ever seen in Arizona, slashing down in bursts. He was shirtless, his swimsuit was already soaked through, and Mom would be furious. He started to run, but three brain-pounding steps into that he slowed to a walk, and that only slightly lessened the pain. His mom had bad headaches. Did her head feel like this all the time? If it did, Michael didn't know how she even dragged herself out of bed every day.

The pumpkin patch was alive with big leaves flapping like sails in the storm, taking the vines with them.

He was pretty sure his window would be closed – if Mom had been able to get up at all today, she would have shut it when the storm came. He considered forcing it open anyway. Things would go much better for him if he had a chance to dry off and get some clothes on before he saw her.

Michael cut through the field and the roiling stems, bristling with their tiny swords, slapped and stung his legs and feet everywhere he stepped.

The blinds were closed. A spark of hope that maybe she had come home and just fallen asleep. But when he made it around to the back of the house, his heart fell again. His window was wide open – just as he'd left it this morning. She would have closed it for the storm if nothing else.

Something was very wrong.

He ran, tripped over a pumpkin and rolled his ankle painfully. He limped the rest of the way up the embankment and hoisted himself up over the sill into his room.

-=.=.=.=.=-

Billy'd hit the jackpot with Brit, all right.

He'd sell most of the pills, but there were plenty of them, and he'd popped a couple, just to see what that would be like, even though he wasn't no hippie doper. They were pretty damn good - *he was flying.*

He wasn't exactly a vodka man either, Jim Beam straight from the bottle being his drink of choice, but the fifth of Popov he'd found in her dresser went down easy enough.

Something popped in a cloud of sparks and paper thin glass that shimmered through the air and it took Billy a full five seconds to realize he'd knocked over a lamp.

When it finally came into focus, a nearby clock read, 5:33.

He should be out of here. Should have been long gone by now.

And even though a good sense of time passed was every bit the virtue patience was, he'd given himself a break today. *He deserved a break, dammit.* He'd planned. *He'd learned.* In Williams, Arizona, he'd followed that girl Karen exactly three times before he'd just lost patience and done her. *That was no plan at all.*

It'd had taken seven years in a stinking hot cell in Bumfuck, Arizona to learn that patience really was the virtue Momma'd always said it was.

You had to plan well and stick to that plan.

This time around he'd done that. Once he'd seen Brit's body, Billy had taken a couple months to figure out exactly what he'd needed to get at it.

He'd learned Brit didn't have a boyfriend or friends of any kind here in town. She didn't talk to her neighbors. She walked that cherry body of hers home the same damn way every day.

Brit's body was piled like raw beef next to the den sofa where he'd left her now. He toasted her limp form with the Popov, again with the now limp form in his other hand – and started looking for the toilet.

"Shit…" he muttered, deciding to forego that formality altogether. Instead, he squirted a yellow-orange stream between her legs, up the walls, and kept it going all the way into the kitchen.

"Weeee –" he snorted. "Weee – weee, momma!"

He jounced his knees, pinched off the last drops, and nearly dropped to the floor.

"Whoa…"

Time is passing.

Shit, what the hell difference did it make?

Seven years ago, Karen's boyfriend showing up had made a difference.

Billy slapped the wall, bit his lip, and then palmed the wall for balance.

Her boyfriend just *had* to come meet her in the park that day. Not that the little shit stopped Billy from getting most of what Billy'd wanted. Not that Billy hadn't made Karen pay for teasing him with that body of hers, the way she would never tease any boy ever again.

But right there at the end her boyfriend happened along. Just when Billy was finishing his business.

The timing of things. Sometimes it really fucked you up. And sometimes, it worked out. If Billy's eighteenth birthday hadn't been later that summer, he'd *still* be in prison.

Brit didn't have no boyfriend. She had a scrawny baby boy who played out in the weeds all day with a fat homo, and a little girlie that was just getting ripe. *That sweet thing's time would be coming soon enough.*

5:40 now. Baby Boy should have been home a long time ago.

Brit moaned, her thigh twitched, and Billy felt himself rising to the occasion.

His plan had been to leave way before Baby Boy came home. But the vodka and pills had changed that, had given a brand new edge to everything and made his new mission clear.

Now he wanted the little punk to show up.

It wouldn't be like Williams, Arizona. Not this time. This time Billy would finish his business. Finish it with the two of them. Then he'd just walk away free and clear.

He fumbled another crushed Lucky Strike from his pocket, licked it together as best he could.

Brit's body spasmed enough to nudge the couch an inch or two. Another moan. Probably cold, being half-naked like that. He found himself staring at the end of his cigarette, and then he had himself a great idea for getting her going again. He'd get her *all heated up all right.*

He dropped the bottle, and nearly dropped the cigarette, as he swayed into the kitchen, then lost his balance altogether. He found his way to the stove on all fours, twisted one burner after another on until most were lit and one was finally close enough. He pulled himself up to it, still sniggering, his Lucky dangling from his lips, the blue flame warm on his face.

And found himself staring up into the big black iron hood over the stove. It was dark and ugly up there, with a mean-looking old fan stuck in the middle. Rain hammered it from the outside, thunder rolled.

He pushed his face forward, tickling the flame with his cigarette; sucked it till a small ribbon of smoke snaked up toward the fan.

A dog barked, somewhere nearby, and Billy started, burning his lip in the process.

"Shit!"

But the bark was coming from over him somehow – coming from that hood. There was no dog in the house. He knew that.

Billy wiped his sore lip with his cigarette hand. The bark echoed and rang a wet, metallic sound. But this time it wasn't really a bark so much as a sort of a snorting sound, then it was a growl, then a bark and thunder all mixed together. All with that weird ringing...

He spun around to see Baby Boy in the hallway staring straight at him.

The boy would scream, and Billy'd cut the scream off with a hand over Baby Boy's mouth and nose. Then he'd tape him up, give him a front row seat while Billy finished his business with Mommy. Maybe Billy'd give Baby Boy a taste of what Mommy got. After that, Billy would slip out the back window, walk past the hills and catch another train. Two, three months from now, once this shitty little beach town forgot all about the stinking bodies they'd found last fall, Billy'd start catching trains back this way again, maybe take another moving job or two – one way or other, he'd come calling again. Then he'd find out what he needed to know about baby boy's little girlfriend.

That was the new plan. It was perfect; it was simple. But somehow, it never got going – somehow, the timing of things got screwed up.

First off – Baby Boy didn't scream. Billy's hand reached out to stop the scream that didn't happen anyway – and then there were *two boys,* one taller, older than the other.

Billy blinked. There was only Baby Boy.

But by that time, *things were just off, and Billy knew he had to move fast* – grab the kid, tape his mouth, bind his feet and hands. He told himself he needed to do these things – and he just couldn't *do* any of them. Baby Boy's eyes, rolled up into the kid's skull, until nothing but glossy white showed between his lids.

Billy was drunk and high on *god knows what those pills were, he was seeing things, but he had his plan.* Billy grabbed the kid's throat and cold bit right back through his fingers. He released him, flapping warmth back into his fingers.

"What the fuck?" His words left puffs of white frost floating in space.

A growl, low and threatening behind him.

He spun, cursing when he seared his hands on the still flaming burners.

Lightning flared. Baby Boy was gone.

Something else was in his place.

It was a dog the likes and size of which Billy had never seen — *never even imagined.* Its chest filled the entryway, a head broad as a steam shovel sat atop a neck bulging with muscles and veins ropey as sycamore roots, its legs ended in hooves, horns protruded from its head like scimitars.

Lumpy butt molasses squirted down the backs of Billy's thighs.

He lunged for the window, but the horns ripped through the meat of his buttocks, and all he managed to do was fling himself across the flaming burners, shrieking and bleeding like a stuck pig.

Outside, rain sluiced down between strikes of lightning and thunder - a storm many times louder than the Hi Fi blasting from the house across the field, even louder than the man screaming from inside the Helm's house.

When a torn, rag doll of a creature flung its head through the window, the *"plink"* of shattering glass was all but swallowed by the storm. The torn doll choked down one last, raggedy breath filled with rain, a breath that hissed and whistled through lacerated lungs, before something ripped it back inside the blackness of the house.

Chapter 14

Sandy had never been to a funeral.

At thirteen, it was hard to get a grip on death. Even her grandparents were still going strong and it was hard to believe you could talk to someone one day, and they could be gone, *truly gone,* the next.

It was strange and unreal, and the service was such a bizarre ritual; everybody knew Pete's body wasn't even in the box under the white tent.

Sacred Cross Cemetery overlooked an ice plant-covered ravine that dropped some two-hundred feet and ended half a mile away in surf and rock. With the ocean behind it, the hillside was beautiful despite the headstones, despite the dark clothes and the tears.

The ocean was Pete's real coffin.

Sandy's stiff dress chafed, her shoes pinched.

Still, she guessed no one was more uncomfortable than Bruce. Standing three rows in front of her, his suit was so tight he looked like a doll made of plump black sausage. Crescents of white salt had crystallized under his fat arms. He was alone, and that was probably a good thing. Mr. Stubik was what Mom called "a good provider," but a thoroughly disagreeable man. He delivered produce to markets up the coast to Newport. Sandy's mom said Mr. Stubik probably wouldn't take a day off work for his *own* funeral, and Bruce's mom never left their house anymore. Rumor was, Mrs. Stubik was three times the size of Bruce and probably too big to leave.

Sandy's parents stood to her left. Her mom wore a smart navy A-line, matching pillbox hat, veil and gloves. Dad, Ken-doll handsome in his charcoal Brooks Brothers, his full head of blond hair just beginning to whiten now. His fragrance of Old Spice was calming. It made her think of happy times, of sitting on his shoulders, laughing and trying to cover his eyes with her small hands.

Sandy tried to find Michael and his mom, but couldn't. A good part of her view was blocked by the Carlucci family. The Carlucci's were Catholic and that meant Mrs. Carlucci couldn't use birth control. There were fifteen kids in all, including two sets of twins, all round as tomatoes. All were present.

Father Moran talked about Pete's industriousness as a student and altar boy - the same Pete she'd grown up with, had learned to *surf* with. The same Pete who'd been one of her best friends until this summer. *Until he'd just stood there and did nothing while her other best friend tried to rape her.*

But what could Pete have done? What happened with Tom had been as unexpected and unreal as this day.

Tom himself was near the front, flanked by his mom and dad. Whatever hit him right before Pete was killed looked like it was still with him; he was a scarecrow in that borrowed suit. She couldn't remember him any other way but sun-bronzed, now he was a sickly yellow-white, gawkier than ever.

Tom's flowers still sat on the table near her bedside. It had been four days since Pete died. In all that time, Michael had never called, and never showed up at their fort. He certainly wasn't here. It wasn't like he and Pete were friends or anything. She'd just hoped.

The La Vista View reported that Pete had been attacked by *a large school of sharks;* they didn't say what kind, where the sharks had come from, or where they might have gone. A marine biologist from the Scripps Institute said an attack like that was an anomaly. She supposed that was the scientific way of saying they had no idea what happened, but it most likely wouldn't happen again.

The beach remained closed.

Sandy couldn't help seeing Tom just standing there, peeing on himself right in front of everybody. Probably *everybody* saw him that way now, and would for a long time. Two rows behind him, the Merrill brothers were sniggering, taking turns poking each other and pointing.

Did he deserve that? Considering what he'd done to her - maybe. But, did Pete deserve not to be here anymore? No.

But he really was gone. He really wasn't coming back. The sun glinted off the sad, empty box and Sandy realized there was something more to all of this, something dark and evil intertwined with the sadness she was feeling. *Guilt.* Somehow, and Sandy didn't know exactly how or why, *she* was responsible for all of this.

The teardrops on her gloves were a surprise at first. She didn't know she was crying. But once she started, she just kept on.

Her dad squeezed her shoulder, gently.

"It's okay," he whispered.

But he had no idea.

When it was over, finally, she walked back to the line of cars in her own silent bubble, removed from everyone and everything else – until someone touched her shoulder.

"Sandy?" Tom's lower lip was tight, and for a second, she thought he might cry. Sadness was an emotion she had never thought Tom capable of.

She should have walked away, probably, but she didn't. She looked in his eyes for the first time since that day in the pool, and for the first time ever she saw something other than arrogance there.

"I'm sorry," he said.

"I know."

"We were all best friends, you know? *Best friends.*"

From the corner of her eye, she saw her parents had reached their car. Her dad opened the door for Mom as he always did, and looked back, expectantly, at Sandy.

Tom looked down at his feet.

"Can I…come over sometime?"

Someone else seemed to say, "Sure."

He nodded, started to say, thanks, and then walked quickly away.

Sandy winced as she headed back up the hill toward her car; a tugging deep inside her. *It was all too much.* This one summer had been like ten years. It wasn't just Tom who had changed. They all had.

And where was Michael? No one answered their phone anymore. She could have just biked over – but she hadn't.

Heavy footsteps and wheezing announced Bruce. His coat was soaked through with sweat, and he smelled terrible.

"Sandy. Can I talk to you?" Bruce glanced around, furtively.

Her mother had seen Bruce, now she sat stiffly in the front seat, waiting for the car to take *her* home. Dad opened Sandy's door, and waited.

Not rushed, no look of annoyance on his face. No look of *anything* really.

Mommy's sharply dressed robot at my best friend's funeral.

God, why was she seeing them this way? It made everything else she was feeling that much worse.

"Okay," she said.

Bruce shook his head, quickly, *"Not here.* There's a place I go. It's out by the backwater – straight back from the second pillar on the bridge - the north end."

"When?"

"Can you be there an hour from now?"

Mommy's robot was walking toward them now, still proper and composed. Simply doing Mommy's bidding.

"Is Michael coming?"

"No!" Bruce ducked his head slightly, as if expecting a blow. "It's *about* Michael."

-=.=.=.=.-

It felt *so good* to be back in cutoffs.

Sandy rolled back the sleeves of her faded red Madras and shouldered the coiled rope. She hopped onto the fence, gripping the smooth beam with her bare toes. The porch window slid open noisily behind her and Sandy glanced back long enough to see her mom, still dressed from the funeral.

"Honey, where are you going?"

"To see a friend."

"Your father and I thought it would be good to spend the afternoon together."

"I'll be back soon."

"Why don't you stay? It would be good to talk..."

"About what?"

"Honey...Pete was in your kindergarten class. You've been best friends...forever."

It wasn't a question, but her mom waited for an answer. Sandy took a deep breath. There was something wrong here, something Mom wanted to say, but wasn't going to. Sandy knew Mom just expected her to step off the fence and walk back inside. But Sandy didn't. She rested the rope on the fence, tied a new knot to the post, tested it, and waited her mother out.

Finally, her mother asked, *"What friend?"*

"A good one," she shrugged.

Her mom smiled. But it was a stiff smile, the one she used when she didn't want anyone to know she was mad. She swallowed.

"Are you going to see Michael Helm?"

"What's wrong with Michael?" Sandy snapped. Her tone took them both by surprise. For a while, they said nothing. Sandy looked down at her bare feet, at the fading red lines her formal shoes had left.

The truth was, she wanted to see Michael. She told Bruce she'd meet him and she would, but it wasn't Bruce she cared about. She had no idea what he wanted to say about Michael, but it couldn't be anything good – that was obvious.

And now, her mom...

"It's not...Michael's fault." Her mom began slowly, trying to be delicate. "But his...situation. Well, it's unhealthy, honey." Sandy shook her head.

"What situation?"

"It's just that his mother..." Her mom's make-up mask was fixed somewhere between a grimace and a smile - a look that meant she had to explain something unpleasant - something that really should be understood without any explanation at all. "Well, you know, his mother didn't just fall..."

"She has headaches, Mom. You know - migraines. She takes medicine that makes her dizzy sometimes. Michael told me." Her mom shook her head.

"She drinks, honey."

"Michael can't be my friend 'cause his mom's an alkie?"

"That's a *vulgar* term," The mask dropped for a moment, exposing something even uglier beneath. But the mask reappeared almost immediately, softened now to a more gentle condescension. "She drinks – there were bottles of liquor hidden all over that house. Hidden in cabinets and –"

"God, Mom! You searched her house while she was sick?"

"She's an alcoholic. She's divorced. For heaven's sake, honey..." her mom paused to deliver the final blow, to say the unthinkable, *"she works at a diner."*

"She has a degree from Boston University, Michael told me so. And she's not divorced – Michael's dad just...went away."

"Honey, good parents don't just go away."

Sandy blinked back her anger, forced to defend Michael's mom, *of all people* - someone Sandy really didn't like all that much in the first place – somebody who didn't like *her* at all.

"But you went over to their house and helped them! You didn't have to do that. You were so nice to her *and all the time* - how can you be so – *fake?*"

Her mom took a deep breath. Sandy turned away, not even wanting to see the mask that presented itself now. She threw the coils over the fence, and leapt after them, so angry now she could barely see straight.

"Honey," she heard her mom say behind the fence. "It was the Christian thing to do –"

The ice plant cracking and squishing under Sandy's feet felt good. Good to work her toes through it as she traversed the hillside over to the stairway.

The *stairway* was really only a drainage gutter that started some four feet beneath her fence with some haphazardly poured concrete and ended as little more than a rust-colored gouge near the bottom of the cliff. There were enough "steps" of dried mud and jagged cement outcrops to take you down to the path if you were careful.

It was a clear and beautiful afternoon. A breeze scented with sea air and freshly cut grass made her close her eyes and dream of summers that had been far better than this one. *Glassy swells, the tang of salt spray, the surfboard rising beneath her feet, ready to fly her to shore, to take her up and away from everything that was wrong in the world.*

It had only been she, Tom and Pete in those days, *and they'd all been happy.*

But now she saw a spidery shadow at the bottom of her swimming pool, saw her legs and Tom's intertwined beneath the inner tube as they floated, Tom pinned against her, touching her...

Then there was Michael. Michael had touched her too, but Michael's touch felt good. She didn't know why exactly, it just had.

Michael had *saved* her summer. If it wasn't for him –

Something fluttered noisily past her, wrenching her from her thoughts, and Sandy clenched the rope.

The bird flew, squawking, straight into the sun, and then all Sandy saw was a black spot in the sky.

She'd seen wild parrots now and again. They were thick shouldered and loud like that. They flew oddly – seemingly hurling themselves into the air rather than soaring over it.

Black wings sprang from the sun. The stumpy silhouette soared, flapped, and dipped. Then the bird dropped straight from the sky. It thudded against the hillside some twenty feet from the stairs, the impact enough to scatter sprigs of ice plant. The sound and force made Sandy's stomach twist.

One dark wing fanned out over the ice plant, then retracted.

It wasn't a parrot. At least not a normal one. Whatever it was - it was injured. It couldn't fly well at all.

The bird was completely under the ice plant. Sandy kept its location in sight as she crab-walked over to the stairway.

Maybe its wing was broken. She might be able to splint it.

Hsssss —

Sandy straightened. She'd never heard a sound like that from a bird.

Her shoulders were even with it now. But her willingness to help the bird had shrunk to zero with that awful sound.

Some of that ice plant began to move and a shudder raced down her spine.

Whatever that thing was, it was coming toward her.

She pushed off, started swinging the other way.

Its progress was halting and clumsy.

What was she afraid of? It was slow and injured, and just a bird. It was nothing she couldn't just kick away or squash if she really had to.

Gray wings butterflied out over the ground-cover. They were big, much bigger than she would have thought. *Slowly, its misshapen head rose above the ice plant* —

Sandy left the rope, jumping three dangerous steps at a leap, flying over them head down, her eyes squarely on her feet, not because the footing was treacherous, which it was, *but because she didn't want to see that thing again.* Not for anything.

Behind her, it squawked and hissed, flapped its useless wings and tried to take flight; and Sandy bit down on her tongue so hard she tasted copper, her watering eyes glued to the tops of her bare feet and nowhere else.

Because she knew exactly what was behind her — and it was something best left unseen.

It was the dog Mom hit with her car and didn't quite kill when Sandy was eight. It was the lizard Tom once decapitated with a rock, the one whose tail kept thrashing anyway; the baby sparrow fresh from its shell that an older kid stomped on the sidewalk in first grade. It was all those things she should never have seen, but did. It was all those and worse!

She hit level ground running way too fast, leaning way too far, and she fell, screaming, to her knees.

To her absolute horror, she heard it take flight once more. It flapped over her shoulder, crashed through the backwater reeds in a yellow cloud of dust and dandelion spray. Sandy was up before the dust settled, ignoring her skinned shins and running *fast*.

Beyond the bridge, the cobalt sky turned a hazy burnt orange where it drained into the ocean. Mosquitoes buzzed Sandy's ears.

On the backwater side of the bridge, the water stank. It wasn't an unnatural smell. If anything it was *too natural and earthy*, the musky, yellow underbelly of animal life. Her science teacher had said life began in a fermenting, protein soup. Sandy figured it probably smelled a lot like this.

Plenty of primordial soup here in the backwater. It was an area she usually avoided.

The bird was most likely still struggling where she'd last seen it crash. When she was good and ready, she'd walk the *long* way back home, across the bridge, up the streets and far away from the backwater; she didn't care how long it took.

She found herself even with the second pillar and a breeze carried with it a hint of a voice so pure and sweet that, for a moment, Sandy forgot the bird, forgot how smelly and spooky the backwater was. She stopped and listened, gauged the position of that beautiful sound, and started that way.

When she found Bruce, he stood with his broad back to her, singing "Surfer Girl" by the Beach Boys. If his sides hadn't been working like a bellows, she'd never have believed it was actually Bruce's voice coming out.

"*Wow...*" she said, without thinking.

Bruce whirled and nearly lost his balance. His face and neck went bright red.

"*Wow,*" she said again. The bird, the mosquitoes and the smelly backwater receded into nothingness. "*How can you sing like that?*"

Bruce looked like someone who'd run into a room with a specific purpose in mind, but forgotten what that purpose was. Then his big moon of a face brightened with a confident smile. The blush faded.

He shook his head, "I don't know. Just always have. I used to figure *everybody* could."

"They can't. I know *I* can't."

Bruce grinned, beaming. Then, just as quickly, the confidence seemed to drain away, his purpose suddenly remembered.

"Sandy," His voice was quiet and low now. "When Pete died —" It trailed off like a question and Sandy nodded. In her head, she saw a shiny box and flowers, the ocean rolling calmly behind. Would she always think of Pete that way?

"You know it happened right after Michael got hit."

Sandy waited for Bruce. His thought was obviously traveling somewhere and he'd expected Sandy to go right with it, but she had no idea where that train was headed. She saw Mom casually casting Michael from her life, and tried to think of something else.

Bruce said, "Did you see those...*things* in the water? I mean, did you get a good look?"

Long, tan streaks in the blue-green water. So many, swimming so hard the water looked like it was boiling.

But that's all they had been from her vantage point – tan streaks in the water. Finally, she had to shake her head, "no."

"I did." Bruce said, "I just didn't believe what I saw. I mean...until Mark said what he said."

That cold shiver ran between her shoulder blades again. She'd started her morning preparing for a funeral, and somehow the day had gone south from there.

Bruce hitched his shoulders, as though shrugging off the same chill she'd just had.

"Mark said they weren't sharks, and he was right. I know the papers said they were, but what do they know? They weren't there."

"So maybe they were rays or something else - what does that have to do with Michael?"

"It's just that - I mean, the way it happened, and when - right after Michael got hit and everything, and..."

"And what?"

"Remember how Ray's surfboard looked?"

Chunks of board rolling in the surf. Gouged across and through.

It was an image Sandy wanted to forget, because somewhere out there, *she knew Pete looked the same way.*

"Rays don't do that – and it didn't look like shark bites either," Bruce went on, "I mean, *look –* "

He pulled a wadded magazine picture from his pocket and unfolded it.

It was a photo of a surfer who'd been bitten. It was mean and nasty and hard for Sandy to look at. This surfer wasn't dead, but he should have been. The hole in his side had healed, at least the skin had closed over it, but there was a huge sunburst shaped chunk of him missing.

She couldn't look anymore.

"The holes in the board didn't look like that. Do you remember?"

She winced, "what do you mean?"

"I mean, the gouges weren't even like that. They were really big and deep at the corners. Like the teeth were a whole lot bigger there. *Like fangs.*

Like this –"

He pulled out another picture. This one was all smudged and wrinkled, from one of those monster magazines Bruce and Michael loved. She knew the monster; it was Lon Chaney, Junior as the Wolf Man. His lips were pulled back in a snarl, the teeth in the middle looked sharp and dangerous enough, but the ones on either side were long and curved like a dog's.

"You're saying Pete was killed by the Wolfman?"

Bruce shook his head.

"No. But it was something with teeth like that; maybe claws too. I've been looking through *Outdoor Life* for attack pictures from other animals, you know, like bears and stuff –"

From his pockets, he pulled wad after wad of nasty black and white magazine photos. All hideous.

"Bruce. These are really gross."

"Yeah, but."

"I can't remember what I saw," she said at last. "I don't even *want* to."

He nodded.

"I knew you wouldn't. That's why I went back and got this."

Bruce squatted next to a tangle of weeds, and pulled them away.

Sandy blinked back tears when she saw the pinstriped surfboard. This piece was less than a foot across, but the bite was clear. The gouges on either side were huge. It was exactly what she'd wanted to forget.

"How could you keep that?"

His face blanched.

"I – I had to know."

"It was sharks! And Pete's dead and that's just the way it is!"

She moved to kick it away, but her foot stopped short. She couldn't even touch it.

Bruce shook his head. When he spoke, finally, his voice was quiet and even, the way adults speak, and Sandy couldn't help but listen.

"No, Sandy. It wasn't sharks. It wasn't even a fish. I mean, *most* of it wasn't."

He unfolded one more picture. This one was a drawing, a silhouette of a creature with the wings and the head of an eagle, the body of a lion.

"They call this one a *Griffon*, but there are different kinds of these things. You see 'em on old armor and stuff. *It's like those pictures at* Michael's house. The ones his dead brother painted."

"This is stupid –" But even as she said it, she felt something like cold foam pumping into her stomach and lungs. *Wide, gray wings spreading over dead ice-plant, a strange, misshapen head rising above those wings.*

And now she saw what she wouldn't let herself see before: the bird's head wasn't misshapen – it was simply wrong – not the head of a bird at all. *The head of a lizard.*

"What do we really know about Michael?"

Sandy started to answer. Then something inside her snapped shut.

The awful images went away. She shook her head, "I know...I like him," she said, softly.

"Yeah. I like him to..." Bruce flushed, understanding now the depth of what Sandy meant, and that it was very different.

"Oh," he said. He rocked back a little on his heels and stared down at his feet. And then he didn't say anything, as if everything he'd been trying so hard to tell her just wasn't important anymore.

"What's wrong?"

Bruce lifted his face into the sky. She thought she saw something flash at the corner of his eye, but when he turned back whatever it had been was gone.

"Nothing. I mean...I guess I sort of figured. Nothing."

There was a tug in her chest that wasn't quite pain. For a second, Sandy saw herself and Bruce from somewhere above; she saw the reeds and sand around them, and the distance between them. The realization came a moment later: *I've hurt him.* She wondered where had it come from, this awful power she had.

And, just like that, everything changed again.

"You're right," Bruce said, "it was stupid. I mean, it *had* to be sharks didn't it? I've got a real imagination - my mom even says so."

A breeze rose up with the bad smell from the backwater. She avoided looking down at the piece of ruined board down in those reeds.

"I should go home," she heard herself say, "Mom's expecting me," even though she really didn't want to go home, and she *really* didn't want to see her mom. And then she said something, she hadn't said for the longest time, "Big Jerry's tomorrow?"

Bruce nodded.

Chapter 15

The Priest

The house was small and poorly kept. St. Bartholomew was a "well-to-do" Parish, school tuition was not cheap. This home was nothing like the one the Helms must have enjoyed in Phoenix. The priest checked the address again.

He was at the right house, but it looked abandoned. The dust-blown car parked out front hadn't been used in some time; sand had drifted halfway to the hubs. Eventually, it would rust and crumble like the junker truck decaying in an empty lot next door.

A terrible mistake, this destructive quest of his.

If the Helms had been here, they were certainly gone now. The trail was dead, there was no more information in the files and he would look no further.

"Thank God," he whispered an almost overwhelming sense of relief.

As much as he felt the need to confront Michael, he hadn't known just how badly he had dreaded it.

He closed his eyes, took a deep breath, and prayed silently.

Perhaps he had achieved something in trying – what psychologists described as "closure." He would go home to his Parish now and do his best to forget and move on.

The sound of footfalls in the sand shook him from his reverie.

A glimpse of a white T-shirt and blue jeans. A boy scurrying around the side of the house. His heart seized, a breath frozen in his chest.

He let his breath go, slowly took another and swallowed. It could be a neighborhood kid checking out the abandoned house. Up to no good, certainly, but not worth a heart attack. He was okay.

So why was the slish-slosh of his own blood so loud in his ears? Why was his heart pounding so wildly now?

A high-pitched giggle – it cut off quickly. The universal sound of children doing what they shouldn't be.

And Father Mulhenney, unsure and awkward in *plainclothes* - jeans, a work shirt and no white collar - realized he was the total mark standing there petrified in front of an abandoned shack. Kids sensed weakness far more acutely than adults. And were much less restrained than adults in taking advantage of it. What was coming next? A water balloon?

He stepped as quietly as possible around the side of the house.

No one there.

But there were fresh footprints in the sand. Prints everywhere you could actually *see* the sand. Pumpkin vines had spread from the empty lot next door to cover most of the ground all the way up the side of the small house.

Mulhenney picked his way to the nearest window, tried to peek inside. The window was partially open, leaving the afternoon breeze to gently push the shade away.

But all he could see was darkness and his own reflection; a man much older than his years, haggard, gray, and weary.

Another pair of eyes appeared next to his.

"God!"

Mulhenney tripped on the vines and pain blazed up through his ankle to his hip as he fell into the pumpkin patch, his skin chafed by a million pins.

The boy giggled freely as he ran to the truck.

Mulhenney choked off an expletive, and managed to stand. His ankle protested, but held. He gingerly touched the scrapes on his cheeks, and angrily brushed the traces of blood onto his jeans.

"Michael?"

Mulhenney followed, vines crunched beneath his leather shoes, bathing his soles in their slimy juices.

Deep inside the pumpkin jungle, rusted metal creaked and crumbled. The door swing out, dropping a shower of bright orange dust that billowed over the patch. When was his last tetanus booster? Could have a problem there.

"Michael I only want to talk to you. *You're not in trouble.*"

.-=.-=.-=.-=.-

Sandy had charted a long route home for certain, one that took her along the backwater and brought her even with her house before turning back toward it. Very close to their fort.

More importantly, the fort was not far from Big Jerry's Market. And straight up from Big Jerry's was Michael's house. She accepted that was exactly why she'd headed this way in the first place, even though she'd told herself it wasn't when she started.

And now her heart was pounding like crazy. Usually, when she wanted to do something, even something that might just get her in trouble, she didn't hesitate. Sandy hesitated now. She even took a couple steps back toward her own house. But then she turned around.

From here, Michael's house was just a patch of shingles worn gray by years of sun, salt, and neglect.

Sandy took a deep, calming breath. The day Pete was killed she'd called Michael the second she'd gotten home to see if he was okay. No one answered. No one had answered for days.

Neither Michael nor Bruce had met her at Big Jerry's. She'd even stopped at the fort, just in case they'd left a message for her.

They hadn't.

She'd learned from her dad that every head injury was serious. The real effects didn't always show up right away. Michael could have collapsed on his way home, or even the next day.

Tom might really have killed him with his surfboard.

She didn't know why, but that just didn't feel right. Somehow she was sure Michael was okay.

Instead, Tom's best friend was killed.

It happened right after Michael got hit...just like Bruce said.

"That's stupid," she said, and her own voice startled her.

What do we really know about Michael?

She could kill Bruce for putting those thoughts in her head. Bruce and his stupid monster pictures – he was just jealous. He wanted her to be his girlfriend and he knew she liked Michael. That was obvious enough.

The sun had crept closer to the water; the shadow from the bridge had crept closer to her. She hadn't moved any closer to Michael's house.

Somewhere, a dog barked, a hoarse and choppy sound. Dogs barking should be a familiar neighborhood sound, a normal sound. She didn't know why it wasn't.

It sounds weird because Bruce showed you that stupid wolfman picture and a grody shark-bite photograph right after.

Seagulls shrieked overhead. They were flying in from the ocean now, better pickings at the garbage dump than the beach this time of day.

The flutter of huge wings. A squawk. A hiss. Something awful raising its head from the groundcover.

Sandy didn't like being scared. It didn't happen often, and the very idea of it made her angry. She was mad at Bruce for planting the seeds about Michael and the animals with all the different parts.

But the sharks had been swimming all wrong that day, she knew that much – up and down, not exactly like the graceful rise and fall of dolphin – but really more like a dolphin than sharks. They were sea creatures of some kind, but maybe Bruce was right and their teeth were like wolves…or lions.

Sea-lions…

"They call this one a Griffon," Bruce had said, *"but it's pieces of all sorts of animals."*

Wolf-man. Sea-lion.

Stupid. It's all stupid. It's those dumb *Famous Monsters* magazines.

But there was something about sea lions that wouldn't leave her.

Where was it coming from? She shook her head.

Her heart was still pounding. She was scared, and she was angry.

It was the anger that made her start walking again.

-=-=-=-=-

"You're not in trouble at all, Michael."

More giggling from inside that truck.

More than one child. There were at least three voices.

"Duh – don't do that," A girl's voice.

My God, were they playing dirty games now? Right here in front of him? *Sex destroyed the best of young lives.* Mulhenney pushed himself forward, ignoring the pain in his ankle. Another vine caught his heel, stabbing more pain into his leg.

"Damn!"

The cab of the old truck was tall; the windshield was blocked by broad leaves and vines.

"Stop it!" Mulhenney shouted. "In the name of God! Stop!"

The boys giggled louder than ever, but not the girl.

"Please. I don't want to –"

Mulhenney stopped dead in his tracks beside the truck. He recognized her voice.

He recognized all of their voices.

Mulhenney wrenched the door open. It fell at his feet with a metallic shriek and a choking dust-devil of rust.

The truck's upholstery had long since crumbled away to the elements, still Mary Clayton's rotting body lay stretched across its front seat, the tattered remains of her blue-plaid skirt hiked to her waist. Two rusty springs had twisted their way through her bloated flesh.

Will Barton, dressed in the Boy Scout uniform he'd been buried in, straddled her. He'd turned to face Mulhenney when the cab door ripped off. The ruin of his brain puffed through the star-shaped crater that had been his left eye socket.

Nicholas Helm, his own face a patchwork of suture and wax, knelt in front of Mary near what had once been the passenger seat. He looked up to Mulhenney and smiled.

"Hey, Father, you want a piece of this?"

Alec Mulhenney blinked the sun, the terrible vision, from his eyes. He was still several feet from the truck. He'd never reached it, had never looked inside at all. His knees failed him; and Mulhenney barely saved himself a face-plant in the sand. No sign of a boy in the pumpkin patch, no one here but a foolish old priest on a fool's quest.

The vision had been so real.

Maybe he was crazy after all.

No. He'd seen what he'd seen. *What God had intended him to see.* There was a reason for all of this. Just maybe he was closer now to understanding *everything.* Saving Michael wasn't his mission alone, it was God's mission. Every moment in pursuit of his quest drew him closer to the Divine.

Surely shadows would fall across his path. Alec Mulhenney had just stepped out from one of those shadows now. It was all becoming so clear.

What had been a matter of faith was becoming a matter of *understanding.* God had chosen *him,* as he had chosen so few, to be touched by the miraculous. Yes, Mulhenney understood it all now. *Truly understood.*

He wiped the tears of rapture from the corners of his eyes in time to glimpse a white bird flying past him to find a perch within the rusted-out cab of the truck. *A dove?* Of course.

Miracles were the *power to change the very elements of the world.* They were the manifestation of God's touch on earth. Forged by the Divine and channeled through mankind, through those who opened themselves to the Divine. Mulhenney had seen that power with his own eyes.

But mankind was imperfect. Only a select few, only true saints, could channel that power and resist the temptation to abuse it.

When channeled by the imperfect, the impure, war happened, famine happened...*Michael happened.*

Mulhenney alone had made the connection. The animalistic destruction of the innocents of his Parish; Mary Clayton, Will Barton, and Nicholas Helm.

The connection was Michael Helm.

From deep within the truck, the bird flapped its wings, strong and loud.

The tears dried on Mulhenney's cheek. How could he have mistaken a gull for a dove?

A rusted panel fell from the truck and powdered. The beating of wings impossibly loud now. The truck creaked with the percussive beats, shuddered.

A new vision?

Mulhenney withdrew his rosary. His thumb rubbed the silver crucifix reflexively, as he approached the old truck. *What would this vision reveal?*

Something plunged through the window so fast he felt the white heat of pain knifing into his wrist before he saw –

Talons. So long and sharp that one split the bones of his forearm cleanly before the pain could hit him; hot red fluid geysered up, spat into his eyes –

In the vine-choked lot beside Michael's house, the junker rocked as if to shake off its own skin, to be reborn, a bright orange cloud of rust billowed into the afternoon sky, followed by the winged shadow of an eagle in flight, and the deep-throated roar of a jungle cat.

A blood-streaked hand thrust itself out the driver's side window; the silver cross hanging from it rang against the frame. The rosary dropped soundlessly to the broad leaves and sand below. A heartbeat later the hand slipped back within the cab. The truck settled back and went silent.

-=-=-=-=-

By the time Sandy reached Michael's street, the sun had drifted beneath the hills well on its way to the water.

It was a long way till dark; still, most of the windows she'd passed were lit, giving her a clear view into the kitchens and dens. Mothers were cooking, and somewhere, one of them was baking fresh bread. Sandy's stomach growled.

There were no lights on at Michael's house.

She just wanted to see him, just talk for a few minutes and see what was going on. Then she'd head home. She'd take the bridge this time.

Sandy wasn't going anywhere near the backwater tonight.

Now she wished she'd ridden her bike.

The Helm's car was home, but it was pretty clear his mom hadn't driven it for a while; the sand seemed to be holding it place. Would they have left town without it?

A lot of the houses on this side of the backwater were showing their wear, but the Helm's roof was balding and down to tar-paper in spots, its eaves were warped and peeling. It looked empty.

Sandy found a part of the front door where the paint wasn't peeling and scratchy, and knocked.

Nothing.

She put her ear close to the door, and held her breath to listen.

When someone stepped from the side of the house; Sandy flattened against the door, her heart thumped. For the first time she admitted she was *afraid* to be here.

But it was only Bruce.

"I don't think anybody's home," he said.

"I was supposed to go home. I started to go –" She explained, and, as lame as it sounded, that was mostly true.

Bruce nodded quickly, too nice to catch her in a lie.

"Me too. I mean, I did go home…then I sort of figured I should just come out here and talk to Michael."

"Well…" She felt stupid and totally off-balance.

"I walked around the back. I didn't see anyone," Bruce shrugged.

I should leave, and leave now, she thought. Still, Sandy couldn't bring herself to walk away. She'd come this far. "Did you check Michael's window?"

"No." Bruce glanced around quickly, as if someone might be listening. "The kitchen window's broken and there's glass all around it. I went back to Michael's window – but I didn't climb up and look in."

Sandy glanced across the pumpkin patch at the houses beyond, then looked carefully both ways up the street. The houses were haphazardly arranged, there were certainly windows with views of Michael's room, and they'd be taking a chance.

"Maybe we should."

The vines snaked all the way up the side of the house. A decent-sized pumpkin peeked out from wide leaves beneath Michael's window.

The shade was down, but his window was open.

"I'm just going to look in and see if he's there," and even as she said it, Sandy knew that wasn't true. *She meant to go inside.* One way or the other, she'd meant to get inside his house from the moment she'd walked up the driveway. Fear stood at the doorway of most good things. A thrill was beginning to build. *She'd caught a perfect wave just starting to curl.*

"Watch out for the army men!" Bruce warned.

She pushed the shade back and poked her head in. His bed was made. His door was shut and the room was mostly dark. There was a tang of cleanser in the air; an even stronger and welcoming aroma of fresh paint. At least Mrs. Helm cared about how the *inside* of the house looked.

Michael's room was all boy – plastered with monster pictures except for one big poster of some guy from the Los Angeles Rams. She'd never been in here before – Mrs. Helm would never have allowed a girl anywhere *near* Michael's room, and despite Sandy's concern for Michael, she couldn't deny the sense of victory she felt right now.

Not a sound from inside the house.

True to Bruce's warning, two green riflemen guarded the windowsill. She crawled straight onto Michael's bed without upsetting the soldiers on the sill, and swung her feet away, careful not to get sand all over his blanket.

She didn't even notice the two other riflemen her ponytail knocked off his pillow.

Outside, Bruce walked in compact circles, keenly aware of his over-sized visibility, of how wrong this was, and how much trouble they were in. He saw himself mortified at the police station, hands pink and fat as party balloons encircled by cold steel cuffs, just waiting for his dad to come and give him Hell.

He counted four windows down the street, two more across the lot. Someone could pass any one of them at any moment and see them breaking in.

We're not breaking in – the window was open.

It was still wrong.

We're looking out for Michael. But in a big way they were spying on him too, and Michael was the best friend Bruce ever had. He'd sensed a basic goodness in Michael from the start – once he'd gotten over being embarrassed, anyway. He had the feeling that Michael liked him, that he didn't even care how big Bruce was. No one else was like that – not even Sandy, really.

Bruce squinted at all the windows, and took a deep, wheezy breath.

He backhanded the sweat off his forehead.

It looked like Michael was gone – but what if he wasn't? Or what if Michael just walked up the street and found them? What then? What would he do?

Bruce saw the seawater roil; saw surfboards flipping fin over nose, dumping their screaming riders, and as the surfers fell through the air, gigantic, toothy lion heads broke from the chop to catch them. What if he'd been right and Michael really was responsible for those things?

He shut the image off, his eyes darting from window to window now.

It didn't help that he felt as big as these houses. *With stupid, ugly red hair* that stands out like cherries on a police wagon.

What would Michael do to them?

What was really on the other side of Michael's shiny coin? That was the side Bruce was *really* here to see – it was the dark half that Bruce somehow needed to get a handle on. Sandy felt it too, that was obvious. And that was why they were here – *spying on their friend.*

What could Michael do?

He imagined the sand shifting, falling away beneath his feet, a huge serpent rising from the darkness below with a cavernous maw armed not with two long fangs but hundreds, rows and rows of 'em, a whole cavern filled with shark teeth –

"Sandy –" he hissed.

She didn't answer.

"Come on, Sandy –"

She poked her head out from under the blind, sending one of Michael's soldiers spinning into the air. Bruce tried to catch it and missed. It hit a wide pumpkin leaf and disappeared.

"Geez – be careful with those!"

"Coast is clear! Climb in."

Bruce spread the leaves apart where the soldier fell, but under those leaves were even more leaves, and thick, twisting vines full of sharp spines.

"Bruce, we don't have all day!"

"But he'll know we were here! I bet he sets those guys up the same way every time he goes out!"

The soldier was a prone sniper with a long rifle. Now he lay upright over a leaf stem, his rifle sighted straight up into the air. But his feet were buried in sand next to a trio of fresh cigarette butts.

Who would be smoking outside Michael's window?

Bruce picked up one of the butts along with the army man.

It wasn't dried out or faded. It hadn't been there long at all.

"Come on, Bruce!"

He threw the butt away, hanging on to the sniper as he squeezed himself through the window. Sandy was already halfway down the hallway.

Bruce quickly replaced both men on the sill. He aimed them outside.

But was that right? Was that how they were?

He faced them roughly toward each other. Crossfire. Anything bad that came in *(like us)* would be in for a crossfire. That was probably the way Michael had set them up. *Or was it?*

Sandy was completely out of sight.

This is bad.

He bounced in place, caught halfway between following Sandy down the hall or just climbing back out that window and running.

"Come on!" She hissed.

He bounded toward the door like an obedient dog, and something rubbery squashed beneath his shoe. His foot shot straight up like he'd stepped on a nail.

A green rifleman, whose rifle would never again be straight, rolled out from beneath his shoe.

"Ohhh nooo –"

Bruce snatched it up, tried to fix it, and the barrel came off in his fingers.

This is very bad.

"Bruce!"

We shouldn't be in here! We shouldn't be in here!

He tossed the soldier and his nub of a rifle out the window and into the vines.

We shouldn't be in here!

And he never would have come in if it hadn't been for Sandy, but the truth was he wanted to be there as much as Sandy did – maybe even more. He had to see those paintings again; to see them up close without Michael around.

And this was the only way to do it.

So he lumbered down the hallway as quickly and quietly as he could, trying not to punish the floor with his weight. One doorway in the hall was shut, and that scared him a little, but by the time he got to it, Sandy was standing in the den, and he had no choice but to go there too.

The den was murky and gray with the dusk filtering through the curtains. In that dim light, all he could see in Nicky's paintings were the whites of tiny eyes. *So many eyes.*

To his horror, Sandy reached for the lamp.

"No!"

But before Bruce could stop her, she'd twisted it on.

But it wasn't that bright. The lamp threw a weak cone of dinge against the wall, and shadows everywhere else. Just enough light to bring the paintings to life, to make Nicky's creatures leap from their strange forest. There were three paintings, one very large bracketed by two thinner ones, that might close over the main one like shutters...or open to reveal another world. Bruce tried to think of where he'd seen that before, and finally it came to him – in Church. There were pictures like this of the saints.

In a weird way, he thought, *there is a holiness about these too* – a reverence to detail, the way feathers gave way to hide, to scales; the way lifelike eyes peered from endless depths. Impossible beasts, fashioned from various parts of others.

Just like those things in the water...

All but one. A doe stood at the water's edge – an actual deer, no extra parts that he could see.

"Sandy – look..."

But then an explosion of bright light filled the room and Bruce's heart slammed his ribs so hard it took his breath away.

Bruce froze. Sandy's shoulders nearly shot up past her ears.

A growl that seemed to come from a gravel pit, "Do you have any idea how much trouble you're in?"

It had been an overhead light, not an atomic blast, but Bruce would have welcomed the blast. The overhead switched off; the shadows became darker than ever.

Michael's mom stood in the kitchen – *it had to be Mrs. Helm, didn't it?* He could only see a silhouette against the kitchen window. She wore a rumpled bathrobe, her hair seemed a mass of tangles over the rest of her face, the white of one eye was the only feature he could really make out, and it seemed to glow in the gloom like the eyes in Nicky's paintings.

"The window was open –" Bruce started.

Her eye was fixed and unmoving, and Bruce suddenly knew a fear way beyond that of being arrested, of the beating his father would surely give him, and his throat locked up tight, shut off any further chance at explanation.

"Get out of here," she said softly.

Bruce blinked as if golden sunshine had just rained down from a stormy sky. He and Sandy spun on their heels, nodding like bobble-head dolls.

"Not you, Sandy."

Sandy stopped so fast it was like Michael's mom had pulled an invisible string and yanked her backwards. *They'd been so near escape.* Sandy's eyes implored Bruce, *don't leave me alone with her.* Bruce had never seen her frightened before, had never even considered the idea Sandy *could* be frightened, and that scared him even worse than Mrs. Helm turning on the lights.

"Bruce. Out, now!" Mrs. Helm commanded, the gravel rattling in her throat.

He bolted the way they'd come, toward Michael's room.

"The front door!"

Bruce about-faced and slammed straight into the door frame, rattling everything that wasn't nailed down in the house. He swung the door open and plunged outside. When he hit the road he sucked his breath painfully back in and kept running without looking back.

-=.=.=.=-

"We weren't going to take anything –"

Sandy's eyes were adjusting to the dim light. Now she saw the house wasn't really clean at all, it just *smelled* like cleaner and paint. The furniture had been shoved off-kilter, one of the sofa's pillows rested beside it on the floor. It looked like there *was* fresh paint on some of the walls, but the job had been sloppily done; a darker color showed through in patches. The sour sweet scent of rotten food was beginning to emerge beneath the assault of paint and cleanser.

There was something much worse here than the trouble she was in. An impossible notion –

This isn't Michael's mom.

She should run, get the hell out of here now. *But it was Mrs. Helm, it had to be.* She hadn't broken in, not exactly, but Mrs. Helm could say she had – there was that broken kitchen window. If she just ran, she really would be in serious trouble.

The woman didn't say anything, at first. Her eye traced a line of ice over Sandy's body, then roamed the worn-out rug, the haphazardly painted walls.

"No, of course not. What would a kid like you want from a place like this?"

Sandy shook her head, her voice barely came out.

"I didn't mean that."

But Mrs. Helm didn't seem to be listening anyway. Suddenly, Sandy had the creepy feeling she was alone in the room. She pushed that thought aside.

"We were worried about Michael. He got hurt at the beach last week. We called – we've both been calling and no one –"

"You wanted to see the paintings, didn't you?"

Sandy shook her head *"no"* even though they both knew that was a lie. She did want to see those paintings again. *Wanted to look hard and long at them.* Bruce had planted a seed in her head she couldn't dislodge.

"Where's Michael?"

"He's not here."

There was no use asking exactly where he'd gone. The woman was on an entirely different track.

Mrs. Helm stepped past her to the wall, and Sandy jumped, the skin seeming to roll across her shoulders and back.

"They're *incredible*, aren't they?"

The way to the door was clear. It was maybe ten steps, no more, and if Sandy bolted she'd be free and clear outside where the air was fresh and she wouldn't have to be creeped-out by this woman anymore and she would never come back. She'd explain it to the police later.

She didn't do it. As queer as Mrs. Helm was acting, she *was* Michael's mom after all. She was medicated, she might even be drunk. But she was just a woman, not a witch or some sort of monster, and Sandy had come here for a reason.

Mrs. Helm stood close to the paintings, so close that those red hawk eyes, and the yellow lizard ones, all those other eyes seemed to be watching *her*, waiting for her.

Those impossible creatures were *so real* in all their strangeness, and odd combinations. When Michael's mom turned back to Sandy, her head tilted a certain way. There was something so familiar in the pose Sandy couldn't look away.

"They're amazing."

"You don't know *how* amazing they are," Mrs. Helm said. "*How amazing he is.* If he'd only paint again, I think everything would be all right."

She had really snapped. *How could Nicky paint again, ever?*

"Nicky's dead." Sandy heard herself say, "He fell off a cliff."

Mrs. Helm tilted her head, and when she did, the hair fell away from a dark and terrible bruise on her cheek.

"Is that what Michael told you?"

Sandy's entire body seemed to blink. It was the slip and fall in your dreams – a piece of reality breaking off high out of sight and smacking you square in head.

Right in front of her, alligators with wide, white wings soared between the vines and broad leaves of a tropical a rain forest, while below, leopards waited in the coils of their rattlesnake tails. And from just beneath the surface of a river, a very special animal peered directly at Sandy. It was a lion, at least, it had the head of a lion, but fading into the darkness of the water, its body tapered into the sleek, gray hull of a dolphin.

Sea lion.

Inconspicuous and small, a signature was scrawled in dark green oil at the bottom of each painting. Barely readable, but very clear to her now.

The jagged scrawl after the letter "N" for Nicholas wasn't simply a flourish – it was the last curve of the letter "M" for Michael.

"Nicky didn't paint these?"

Mrs. Helm laughed painfully.

"Nicky couldn't do a damn thing. Except be mean." Tears collected in the lines of her smile.

"I just didn't know how mean he could be. God, I don't know, maybe I did. Maybe I ignored it – I just, can't remember anymore. I've lost so many…moments. I –"

She stopped, looking blank and lifeless as a wind-up toy whose spring has suddenly broken. A moment later, she started where she'd left off.

"I just let Nicky do what he did…I just let it all happen."

"Nicky's accident..." Sandy said.

The woman visibly shook, she laughed again, nearly slapping herself covering her mouth.

"There was no accident. Michael killed him. He killed his brother."

Sandy wanted to hit her. No, to pound the life out of her and scream that only a horrible, horrible mother would say something like that about her son. Michael was good. He was her friend. He deserved a better mom, not someone doped up on pills, not this miserable drunk of a woman.

But Sandy couldn't say anything.

Mrs. Helm looked up at her suddenly and the hair slipped away from her face. The woman's left cheek wasn't only bruised; it was shattered, so swollen her dilated left eye had nearly left its socket.

"Get out of my house."

Sandy's knees buckled. The threadbare carpet was real beneath her bare feet. It covered a floor made of concrete. The concrete floor was attached to this planet. *So how could it be dropping away from her now?*

How could she be falling so far away?

Sandy's feet slid over the abyss, slip-sliding over nothing and to nowhere, then they made contact with the solid world and the next thing she knew she was flying through the front door and back into the real world, her chest and stomach heaving.

Behind her a voice like a cold, chafing wind.

"I knew," it cried, "I think I *always* knew.

Chapter 16

They Usually Don't Stay

Sandy's view of everything had changed – even their swimming pool. The gleaming white vacuum hose coiled cobra-like on the terrazzo near the cabana; there were evil, broken faces in the flagstone and mortar of their barbecue; their redwood fence was a jaw bristling with sharp red teeth.

Beyond, were darkening skies with ever-shifting clouds.

Her mother's knock at the door seemed far away and pointless, she shook her head, "no," before her mom asked,

"Honey, aren't you the least bit hungry?" *No. Not the least bit.*

She had carried the storm clouds with her through the house tonight, and her parents had seen them, and kept their distance.

As far as they were concerned she'd seen her best friend buried today. She had a right to be moody. She was sure that's what they thought.

They had no idea.

"There was no accident. Michael killed him."

So many thoughts and images to sew together. So much to understand.

What had happened to Mrs. Helm? Did she believe Michael had done that too? *Was it possible he had?*

Sandy watched clouds shape-shift over the valley; they grew from formless blobs to horses, to bears and elephants, and combinations of all kinds of things, creatures she'd never seen before. *Creatures never meant to* be.

What terror had his mother only barely survived? And where was Michael now? Had he survived?

It was the bottle rocket.

It was what happened when you had something awesome inside, something that had to come out. You soared like a rocket, or you blew up.

You and everything, *everyone,* around you.

Michael was talking about Bruce then, at least Sandy thought he was. But even that picture was different now, as different and strange as any of *Michael's* paintings.

It had always been Michael. *All of those magical, thoroughly frightening creations were his.* And, one day Michael must have stopped painting altogether. Not only stopped – *began lying that he'd ever painted in the first place.* He'd stuffed the neck of his own bottle.

Why? What was he scared of? What had Nicky done to *him?*

What made him explode?

The possibilities of Nicky's demise made her shudder, and brought a much closer horror near the surface: she hadn't witnessed Pete's final moments, and hadn't seen the aftermath – only the collateral damage done to his brother's newest surfboard.

Thank God.

Nicky's murder opened imagination's window to the tan streaks in the water, *to snarling faces and gaping jaws breaking through the surface.* Faces of a terrifying and terrible death, faces all the more horrific because they didn't *belong* there. *Another world had formed where anything was possible – no matter how awful.*

"There was no accident. Michael killed him." Pete too.

Impossible. As detailed and lifelike as those paintings were, painting fantastical beasts on a canvas was a far cry from creating something that lived and breathed...*and murdered.*

The clouds had encircled the moon. The blue, moon-dog eye stared down at her.

Moon-dog.

Sea-lion. It had been that easy for him. *Bible* - easy. *The word was said, and the word was made so.*

Was it really possible Michael was capable of something far more powerful than making a painted image lifelike? Seeing the painting today had nearly brought it all back to her, but his mom had scared Sandy nearly to death and broken the thought mid-flight.

Now she saw herself sharing the surf with Michael, talking about Avalon, and the sea lion. She'd given him the words.

Did Michael really only need the words to do it?

Had Nicky tortured him until Michael had somehow crossed that line?

Her mind was racing now, going places she never intended to go. She'd trained herself to fight her fear, the most dangerous waves were always the best ride, and now she couldn't stop herself.

What had happened next?

Once Michael saw the raw power unleashed, he'd shut it down. Shut it all down.

Or tried to... but maybe he'd only choked-off the bottle rocket. He'd made it worse. Even more powerful.

Impossible. But her fingers trembled at the thought, her stomach rolled softly. It must have seemed impossible to his mom too.

Until now.

That wretched voice of despair, leaking through the walls of Michael's home, *"I knew. I think I always did."*

And once his mom had seen the truth, she'd blown up right along with the rocket. Now she was gone, body and mind.

There had been one animal Michael had left unchanged in his paintings, Bruce had noticed it too: The doe stepping one tentative hoof from its hiding place in the forest, its innocent eyes wide, awed by the strange beasts around it. Sandy now understood just what it was about that particular animal that seemed so familiar. The answer had crept close enough to touch her as she'd stood with Mrs. Helm, viewing the paintings tonight as if for the first time. But Sandy had been way too frightened to recognize it then.

The doe was Michael's mom.

-=-=-=-=-

Bruce whispered a song through air heavy with the gummy smoke of frying pork and scalded cooking grease. Breaded chops, a staple of Momma Stubik's breakfast menu, was soaking up everything that didn't burn off her two blackened skillets – both of which she worked with the urgent efficiency of a short-order cook as she sat, butt billowing over two well-placed stools.

Dad was hunkered down at the kitchen table, working his pencil over the daily scratch sheets from the Del Mar racetrack. The effluence from his cigar mingled with the greasy cloud over the stove, adding a cloying sweetness to it.

Bruce sang, barely making a sound, but exercising his lungs, throat, and diaphragm just the same, working on his breath control.

The *magic* was there. Even whispered, with a pillow inches from his lips, he could feel it.

Whisper-singing was a technique Bruce had developed out of necessity. In the years following Bud Stubik's infantry stint in the Korean War, *produce supplier* had been the *steadiest* of his professions, at least the one that looked most presentable on his son's school paperwork, but not the most profitable. But even Bruce knew his real job title included the word *shark,* and often required the use of sticks, saps, or fists; it was a trade plied in places of business even smokier and darker than the kitchen where he now sat. *"My son sings,"* was not a phrase uttered with fatherly pride in the Stubik household.

In his own home, Bruce had learned to exercise his vocal equipment in near silence. And right now, anywhere beyond the walls of his own home was the last place he wanted to be. He sat at the head of his lumpy, too-small bed; arms crossed over his pillow, and sang straight into the smoke-stained wall.

He'd chosen *Wild is the Wind,* which he knew was one of his mother's favorites – at least when Johnny Mathis sang it - as his ticket for winning the talent contest. Winning that contest would take him far away from the skinny kids on the beach, far from the local bullies, and farther still from the ridicule and fists of his father. Just as singing this song over and over, and over again ever since he'd shut the door to his room and caught his breath tonight, had taken him away from his fear, and from something far worse than fear: his thoughts about Michael and Sandy *and how he truly loved Sandy,* yes he did, yes he did, he admitted it, and how she'd never care for an ugly fat freak like him, and how he was finally made to understand that today –

And yet he sang about the desperate love in his heart, a love that was like the wind, wild and untamed – whisper-sang in that beautiful voice that was, in at least one way, like the proverbial sound of a tree falling in the forest, not a sound at all because Bruce was *no one,* and only Bruce heard it – *and thank god for that now, yes, thank god for that because if Dad hears me sing –*

But now, his whispered song took him from thoughts of just how close he'd come to *real trouble* for breaking into Michael's house, and just how scary Michael's mom was, and *Jesus Freaking Christ where was Michael and what had happened in that house anyway?*

So he sang almost silently, keeping his thoughts, hopes, and misery very much to himself, very much in the neck of the bottle.

And yet his love was wild, wild as the wind...

Only the tears, falling so hard he could hear them tap his pillow, would betray him, and no one would hear those either.

-=-=-=-=-

She shouldn't have come here. It was wrong. *Everything was wrong.*

Her parents were asleep, just as Sandy had been before she'd gotten the call. She was wide awake now. Or was she? The flowers, her desk, the moonlight through her window – everything was clear, everything was as it should be. And yet…it wasn't exactly. Such an odd bubble of numbness around her, a feeling that her feet didn't quite reach the floor, that her fingers didn't quite touch the sheets as she slid them away. And it hadn't been a call exactly that roused her, at least not a phone call or anything; it had been more of a thought.

Michael put that thought in her head, she was sure of it; his voice had been clear, and he'd asked her to walk into the night all the way to the backwater and badlands beyond.

But it wasn't walking really; it was more like flying, as though she were soaring high above it all, until finally, she plunged deep into to the cool, dark, heart of Michael's world.

The sulfurous primeval stink of the backwater was gone. There was no scent at all. And here, in Michael's world, the darkness wasn't black like night, but rich and saturated with cool violets and blues; the reeds, grass, and tumbleweeds, even the ice plant, were vibrant with hot greens, warm pinks and burnt orange. *A dream surely, there was an unearthly neatness about this place, with freshly mowed grass in the hollows, marble benches to rest on if you wanted. But she wasn't tired at all.*

She felt Michael's presence, knew he would be with her soon. She felt safe and at peace.

And with the thought, came the wave and rustle of tall reeds. But it wasn't Michael who came through to see her now, but a big dog, spotted white and black. It was more than big; it was huge, but sweet and cuddly.

She scruffed up the softness behind its ears, and...it purred like a big cat. There were more creatures now, watching her through the reeds, or approaching slowly to be pet. Here was an ostrich, no, not an ostrich but a giraffe with two long bird legs, its long neck craning out to gently brush her cheek with his own. Small dogs that, like the big one, acted more like cats, curling their smooth flanks against her calves, other furry creatures that seemed to be as much rabbit as squirrel, their long ears and noses twitching. One by one they came from their hiding places to greet her. The reeds had given way to evergreen and ferns, and now to marble benches and small pyramids of granite, beautifully sculpted angels and crosses.

"Some of them work, and some of them don't."

Michael's voice floated to her on a gentle breeze.

"When I make them, I don't know how they'll do. All I can do is try.

"They usually don't stay very long though."

"They're so pretty."

"Yeah - most of them are. Thanks."

The colors cooled, still vibrant but dominated by blues and violets, the warmer colors fading to gray. Some of the animals curled up on the grass, and soon they were fast asleep.

No. *Not asleep, not exactly. They were too still for sleep.* The breeze played with the feathers of a sleeping bird-creature, and some of those feathers floated away. The fur of a sleeping cat-dog lifted off in dandelion-like tufts.

Bodies thinned before her eyes, ribs appeared, small puddles, dark and shiny as molasses spread beneath the decay.

What had he said? *"They usually don't stay very long..."*

Now she saw where she was, what the badlands had really become.

What Michael really was.

"I don't want to be here."

"But you are here."

She had come on her own. She could leave on her own. She could float, soar, fly her way back home, back to her bed, the same way she'd come.

But she couldn't.

Purple clouds slid, and then raced across a black sky.

A stone angel stood in the shadows of a small bronze house. And beyond the house, row upon row of headstones.

"Please let me go," she pleaded, *"Everything you change dies."*

The angel said nothing.

-=-=-=-=-

"They found Alec."

It wasn't a surprise.

"I'll make coffee."

Deanne watched her cousin freeze right before her eyes. He was still dressed in what she called his "uniform" the white square at the center of his collar gleaming blue in the moonlight.

"Pat, come in."

"I..."

"It's late Pat, and it's cold. Come in, I'll make coffee."

She pushed the door wide and held it until, finally, he shuffled by her toward the kitchen. She waited till he was long past before she bit the cry from her tongue. Beyond her doorway, the dark hump of Camelback Mountain blotted out most of the stars. From here, she could see the tall, narrow rock Phoenicians call "The Praying Monk."

She closed the door softly behind her.

"How did he do it? And yes, I want to know."

She had waited till the pot had finished its job, until they were both holding the warm mugs in their hands before she'd asked; before she'd said anything at all. Her brother, her poor, self-centered, self-righteous, brother had finally accepted he wasn't God's hand on earth. He'd been setting himself up for this fall for years. It was only a matter of time.

Pat, sweet, innocent Pat, sat slack jawed across the table from her – she'd shocked him wordless for the second time tonight.

"Come on. You saw this coming. We all saw this coming. He was half –"

"He didn't kill himself, Deanne. He was murdered."

She heard herself ask, "Where? How?" with the same cool detachment she normally reserved for her sources. But this wasn't a story she was tracking, this was her brother; could she really have uttered those words just now? And then the tears came freely, the first she'd cried in years. The first ever for her brother.

Chapter 17

Sandy sat atop her bike, one leg rooted in the sand, and stared at the dilapidated little house next to the pumpkin patch; at the vine-covered window, now closed tight, at the top of the sand hill. It was her first time back to Michael's since she and Bruce had boldly slipped through that window only to land squarely in Hell.

Weeks had gone by, school was in session, and the excitement of finally being an eighth-grader, had eclipsed the strange events of summer for most.

At least it had made them seem farther away.

Next year she'd be a freshman at Vista High. Hard to believe.

The morning after her nightmare about Michael's world she'd ridden her bike across the bridge on her way to meet Bruce at Big Jerry's. It took most of that ride, a mile as the crow flies, to realize she was wasting her time. She turned back and went home.

She hadn't seen Bruce until recess a week ago. He wasn't looking in her direction; she didn't bother getting his attention.

She'd spent the last days of summer making up for lost time at the beach surfing with Tom and all the other boys. She never went back to the fort, had never even come close to Michael's neighborhood.

Till now.

There wasn't a lot of news about Michael. Not many of her friends even knew who he was or cared. Big Jerry hadn't seen him since the last time they'd been to his market together. At one point, she'd ridden to Joe's Diner on the north side of town. Mister Romani said that Michael's mom came in the day she'd been sick, but never again. She never called, never even cashed her last paycheck.

It was still mid-afternoon; it had only taken a few minutes to get to Michael's from school. Blinds kept the day outside. The Plymouth still sat out front, but rather than making the house looked lived-in, it was so dusty now it made the house look even more lifeless. Sand had drifted nearly to the hub caps on one side. She supposed, if the neighbors hadn't complained about the rusted-out truck in the pumpkin patch after some ten or fifteen years, the car could sit there for quite some time, used or not.

Would they have moved without taking the car? Maybe. Maybe it didn't work anymore – but it wasn't old.

Sandy pushed off, riding slowly up the driveway, her heart suddenly pounding. It had taken a long time to get up the nerve to come this far. That was the truth of things. For weeks she'd been too scared to come back. Too scared to go anywhere near the badlands. Fear had always been a momentary thing – a springboard to fun. Not this time, this time she'd let it rule her for weeks.

If it hadn't been for what she'd seen at recess today she wouldn't be here at all.

Thought she'd seen. *It couldn't be real.*

The word at school was there'd be a marble toss today. That meant everyone would gather round, and a few kids would climb to the top of the monkey bars with a big bag of marbles. Once perched, they'd fling handfuls of marbles, boulders, half-pints – even steelies, which were essentially shiny steel ball-bearings – out into the crowds below.

It wasn't that Sandy was into marbles so much, even though some of the agates – the opaque ones with color swirls – were pretty. Most of the marbles that got tossed were cat eyes – clear glass with a tiny ribbon of color down the middle, and very common. The draw for her was that marble tosses were more than a little dangerous, which made them fun to watch. It was pretty easy to get conked on the head – but the bravest kids shoved and fought their way to the front anyway, stuffing their pockets and cloth marble bags until they were ready to burst. Some kids crystallized their marbles – which meant they'd boil them for a while – then stick them in the icebox sending tiny glittering fractures all through them. The crystallized marbles would shatter like little ice bombs when they hit the ground. *That was bitchin'.*

She'd left the cafeteria on her way to the playground, cut between the North hall, which held the seventh-grade classrooms and the South Hall where her homeroom was. She could hear excited shouts and laughter from the playground; the kids gathering around the monkey bars.

A hedge of oleanders flanked by jacarandas separated the two halls.

The hedge was so tall and thick, that standing five feet from it, you couldn't even see the hall ten yards behind it.

It was the odor that caught her attention as she walked near the hedge. Musky, foul. That same stink of nature gone awry that hit her in the wetlands as she'd run from that horribly deformed bird at the end of summer.

That smell stopped Sandy in her tracks, sent an icy spike up her spine.

Something dead, deep in the oleanders. Something big – no sparrow or pigeon - had to be a cat or dog at least, to send up a stench like that.

A couple other kids ran by, and Sandy picked up her step and followed them. Halfway down the mall, the odor came back, as strong as before.

What were the chances two cats, or dogs, or whatever, had died in the hedge?

Loud cheers from the playground. The toss had begun and she was late for it. She trotted now, eyes on the jacarandas at the far end of the hedge. *Why did the trees and the playground beyond still seem so far away?*

She broke into a run, humming softly to herself, keeping herself company, the jacarandas getting closer, but not close enough. The smell wasn't fading.

She had another thought: whatever it was wasn't dead at all.

It was moving right with her, pacing her.

Goosebumps rose on her arms and neck. She ran full out for the end of the hedge, biting into her lip, humming out loud. Something rustling the leaves of the oleander beside her, bending the branches. She could hear it, but she wasn't going to turn her head that way. *Wasn't going to. Not for a zillion dollars she wasn't.*

Five yards from the end of the hedge – she turned and looked.

Cat eyes stared back from the shadows.

But no cat owned them. The eyes were too large, too widely separated, and whatever it was, it stood way too tall for a cat. *Nearly eye-to eye with her.*

She didn't stop running again until she was in the middle of the playground, smack center in the crowd of a couple hundred kids. Happy enough to be pushed and shoved and take a marble to the skull if she had to.

Sandy wasn't going to live in fear anymore.

She stopped her bike near Michael's front door, swung off, and heeled the kickstand down. Her heart hadn't quit pounding since she'd reached his street.

The sand felt oddly light and unstable beneath her. Surfing up and down the California coast since she was six, twice in Hawaii, and once in Montego Bay, her feet had felt everything from pumice, to gravel, to pure white heaven. This sand puffed and parted underfoot the way she imagined snow might.

By the time she reached the door, it felt more like quicksand and her heart was thrumming like a hummingbird's wings.

It's not the sand. You're just freaking spooked. Get over it.

She raised her fist to knock, couldn't bring herself to touch the door, and then pushed the doorbell instead. It rang much louder than she'd expected. She fought the urge to "ding-dong ditch," to just turn around and run.

There was nothing but the echo of the doorbell from within.

But what had she expected? An invitation to come inside for supper?

All right. She'd done it. She'd faced her fear. Michael was simply gone, gone forever.

No. Pete's gone forever. Michael's just…disappeared.

And that was okay. It had to be, there was nothing she could do. She started back, and stopped. She was breathing normally now, thinking clearly again. She looked at the narrow, brass-covered slot in the door.

Mail wouldn't stop coming. Not right away. If they were still living here, they'd pick it up. If there were a bunch of envelopes piled just inside the door then Michael and his mom had moved. Simple as that.

All she had to do was squat down, open that mail slot, and have a look.

Then again, Michael's mom was more than a little loony. It wasn't so hard to believe she might be hiding deep inside the house with the lights off and the blinds closed. *Or standing just behind the door...*

If she did it, she'd be quick about it. Just flip the tiny door open and look inside. Sandy squatted down, reached for the brass cover – and her hand just seemed to hover there for the longest time.

Finally she grabbed the cool metal, but it was like gripping a Band-Aid you couldn't quite bring yourself to rip off. She crouched closer, put her face next to it – *and imagined two widely-set cat eyes staring back her from the darkness.* Her hand shook, then let go of the metal slot altogether.

She looked back one more time at the windows, at the warped and worn door.

"I'm sorry, Michael."

She didn't know why, or what she had to be sorry about. It was herself she'd failed, not Michael as she kicked the stand back up, and pushed her pike away from his house for the last time.

She hadn't conquered her fear at all. Quite the opposite, s*he was more frightened now than ever.*

Sandy slowed when she reached Big Jerry's above the ravine. You couldn't exactly see Michael's fort from the road, but she knew generally where it was amongst the tumbleweeds and tall grasses.

She stopped, and had to look again.

The badlands were greener, lusher than she'd ever seen them. *No, not the entire badlands. Just there, the part of it that hid their fort,* the vegetation was thicker, greener, and higher than anywhere else.

Michael's world.

A musky scent seemed to rise up from the badlands, that terrible concoction of life and decay... She saw the tall, sheltering oleanders at school, two eyes peering out from the shadows...

"Some of them work...and some of them don't."

She slammed her pedal down, sped off, and didn't look back that way again.

-=-=-=-=-

The Cove Theater was decked out proud enough for a Hollywood opening.

Bruce's opening.

At least that's how it looked to Bruce. The big Marquee still read, "The Thomas Crown Affair" in big letters, but small letters beneath read, "Ed Sullivan's Search for Young Talent." There was a long, red carpet in the lobby, and a large poster of Ed with big blinking lights all around. Ed wouldn't actually be here, Bruce knew that, but he'd be meeting Ed soon enough. Soon they'd be best buddies.

Bruce was going to win.

Best yet, all of La Vista was crowding in. All those classmates who called him names if they even looked his way at all. Every teacher and coach who'd been mean to him. Everybody in town except Bud and Linda Stubik, and that was just fine with Bruce. He hadn't told his parents where he was going. Had never ever told them there was a contest. This afternoon, he'd simply folded his suit and best shirt and stuffed them in a shopping bag, and sneaked out the back door. He'd changed behind Big Jerry's. His parents would know about it once he was famous and they saw him on TV. Nothing was going to wreck his day.

Sandy would be here too.

She was an eighth-grader now, which was like being in another dimension to a seventh-grader like himself. Still, he saw her at recess a lot, and sometimes at the bike racks after school. She always seemed to be looking the other way.

She'd be sorry when he was a star. She'd be real sorry, just like everyone else. *Nobody could do what he did. Nobody sang like Bruce Stubik.*

He was sorry Michael wouldn't be here though. If it hadn't been for Michael, he'd never have done this. He'd just be singing to the backwater or into his pillow forever.

He'd never get everything that was bottled up inside him out.

On some level, he understood "not getting it out" his whole life had made him fat. It wasn't that he loved eating – not the way he loved to sing.

Eating just made him feel halfway okay.

And he'd finally come to realize that even *singing* was no good if nobody heard you.

It was the same suit he'd worn to Pete's funeral, his one and only – but it would stay unbuttoned today. He'd knotted his tie but kept it loose, with the collar open. Maybe he didn't look so good, but his looks weren't going to win him his freedom. *His voice would.*

"I'm gonna win this thing," he sighed to himself, beaming. His star was on the rise.

Bruce had never been backstage of the Cove Theater, and to be sure, he hadn't missed much. Not having been built for live theater, the backstage was a dark, narrow place with a high ceiling that held a black catwalk and some big spotlights suspended from black pipes. There were two sets of stairs to the stage, and a long room in the back, now crammed with kids – some in shiny, spangle-covered costumes, others in suits and formal dresses.

He knew some of them – Mark D'Arcangelo, who everyone called "Mark Dark" would be playing banjo, and Danny Tarajcak (<u>Tear-shak</u> – soft "j" and the "a" and "c" were silent, he'd always say). Dan was the pianist for the church choir – Darky played for parties and school functions. They were good. Then there was Cindy Taylor, one of several girls in spangles and tights, who would be tap-dancing. She was annoying, but Bruce couldn't help but notice her legs, which easily took up three quarters of her body and actually weren't bad to look at. Shirley Davies, in a shapeless, forest green dress, granny glasses and white socks, would sing folk songs and play guitar.

The rest of the kids came from schools up and down the coast from Oceanside down to San Diego.

A woman in a bright blue jacket checked names off a clipboard. It took forever to get her attention. He pretended not to notice the look of disbelief on her face when he pointed to his name on the sheet, and announced, "Bruce Stubik, *vocalist.*"

"Well…Bruce. Is your accompanist here?"

"I sing a capella."

"Oh. I'm sorry. We don't have *a capella* singers on the show. All singers must have accompaniment."

She moved on. The entire backstage had turned into a tunnel, a very, very small tunnel with her moving toward its inevitable, impossibly far away end.

He swallowed, and his Adam's apple just seemed to keep sinking into some bottomless pit, taking his heart right along with it.

"But – ah… Miss? Ma'am… I don't need music. I can sing…"

"I'm his accompanist." Danny said, raising one amazingly long fingered hand as he slouched in his folding chair.

She looked down at her sheet, "You're…"

"Dan Tarajcak. Tear-shak. Soft "j," the "a" and "c" are silent. Remember?"

"You're *already* in the show."

"Yeah. And I play for Bruce too." He shrugged, "What's the deal?"

"Me too." It was Mark Dark, a toothpick moved from one side of his mouth to the other, seemingly on its own.

"You accompany him…on the banjo?" She said.

"Yeah." He pulled the pick. "We're his backup band – The uhh… *Driftwoods.* "

She sucked in a breath the way grownups do when they've had enough.

"Fine." She said, and moved on.

Bruce was flabbergasted. In a single moment he'd been to Hell and Heaven. *No one at school had ever done him a favor.* No one ever even looked at him except to make fun.

Then a whole new fear shook him.

"But – you won't know my song…"

"What's the song?" Mark Dark asked.

"Wild is the Wind."

"You're right. Don't know it."

"Relax," Danny said. "You came to sing by yourself, right?"

Bruce nodded.

"So they call your name, we go up with you – you nod your head like you're ready – and then you sing and we just sit there and watch. Screw 'er."

"You guys would do that?"

"Heck yeah," Danny said.

Mark nodded. He pulled the shattered toothpick from between his teeth and added,

"She's a dick."

-=.=.=.=-

The last time Sandy had been to The Cove, Michael and Bruce had been with her. They'd been so close then, watching *Planet of the Apes* twice in a row, chomping Bon Bons and popcorn like the stuff was going out of style and having a great time. It was only last summer, and now it seemed like years.

She didn't look back at that time with longing anymore; it was just a passing thought, not nostalgia for better times. She was an eighth grader after all, one step away from High School. Everything would change for her then, everything *always* changed, which was the way of things. It was too bad Michael hadn't hung around longer, but there was nothing she could do about it. She had no regrets.

Only fear.

These days, she found herself looking around more and more, checking who, *what*, was around her. Even here in a crowd of noisy people waiting for a stupid talent show to begin, she couldn't help feeling watched. Not the sheep-eyed sort of way boys watched her these days. She'd come to accept that like she accepted most things now. Eventually she'd find the best way to use it.

What she felt now was something very different. *A presence.*

"What's up there?" Tom asked, already bored.

She'd been staring at the bright gold valance above the curtains. She hadn't even realized it until Tom spoke.

"Nothing. When is this supposed to start?"

"Should have started five minutes ago. I don't even know why you wanted to watch this stupid thing."

She shrugged. She didn't quite know herself. To support Bruce, would have been her first answer. But that wasn't it. They didn't hang out anymore. She wouldn't even if he wanted to. Michael had been the glue holding them all together, and Michael was gone. In science, they talked about things some animals still had after all the years of evolution but didn't need anymore – things like that little sprig of bone under your butt that might have been a tail a few gazillion years back. She was pretty sure the term was "vestigial."

Her friendship with Bruce was like that now – vestigial. Still there, she supposed, but unformed and unneeded.

The lights dimmed, a spotlight hit the curtain.

"Finally," Tom said.

"And now, Ed Sullivan's Search for Young Talent!"

"Good luck finding it here," Tom muttered.

Sandy smiled at him the way she was supposed to. The way her mother might for something stupid Dad said. But her eyes and attention were in the darkness high above the spotlight, high above the stage.

"The Search" itself seemed endless. And Tom's comment had been right on the mark – there wasn't much talent to be found. A lot of whiny kids, a lot of screaming, cheering parents. A lot of out-of-time tap-dancing, sloppy baton twirling and thoroughly abrasive singing. Very little talent. At least, once Bruce appeared – if they ever got around to him, Sandy knew the singing would be good.

That boy can sing.

Fat as he is.

She'd grown more and more uncomfortable as the show wore on. Not from the seat, nor from her clothes. She'd dressed in her favorite jeans, a Madras shirt, and sandals she'd slipped off the moment they'd found seats. *It was that presence high above the stage that weighed down on her.*

Something watching from the edge of the light.

"And now, Ed Sullivan presents: the vocal stylings of Bruce Stubik, with...The Driftwoods."

Finally, her "vestigial" reason for sitting through it all had appeared:

"The Driftwoods?" Tom said. "Porky's got a band?"

She shook her head. It was the first she'd heard of it.

Danny T and Mark Dark came out and sat – Danny at the piano, Mark slinging his banjo. Then came Bruce, big and white as a mountain of raw dough, carrying his coat over one shoulder, his tie undone.

There was a collective gasp, from the audience.

"It's *Fat* Sinatra." Tom muttered.

Sandy shushed him, "Wait'll you hear him."

Bruce folded his coat over a chair at the middle of the stage, and stepped confidently up to the big microphone. He nodded to Danny and Mark. They nodded back, and Mark looked to Danny. Danny spread and clenched his fingers twice, raised his hands over the keyboard, then folded them across his chest. He turned back to Bruce.

Bruce closed his eyes, opened his mouth, and the sweetest sounds Sandy had ever heard, swept through the sound system and immediately, the crowd was silenced.

A woman in a blue coat who had stepped out from the curtain on stage right, stopped suddenly, she backed off the stage awestruck. Even Danny and Mark looked stunned.

His voice lifted and fell, soared above them all.

The sight of Bruce, his eyes narrow slits in that dough-boy face, and the sweet tenor of the voice coming over the PA was so striking – so...*unbelievable* –

"It's a joke!" Tom guffawed. *"It's a record!"*

There were giggles. Then, to Sandy's horror, laughter broke from small islands in the darkness.

"It is! Oh – that *is* funny!"

"He really looks like he's singing!"

And he sang about love, a love so deep, so uncontrollable –
Bruce pushed on, his incredible, sweet tenor convincing even
more people…*that it was some weird joke. That he was singing to a
record. That he was fooling with them. It didn't even matter that there
were no instruments playing in the background – no music at all but his
own, clear, magical voice.*

Laughter, coming from everywhere. No longer
islands, the entire audience was bawling with laughter.

"SING IT OUT FAT BOY! Sing it, FAT Sinatra!"
Tom shouted, and the *chant picked up.*

"FAT Sinatra!!! FAT Sinatra!!!"

"Let him sing, you idiots!" Sandy shouted at Tom – at
everyone around her. "LET HIM SING! *Please let him sing!"*

And now, they were pointing and laughing *at her* – as if
she were either part of the fun - or the only one who didn't
get the joke. A hoot either way.

Up on the stage, Danny and Mark were shouting the
same thing Sandy was "It's him! He's singing! *He really is
singing!"* But they didn't have microphones and their voices
were drowned by the din.

Bruce's lips moved soundlessly. His eyes, nearly closed
while he sang, showed white all around.

The woman in the blue jacket had been laughing with
the rest, but now she glanced at her watch, at the clipboard in
her hand, time was money after all. She walked briskly across
the stage and took Bruce by the elbow.

She waved the next entry on-stage.

Bruce took two sideways steps with her and stopped
dead, nearly toppling the woman in her heels, his eyes darted
from one side of the theater to the other. The streams now
running freely from his eyes to his chin sparkled in the
spotlight.

A shriek of pain soared over the crowd, a sound
nothing like Sandy had ever heard before. Part scream, part
roar, it flooded the auditorium; silenced everyone.

Bruce stood, shell-shocked, half a stage from the microphone stand.

The shriek wasn't coming from him.

It came from the catwalk over their heads.

Two bright almonds of light shown in the rafters. Cat eyes. The same eyes that had followed Sandy near the playground.

A shadow dropped from the curtains, slammed to the floor and sprang across the stage while the spotlight tried desperately to catch it.

The spot raced toward the woman in blue who had suddenly executed a backwards swan dive off the stage, she hung in midair, then came down hard, fast, and awkward over the first row of seats, scattering the occupants and sending up a *snap!* like a hundred wishbones twisted at once.

In the spotlight, her eyes mirrored that same trapped-animal look Bruce had, as she stared, blindly, lifelessly at the stunned faces directly behind her.

The spotlight left her immediately for the rafters. The paralyzed crowd found their own voice. The houselights went on – and just as fast, were extinguished.

Pandemonium.

Sandy knew the word, but she had never *seen it* until now.

Exit doors sent shafts of life over mad rivers of people shoving and trampling each other, sticking in the doorway, only to be crushed and flattened by those behind them.

This isn't happening. This is a dream. Blood seemed to drain from her limbs and ice water rushed to fill that void, dimly she understood she was slipping away into shock now. But shock was a way of protecting you, wasn't it? A way to keep you from pain.

She stood in the eye of the hurricane, numbly watching the storm around her. The storm of Michael. The bottle-rocket had indeed exploded.

An elbow crunched a hot stream from her nose that down her cheek. It was a blessing, *it was real.*

She focused on the word *EXIT* in glowing red and vaulted toward it, and then was smacked straight down to the floor. She rose halfway to her knees only to be whacked from another direction, a shoulder sent her sprawling painfully over the seats, over toppled, screaming bodies. The air grew hot and thick, filled with danger and flailing limbs. The screams were deafening.

Wherever she stepped her feet found flesh and bone, finally, she ignored it, stepped wherever she needed to find balance and move forward. She slipped and came face to face with the woman in blue, still lying broken across the seat backs. The woman's eyes looked straight at Sandy, but they were doll's eyes now, not really looking anywhere.

She half-crawled, half-swam to the stage through the melee, there would be more exits in the darkness there most people wouldn't think to run to.

Bruce was nowhere to be seen – a knot of struggling men on the stage.

Good night La Vista. FAT Sinatra has left the stage.

The clot of men on-stage pushed back and forth as if in a scrum, there was a fight raging. Shrieks came from everywhere. Something insane was going on here, something crazier than the tug-of-war on-stage, and even scarier than the dead woman in the crisp, blue, jacket.

The on-stage scrum exploded, a shadow in its center tossing bodies to the side like a dog shakes water from its back.

The shadow pounced from the stage and straight into the struggling, screaming crowd, and she saw that now people weren't just trying to get out - *they were being chased, pulled down like wounded antelope, and slaughtered.*

Yes, the bottle-rocket has indeed exploded.

When the doors shut again, even the exit lights had given out; the only light now came from those two, almond-shaped orbs. And then, there was nothing at all.

"Hey, kid! Did you see that thing! You must have seen it! You were right there."

It's real. This is not a dream.

But how did he get here? How did he get outside?

A small boy crashed into Bruce's wide, pillowy back, rebounded, and sped off in another direction. Whistles, shouts and screams, a siren blared as an ambulance pushed its way through the scattering crowd outside the theater where he was supposed to show them all, *and ascend to the heavens of stardom.*

Cat eyes. When his whole world had blown up, he'd thought he'd seen cat eyes.

Michael.

Bruce blinked and tried to comprehend what was happening. People were still shoving their way through the doors. Some had bad cuts and bruises. He tasted his own blood now, felt the warm trickle of it from his nose and lip and began to swoon. The sky loomed over him and turned on its side. He saw the dirty back wall of the Cove Theater, saw it spin up and away, and just as his knees buckled, he saw –

Cat eyes.

They watched him for a moment, and then the shadowy form around them leapt into the sky...*or was it the ocean...or the cliffs...or another rooftop, everything had melded into one, swirling mass...*

"I was going to be a star," was all he said before he fainted.

-=-=-=-=-

I AM the eye of the hurricane, Sandy thought. She floated like a ghost through the darkness, between the thumping bodies still struggling like mad to escape the darkness, to escape the horrid creature with the shiny cat-eyes that ripped past them, and into them, tearing them apart.

She passed through the lobby, still feeling as though everything in the world was running triple time around her, ripping itself to pieces in her wake.

Shouts of *"Monster! Maniac!"* and *"Devil!"* words she'd have heard in conversation right here in the lobby any given day of last summer. But that was after horror shows, the kind that starred Peter Cushing, or Vincent Price, not talent shows starring her schoolmates.

She heard her name called several times. She knew people wanted her attention, wanted to talk about the crazy, violent man in the furry black costume, the one who was, at this very moment, killing people in their favorite hometown movie house.

But they didn't know what she knew. They didn't know about the bottle rocket, how it had been stuffed up real good and tight and blown itself up with everyone around it – just like it had at the beach.

Sandy drifted passed the mayhem to her bike, flipped up the kickstand, and when her fingers had quit shaking enough to firmly grasp the handlebars, she rode home.

-=-=-=-=-

That night Sandy had a dream.

Fix it. Set it straight.

It was 3:00 AM. Time to face her fears again.

She pulled on her jeans and her favorite Madras shirt. It was cold enough outside to warrant sneakers and a jacket – she carried those with her as she slipped out her front door.

She'd been afraid the first time she'd stood up on a surfboard; afraid of getting hurt, afraid of looking stupid if she fell. And even once she'd gotten the hang of it, she'd been afraid of every new move – until she'd actually tried it. The world, her world, had been very different then. And as clearly as she was able to see that world now, she had to admit, it was no longer a world she enjoyed very much.

The ride across the bridge to the badlands gave her time to think things over, time to pull out if need be. She biked along on the ocean side of the Pacific Coast Highway, watching the nighttime surf crash way far out where the tide had carried it.

Even now, low tide and all, it was easy to see herself out there surfing with her friends, raising hell and having a great old time. They'd done it day in, day out – summer after glorious summer.

She wanted that again. Something like that again. *Anything.*

Just where PCH curved around the center of town, the marquee of the Cove Theater still read "Thomas Crown Affair" above, but they'd already pulled the "Ed Sullivan's Search for Young Talent" nonsense down.

Bruce had been humiliated in front of the whole town. Would he ever be the same? What had they done to him?

What had *she* done to him? Just by being his friend…and then letting that go.

Stuffing the bottle rocket. Right along with everyone else he ever met.

There was no real sadness that went along with the thought, and *that* she realized, as she pulled across PCH and took the dirt road alongside the badlands, was *exactly* her problem. *There should be.* Whether it was her fault or not, there should be some sort of feeling walking hand in hand with it. *Sadness, anger, regret. Something.* But somewhere along the line the feeling part of her had left. Even Pete's death had become little more than a footnote in her heart's *"What I Did Last Summer"* essay.

All she had now was fear.

But she would take care of that tonight once and for all. She'd failed at Michael's house. And Michael hadn't even been there, she *knew* that now.

But she knew where to find him.

None of the usual cricket and frog sounds as she straddled her bike and stood looking out over the badlands.

But there *were* sounds.

Chittering and croaking for sure, but their timbre was way too deep even for toads, too uneven for crickets. *What was out there?*

The moon had painted everything silver or black. Not the violets, pinks and oranges of her dreams, and as scary as those dreams had been, she found herself wishing for the worst of them. There would be no waking up from this.

Sandy laid her bike just over the side of the bank and out of sight from the road. *As if anyone would be coming by here right now to steal it…* She picked her way carefully down the bank, feeling clumsy and loud and altogether too real. The sand crunched and moved beneath her feet, reeds brushed her face, rustled around her in the night. She heard these small things clearly. Everything else, the bullfrogs *that aren't quite bullfrogs,* and all the chittering of the insects *that most likely aren't quite insects,* had gone dead. Whatever lived in the badlands now had stopped to listen to her.

If she ran. If she just turned around and ran now…

From where she stood, halfway into the badlands, her bike looked a mile away. Whatever had been pacing her at school, whatever had rushed through the theater, would run her down before she got anywhere near safety. She was past the point of no return.

But this was about facing fears, not running away.

And chances are, nothing is really out here anyway.

Michael had moved on with his loon of a mother. There were never any werewolves, or griffons, or chimeras, or whatever the heck Bruce had said.

She had almost succeeded in convincing herself of that, and then the scent of decay and festering life drifted by.

A shadowy form slipped away from the others in the tumbleweeds. A shadow with two yellow cats-eyes perched high on its head. It was about the size of a cheetah, much taller than she was, as it stood upright on its hind legs as it watched her.

She forced herself on, aware of other shadowy *things* out there now, *other eyes.* These belonged not to the cuddly cartoon-like creatures of her dreams – walking stuffed toys waiting for their turn to be pet and loved – but to ugly things with scaly, plated lizard backs, and rows of shark teeth. Things built to last now, *to survive,* because Michael had finally quit stuffing the bottle rocket. *Now he was streaming that fuel out the bottle's neck.*

Michael had launched.

She walked between them toward the old fort, some of them striding, padding, slithering right along with her, flanking her.

She'd been wrong about nothing. Whatever happened now, she knew what was here, and she'd come anyway. But she realized, as her heart began to beat far too quickly, and her breaths came fast, uneven, and shallow, that her fears hadn't been conquered, only justified.

Blood pumped noisily in her ears. She stopped a short way before reaching the fort, sucking in breaths that seemed to draw frost through the soft tissue of her lungs. She couldn't even *see* the fort.

The area around it was a jungle now, with thick growth everywhere, bamboo, small trees, and ferns. A million places for creatures of all kinds to grow, to hide, and to thrive.

She pressed on, into the heart of it, and was thankful to see the fort had not been replaced by a cemetery, it was not a crypt guarded by the angel of death.

Or was it.

There was a guard. One of the creatures Bruce had shown her. Fanciful and strange in the drawing, but sitting in front of her now, sizing her up with cold, piercing eyes, it was the most frightening beast she'd ever seen, and easily the biggest of any of the creatures here. It was winged, with a wicked beak and feathers like an eagle in front, its gigantic talons rooted firmly in the sand before it. The beast rested on haunches like that of a great lion, a long tail curved around it ending in a tuft. A Griffon. That's what Bruce had called it.

Its eyes hadn't shifted from her since she'd stepped into the clearing, only its sharply pointed ears tracked her movements.

A light snapped on inside the fort throwing shadows against the grass walls.

A paper thin voice whispered, *"Sandy. Come in."*

The Griffon stood the spread of its wings made the *snap!* of a great sail unfurling in the wind. The force of its wings as it rose into the night threw back her hair, made her knees buckle.

Its silhouette flew straight into the moon before it disappeared.

No. This is not real. *None of this can be real.*

She found the strength to move again, to pull back their makeshift door, and step through.

Mrs. Helm, not Michael, sat at the head of their little table, a bandanna tied around her head, pulled over most of her face. Her long hands covered the rest.

Sandy turned for the door, started to open it —but it wouldn't budge. And she realized, with growing terror, that Michael was leaning against it, *holding it shut.*

"Sandy, stay in there. Okay?"

"I came to see you! I can't stay in here with her!"

"Sandy, please. You can't see me now."

His voice was so plaintive and sad. Sandy looked back at the woman at the table. Mrs. Helm hadn't moved. It was too creepy. Sandy couldn't stay here long.

"I *have* seen you, Michael."

"Not like this."

"I saw you at school." She swallowed hard, *"I saw you...at the theater."*

"I thought...if Bruce just sang...you know? Let it out a little. He'd be okay."

He didn't say anything for a while. She could practically feel him pulling syllables together, as if forming each word was an effort, like lifting a heavy weight.

"I got mad, Sandy. *I got mad...*"

"I know that."

"Someone hurt my mom, Sandy. He hurt her really bad, and once I started...I got mad and I couldn't stop..."

The thing that had been Michael's mother still hadn't moved. Again, the hope that *this isn't real. None of this is real. It can't be.*

"My mom's broken!"

Michael choked, the sound was wet, deep in his throat, he was trying to cry but...couldn't somehow.

"I tried to...fix her, I wanted to fix things. All I wanted to do." An insane dream. Just a horrible, horrible dream.

"Michael, I thought I could do this. I thought if I just came here and saw you – but I can't. I thought I could stop being scared, but I am scared, Michael, I'm really scared and I have to wake up now, I have to go home!"

"Sandy...you can't! *You came here to be with me."*

A creaking sound from the head of the table. His mom had stirred; now she rocked back and forth in her chair, going further with each push.

Hot bile rose up Sandy's throat. A few more rocks and she'd have to take her hands away from her face for balance – and Sandy wasn't about to look into that ruined face again. How do you wake up from a nightmare that doesn't want to end?

I came here to be with him? God, no. She had come here to face her fears. That always worked before. So why was her heart still racing? Why couldn't she breathe? Why couldn't she just settle into the fear and ride it – dive through fear's doorway and collect the thrill that always waited behind it. *Think.* Think and ride this through. Think about what he just said, *he thinks you want to be with him. He's a boy.* He wants me *just like every boy does.*

The answer was always there, and always more simple than it seemed.

"I like you, Michael. I like you a lot, you know that don't you?"

She put her shoulder against the door. She could feel his weight, his heat from the other side.

"Out on those waves – when you kissed me, *you liked that didn't you?* You wanted to kiss me again. "

She felt his weight shift. Behind her, the chair stopped rocking, she could hear the table sliding forward, scraping up gouts of sand with it. *But I am not going to look back there; I am not going to look!*

"Michael, you want to kiss me now, *I know you do.* Then I'll go home, okay? I'll go home and you can come over later. Okay? *My mom won't even be home this afternoon.*"

Nothing. Her heart dropped.

And then the weight beyond the door was gone. *She'd been released.*

She threw the door wide open.

Michael stood just outside on what could only be described as hind legs. He had no face at all, only a depression within a mat of black fur remained. From the center of that horror of emptiness, two yellow cat-eyes blinked at her.

And Sandy felt herself falling, falling with her own scream ringing in her ears – and before the darkness came, she saw Michael's mom struggling to stand, both hands clutching the sides of the table...

The woman's cheek was no longer shattered; her eye no longer bulged from a broken socket, because it was no longer her face, but Michael's that stared from beneath her bandanna.

Chapter 18

Cross the brightest hues of Monet's palette with the deepest tones and moody brushwork of Winslow Homer, and you have an Arizona sunset.

Father Pat Mulhenney, newly installed Pastor of St. Bartholomew's, sat facing that sunset as Deanne wound her way to him through the tables surrounding the Biltmore's tiled pool.

She hadn't seen her cousin in weeks, and the amount of gray now peppering his hair was startling. Still, she said he looked good as she kissed his cheek, ordered a Manhattan, and sat beside him to watch the last brilliant rays of the daylight.

"So, what have you got?" she asked.

He set a manila envelope on the table, right beside the remnants of his drink, also a Manhattan, she noted. A small dark, ring of wetness where it touched his glass. She wiped the envelope, slid it into her bag.

"Do you ever stop being a reporter?"

"Do you ever stop being a priest?"

"I'll drink to that."

They clicked their rims, then savored the warm sweetness.

"You have a Parish to run now."

"I didn't ask for that."

"Umm."

"You know you didn't get that from me."

"An unnamed source."

"And not within the Catholic Church."

"Pat, I get it. But it's a pretty safe bet they'll make the connection."

He nodded.

"Then, you may as well have this too."

Pat set a small leather-bound bible on the table. A few pages of folded newsprint poked from the between the tassels.

"This was Alec's – plus a few news stories you might find interesting once you go through it – the contents of that envelope."

Deanne pulled the newsprint and flattened the pages as the waiter arrived with her drink, and Pat ordered another for himself. The pages had come from a small, local press from a California town named La Vista.

Various passages were circled.

"Local Boy Killed in Nightmarish Shark Attack" read one headline, the other read, "Five Killed, Many Injured by Costumed Maniac at Talent Show." Deanne scanned the circled passages.

"Bizarre descriptions of marauding sharks by local surfers discounted by officials. Though more than one eyewitness claimed to have seen claws and fur on the "sharks," these accounts were dismissed by experts. "The most likely explanation is that a school of sharks pursued a group of California sea lions into the shallows," said Dr. Tory Evans, a marine biologist from Scripps Institute. "The panicked surfers apparently saw both – and mixed the descriptions. They described complete mayhem out there."

"A female producer for a national talent show and several spectators were killed, others injured by an unknown, masked assailant today at the Cove Theater. The costume worn by the killer was described as a panther by some, as a wolf-like creature by others, with glowing eyes...costume was very, very realistic..."

Deanne shrugged. "I remember the stories. But this town is on the coast. *California.* What do they have to do with Alec?"

"I know, he was found over in Arcadia, in St. Frances Cemetery. But the police said the body had been moved. *You verified that.*"

"A long way – judging by the loss of..."

Pat was looking at her with that horrified blankness she remembered from the morning she'd learned her brother was dead.

"A long way." He nodded.

How was it that her cousin had been so much more aligned, so much closer to her brother than she *ever* was? Had Pat never looked inside the man's heart?

Deanne paged through the bible. In the margins, line after line of notes, and sketches of strange creatures built from the parts of completely different animals.

"I started checking the papers when I read his notes," he said, "you're not the only detective in the family."

She shook her head, as she paged through the book.

"I'm not a detective, Pat. Just a reporter."

On the inside of the back cover, a drawing that took Deanne's breath away: an image Alec had once described from a dream: *a boy's body, but the face tapered into a cat-like muzzle, the eyes had been left blank and pupil-l*ess.

The costume worn by the killer was described as a panther by some...

Underlined at the bottom, the words, "La Vista."

"Okay. It's crazy, but so was my brother. So why don't you just tell me what you think the California connection is, save us both a little time?"

Pat leaned across the table. Careful of the waitress, of the conversations around them. But it was a beautiful sunset at one of the most posh watering holes of Arizona; no one cared.

"You know his obsession with the deaths of the innocents at our parish."

Now it was Deanne's turn to nod, it had driven her brother from self-righteous to certifiable.

"When Alec disappeared I looked for anything he might have taken with him. In that envelope are copies of *personal records*. Personal information of parishioners which we're unfortunately not supposed to keep."

"Okay."

"Well, no. It isn't. But, when I matched up our copy to our records – this file was missing. It's the Helm file – the family of one of the murdered innocents. After the investigation, the parents separated, the mother, Brit, disappeared with her surviving son. We're not supposed to track them – but they *are* Catholics, still part of the flock. There is apparently a house on the coast that belongs to the family."

"In or near La Vista, the town where these attacks took place, is that what you're saying? And you believe Alec followed them there?"

"Almost certainly."

-=.=.=.=.-

Joe Romani gave the tabletop one last, half-hearted swipe of the towel, and sat heavily at the counter. He'd picked up fifteen pounds since the summer, and he wouldn't be getting rid of it anytime soon.

Even the regulars were less regular these days. Business was in the toilet, and Joe wasn't helping matters. He'd grown grouchier by the day, and the booze only added to it. He reached around the counter, pulled up a bottle of grappa, and poured two fingers into a cup.

"To you, babe. You had me going there for a while."

To anyone looking in, he was toasting thin air with a coffee mug. What he was really toasting was the apron hanging from a hook next to the order wheel.

Brit had never come back. He'd never hired anyone else. And her apron still hung where she'd left it.

He'd been to that house five, six, *Hell – maybe a dozen times,* he didn't know.

Brit had just disappeared with her kid. *No reason.*

And yes, he realized his reaction was dumb. No reason to let things go like he had. *No fool like an old one.*

When the bell on the front door jangled, he waved a hand over his shoulder without even looking back. *Had he forgotten to lock it?*

Most likely.

"Closed. Sorry," he said into his mug.

He was startled when a warm, soft hand gripped his.

"Are you Joe? I could use a job."

He barely found the counter with his mug as he spun around on the stool to see the young woman – she was a looker, alright. With hazel-green eyes, blond hair – *and a body like…*

"Yeah, yes, I'm Joe. But I'm not looking for anyone to –" he started.

"Well, you should be. This place is a mess."

Before he could protest, she'd pulled the sacred apron off its hook. She tied it around her thin waist like she owned it.

And then, he saw *something…*

"Wait – I know you."

"Not likely." she laughed, a pleasant sound he so *needed* to hear, "I just got here."

Maybe so, but he was sure he *knew* her. The body, and that face, he'd seen that face around town before. He was *sure* of it.

"You got a…little sister, or cousin?"

"Hah. I get that a lot. I guess I look like *a lot of girls.*"

Before he could stop himself, he found himself searching for an excuse to hire her – finally, he admitted he really didn't need an excuse. She was right – *he needed her.* His diner and the regulars needed her. The place *was* a mess. *He* was a mess.

"So, you just saw this place…and wanted to work here?"

She dumped the stale contents of both coffee pots, started a fresh brew with one, and checked the bottom of the other for scorch marks.

"I'm a waitress." She shrugged, "It's what I do."

Joe nodded, feeling something like he'd been gut-punched and French-kissed at the same time.

"So…what's your name?"

She blinked.

He gestured for her to go on, making a spinning motion with his hands. She was the most confident thing he'd ever seen – *and this question stumped her?* She flashed a smile that shut the door on his second thoughts.

"...*April.* April Griffin."

"That's...pretty."

"Say, you wouldn't happen to know if there's a place for rent near here?"

"Well...I know there's a house that's been empty for a while. I don't know if it's for rent though... Nobody's using it – that's for sure."

"Do me a favor. Take me to it later on –"

"Look – I don't really know who owns it – or what kind of shape it's in these days."

"I'm sure it'll be fine." She added, "...as long as they like pets."

The End

Books by Steve Zell

Urban Limit by Steve Zell
Pub: Tales From Zell, Inc. ™

Members of an Oregon family move to the mountains hoping
to escape city life, only to find themselves fighting for their
own lives and, possibly, for civilization itself.

Twins Kristi and Reed Carroll could not be more different. While Kristi trains for her shot at Olympic glory in the winter games, Reed spends his days in the cyber world of video games. But something sinister has found its way into both worlds that will soon bring them together, or tear them apart forever.

WiZrD by Steve Zell

Pub: Macmillan, St. Martin's Press, Hodder|Headline

Caught in a centuries-old cycle of boom and bust, the northern Arizona ghost town, Pinon Rim, is booming once more, but ominous signs are beginning to emerge. It's up to newly arrived, Bryce Willems, and his stepsister, Megan, to end that lethal cycle…or not.

Running Cold by Steve Zell
Pub: Tales From Zell, Inc. ™

An ancient gift turns deadly in the hands of a young boy. It's the mid-1960s, and Brit Helm, mourning the recent loss of her husband and eldest son, struggles to make a new life for her youngest boy, Michael, in a small beach town. But lingering suspicions about the horrific "accident" that took her eldest begin to rise, and soon Brit realizes she must control Michael's anger at all costs. A pretty surfer threatens to break her tenuous hold...

About the Author

The kid everyone brought their sick pets to, Steve Zell grew up in Phoenix, Arizona, with a backyard that eventually resembled a small zoo.

He spent many of his childhood summers as a "Zoni" in the beach communities near San Diego. A former cartoonist, animator, and session vocalist in Los Angeles, he now haunts coffee houses in the mythic environs of Portlandia...

For more information, or to contact the author, please visit:
www.talesfromzell.com

CPSIA information can be obtained
at www.ICGtesting.com
Printed in the USA
LVOW10s1706021217
558390LV00014B/1206/P